THE OBJECT

For eight-year-old William, it was a
game. But for Natasha it was a voyage
of discovery, and for Alexis it was the
end of years of waiting. But none of
them had expected it to culminate in a
Soho nightclub!

THE OBJECT OF THE GAME

BY
VANESSA JAMES

MILLS & BOON LIMITED
15–16 BROOK'S MEWS
LONDON W1A 1DR

CHAPTER ONE

THE house was on the fringe of Cambridge: built for a large Victorian family, it was tall, gaunt, of red brick, without charm from the exterior. Natasha, standing at the attic window, drummed her fingers against the pane.

Her room overlooked the large and unkempt garden. Against its brick walls grew a tangle of roses fifteen feet high, now in full bloom. The grass—what was left of it—was scarred by summers of family cricket. Beyond was a small muddy stream; there one of her cousins was attempting, without great success, to launch a punt. Their half-term holiday was almost over; he was already caked in mud.

Beyond the garden walls there were fields: large flat treeless East Anglian fields, stretching away towards the fens; on a clear day you could see twenty miles. Natasha's cousins loved this part of the country. Their mother, Anne, also loved it, and painted it constantly. A number of her water colours, pale, bleached, a series of indefinite washes as vague as Anne herself, lined the stairs and had encroached into this attic room.

Natasha looked at the watercolours, as she did the view, with dislike. She did not like Cambridgeshire; it affronted her nature. Were she to choose where she lived she would select a place altogether more turbulent, she thought. Somewhere wild and remote, such as Yorkshire or Scotland—neither of which she had ever visited—or a great city, vibrant with life and excitement. London, for instance. An hour, Natasha said to herself, often; it is only an hour from here to London.

She had an hour to pass before she went back into Cambridge; she could think of no way to pass it tolerably. She did not want to play rock music extremely loud on the hi-fi, because Alexis was out, and so there was no one to be irritated by it. She did not want to tidy her room which looked like a tip. She did not want to help float the punt, or go for a walk, or chop vegetables for Anne. Above all, she did not want to go into Cambridge and see Alexis, but short of being overcome by an obscure and sudden ailment, she could think of no escape. She banged the door of her room; smells

5

of Anne's cooking—wine and garlic—drifted up to the landing.

In the hall the books were invading again. Alexis was going to put up more shelves, had been going to do so for the last three months. But, since the process involved weeks of agonising over catalogues of shelving systems—Alexis was always about to discover the perfect new system—and then days of sawing and hammering punctuated by plaintive cries as Alexis again hammered his thumbs or discovered his walls were mysteriously and unaccountably resistant to assault with drill and rawl-plug, he had, understandably, postponed the attempt. The piles of books outside his study were now waist-high. In this room Alexis conjured brilliance out of chaos—or so people said.

Natasha entered the drawing-room warily. But there was no sign of Anne. William, Anne's youngest son, was lying on his stomach, surrounded by huge sheets of paper covered in hieroglyphics. He was eight. He did not look up when Natasha came in.

'What are you doing?' Natasha said, without much hope, anxious for diversion.

'Re-programming it.' William sighed noisily. 'Alexis should have got an Apple. This thing's antediluvian.'

'Maybe Alexis isn't very up on computers . . .'

William gave her a withering glance. 'Alexis is living in the print era. What can you expect?'

The sun caught his spectacles as he raised his head briefly. Then, bending forward again he returned to his hieroglyphics. There was a silence.

'Maybe Alexis thought you'd want to play those games with it—you know, like Atari,' Natasha said at last.

'Alexis thinks we're all kids. You too. He'll learn,' William said darkly. He bent his head once more. 'There's been a crisis,' he added. 'The cats opened the fridge again and ate all the fish. Then they were sick in the scullery. Anne's going potty. She says you've got to stop off at the fishmongers on your way to Alexis', and buy sixteen trout and they mustn't be gutted.'

'Sixteen?'

'There's thirteen coming, plus you, plus Anne, plus Alexis. You're having *truite meuniere* with some stuffing she found in Elizabeth David, then *coq au vin*, then vanilla soufflé. We're banished upstairs. Julian is going to fry us some sausages.' He pressed a few buttons, and leaned back on his heels. 'Alexis said at breakfast that it would be much appreciated if you could make a sartorial effort.'

'Oh?'

'Wear a dress. Not jeans. Vansittart's coming.'

Natasha turned round sharply. 'Vansittart? Paul Vansittart?'

William cackled. 'The very same. I said that in view of the moony expression on your face last time he was on the box, *and* the fact that you actually bought his last paperback, *and* because you know Alexis can't stand him, that there was a good chance you would make a sartorial effort. Anne thought so too.'

He ducked expertly as Natasha threw a cushion at his head. It missed.

'What did Alexis say then?'

'Nothing. Glowered. Mumbled. Said the milk was off. Said Vansittart's novels were going off. Made a few trenchant remarks about realism and modern fiction. Left in a hurry and reversed the Morris into the garage doors. I told you he thinks you're still a kid.'

'What's that got to do with it?' Natasha stood up, only half-listening, and adjusted her hair experimentally, peering in the old spotted glass that hung above the fireplace.

'Vansittart's a womaniser. A notorious womaniser. I heard Alexis tell Anne. She invited him. Alexis was hopping mad.'

Natasha grinned at her own reflection in the glass.

'You don't even know what that means.'

'Of course I know what it means. I read.' He paused to consult his blueprint. 'I read one of Vansittart's books.'

There was another brief silence. Natasha looked at him suspiciously.

'You oughtn't to read books like that,' she said at last. 'Where did you get it? Alexis would go mad if he knew.'

'From under your bed.'

Natasha gave him a cold glance. 'You're getting horribly precocious,' she said eventually, with dignity. 'Do you know that?'

'I'm not precocious. I'm just clever.' William had already lost interest and had returned to the computer. 'I can't help it. It runs in the family . . .'

'Not my side of it,' Natasha said glumly.

'Well, no,' William said politely. 'But look at it from my

point of view. Uncle Alexis is brilliant. Odd, but brilliant. Aunt Sophie's the country's leading gynaecologist . . . Anne's clever, she just tries to hide it . . . Not that *you're* dim. Just lazy. Alexis thinks you've got potential. I heard him tell Anne.'

'Potential for what?' Natasha looked at him gloomily. 'I suppose he wasn't too specific.'

'Not terribly. Ask him for yourself. When you go in for your wigging this morning.'

'It's not a wigging.'

'What is it then?'

'One of Alexis' Serious Talks.'

William turned back to the computer. 'Just as I said. A wigging. It's in his rooms at college, isn't it? It's bound to be a wigging. He always does them there. It's because it's more impersonal, I think. It makes him fiercer. Ask Julian. He had one when he said he wanted to go to Bedales not Winchester. He said it was *awful*. Terrifying. You wait.'

'Thanks a lot,' said Natasha, making for the door hastily, before William could notice that he was making her nervous.

'Don't forget the fish,' was William's parting shot.

Natasha wheeled her bicycle along King's Parade, in the direction of Trinity Street. The large carrier bag full of trout was slung over the handlebars, and bumped against her legs. She walked because she was early for her appointment with Alexis, and because she wanted to stop and see if any of the bookshops had a copy of Paul Vansittart's latest novel. It was in hardback, of course, but she'd had her dole come through that morning, and so she thought she might risk getting it, even if it left her short.

She paused at the corner, staring at the windows of Bowes and Bowes. Her heart gave a little jump: it was there—the whole window, a huge display, with lots of copies, and a large black and white photograph of Paul Vansittart. Hastily she parked the bicycle and crossed the street. The novel was called *Couplings*; the jacket was scarlet and yellow, with Paul Vansittart's name in larger print than the title.

Natasha glanced at it briefly, then concentrated on the photograph. The author was leaning against a bare brick wall, smoking a cigarette. He was dressed in worn jeans, a labourer's jacket and an old shirt opened sufficiently to give a glimpse of his quite magnificent chest. His hair, black, untidy, and worn long, blew across his forehead. His mouth, full, with a marked downturn at the corners, was unsmiling. And his eyes! They had met the camera lens with a hard questing stare, emphasised by the straight thick lines of the dark brows above them. Natasha, who at Alexis' behest had read *Wuthering Heights* at the age of fourteen and had still not recovered from the experience, felt now as if she stared at Heathcliff's very face. And he was a *writer*.

She sighed, and clasped the carrier bag of fish more tightly. It was such a fierce face—so uncompromising. It was the kind of face you might expect in a loner, a man who pitted himself against the elements in some harsh unwelcoming corner of the world. She hastened into the shop and spent half her week's money on *Couplings* with hardly a twinge of conscience.

She came out into the sunlight feeling suddenly gay, her spirits soared, the gloom and depression of the morning was fled. Why, if this wretched talk with Alexis did not take too long, she could go home and read several chapters before dinner that evening.

She looked at her watch. Nearly twelve. She was still a little early for Alexis, who had a seminar that morning, but the more quickly she saw him, and the more quickly she left, the more she could read. She would be docile with Alexis, she decided, and not argue as she usually did, but simply agree with everything he said. That way the whole thing should be over in half an hour at most.

There was a new porter on the gates at Trinity, and he stopped her.

'Professor Lydiard,' Natasha said, giving him an imperious stare.

The man looked at her stolidly from beneath the brim of his bowler. He consulted a clipboard with elaborate slowness.

'The professor has a seminar.'

Natasha decided to change tactics. She lowered her lashes and gave him her best smile.

'I know. I'm his cousin. He's expecting me.'

The man's manner instantly changed, although whether in response to the smile or her connection with Alexis, Natasha could not be certain. He at once showed indications of deference. Natasha was amused. At home she was so used to Alexis' eccentricities and vagueness, to his being the butt for his large household, that it always surprised her when she came into college and saw the respect and esteem with which he was treated there.

'Oh, I see. My apologies, Miss. His cousin.' The man opened the flap in his counter and came forward. 'If you'd like me to show you the way, Miss . . .'

'Lydiard. And that won't be necessary. I know the way. Thank you.'

He gave her an odd stiff half-bow, and stood back to let her pass. Without a backward glance Natasha hurried across Great Court, vaguely irritated by this encounter. The man had hedged his bets. He had been polite, yet there had been something in his manner which she had not quite liked. Almost as if he'd suspected her of being an impostor. How absurd! Surely there couldn't be that many young women calling on Alexis in college, from whom he needed protection.

She could have told the man that she was Alexis' ward, of course, and once she would have done so. There had been a period, when she was still at boarding school, when she had boasted shamelessly that she had a male guardian. The fact that she was an orphan had already given her a certain status within the school, which Natasha, who could scarcely remember her parents, had played upon. That she also had a guardian, she had quickly discovered, gave her considerable cachet. Then she had mentioned her 'guardian', her cousin, the brilliant and unmarried don at Cambridge at every opportunity. She had invested Alexis, whom in reality she then saw only infrequently and scarcely knew, with a character and a past invented by herself, which was, she had felt, a distinct improvement upon the truth.

Now, however, she used the tags 'guardian' and 'ward' a great deal more circumspectly. She was not a girl anymore, she was a woman. She was twenty-two, so technically she was of age and Alexis was her guardian no longer. Besides, to admit to a guardian threatened the new image Natasha wished to present to the world, that of an energetic, independent, self-determining young woman. She had not chosen to exercise that independence very much as yet, but when she did—and she felt today as if it were very close that moment—then she wanted no hindrance from Alexis, who irritatingly, and as William had observed, blithely continued to treat her as if she were a child. So, now, she relegated Alexis' role in her past life, and spoke of it to outsiders only rarely. There were advantages to having no parental overseers, she had discovered that already, and she had no intention of allowing Alexis to assume any longer the role of father figure in her life. An orphan, she said to herself a little smugly, as she crossed through into eighteenth century New Court. A young woman free, and without family ties.

She was so deep in thought that she almost collided with the two young women carrying their gowns over their arms, who were coming down the stairs from Alexis' rooms. One was small, dumpy and bespectacled, the other tall, slender, blonde and beautiful. The blonde was in apparent distress.

'Tore it to shreds,' she was saying. 'And I stayed up three nights writing that paper. Isn't he amazing?'

'At least he noticed you,' the other replied comfortingly. 'He just looks straight through me . . .'

'But he thinks I'm a fool . . .'

'He thinks all women are fools. Don't let it worry you.'

'I suppose I could ask for some extra time with him. Say I needed help on the metaphysicals. I'm okay for the novel paper. I think.'

The dumpy young woman laughed.

'Try,' she said. 'Why not? It's been done before.'

'It has?' The blonde looked mournful.

'Sure. Didn't I tell you about Belinda? Well, last Michaelmas term she . . .'

Natasha turned as they passed out of earshot. They were talking about Alexis, that much was certain, and she felt a passing irritation that she would never learn Belinda's fate.

Alexis' outer door was opened, which meant he could be disturbed, and she rapped loudly on the inner door, and then paused. Unaccountably, her earlier nervousness returned, and re-doubled. It was years since she had been summoned here to college, and she hoped fervently that Alexis would not be too stern. At home, she felt, she could have dealt with him. But here . . .

'Come . . .' Alexis' voice was muffled; she opened the door.

The room was empty. The windows overlooking the river and the Backs were thrown open and sunlight streamed in. Natasha paused, looking around her curiously. She had forgotten how beautiful these rooms were, how peaceful. Alexis' voice, still muffled, came from the room beyond, where there was a bedroom—used on the occasions when he wished to stay in college.

'I'm just changing. Is that Natasha? I won't be a moment . . .'

Natasha looked round furtively for somewhere to dump the

fish. She did not want the bag to attract Alexis' attention, on the other hand she mustn't forget it. Where was Alexis likely to sit? It had been behind his desk on the last occasion, so somewhere at the other end of the room perhaps ... She peered around her. All four walls were lined from floor to ceiling with books, there were no cupboards. In front of the fireplace were two large velvet sofas, and a number of deep armchairs—presumably the place where he conducted his seminars. They ringed a large square table piled deep with papers, books and typescripts, and heavily ringed with ancient coffee mug stains. Nowhere there. But beyond the sofas, in the corner by the fireplace the books had overflowed on to the floor; moving quickly Natasha dumped the carrier bag of fish behind the books, and moved hastily back to the fireplace. It was surmounted by a large oil painting of Alexis' Russian great-grandmother, who was of course her great-grandmother too, who had bequeathed her descendants the tradition of Russian names, and in her case, Natasha hoped, her looks. She had been a famous beauty, born in St Petersburg.

Natasha peered at the painting. Her great-grandmother's hair was up, she observed, and she had chosen to wear a dress of deep blue satin for her portrait, which emphasised the startling blue of her eyes, a colour charmingly at odds with the darkness of her hair. Natasha leaned closer. Her own eyes were blue, and she had a blue dress at home—cotton not satin. But still ... Her gaze fell to the mantel. It was dusty, and supported a toothmug filled with cow parsley, an opened book of poems, and a great many impressive-looking invitation cards. Natasha flicked them over curiously: her cousin seemed much in demand, though as far as she knew he rarely accepted the invitations he received. Her eyes fell to the opened book; she read:

I wonder by my troth, what thou, and I
Did, till we lov'd? Were we not weaned till then ...

'Natasha.'
She started guiltily, and turned round. Her eyes widened.
Alexis stood before her, most curiously transformed and wearing an extraordinary garment. It was a sweater, of sorts, a hand-knitted one, dark green. Something had gone badly wrong with its sizing. Large and very loose, it hung on his tall frame as far as his thighs. The sleeves were as inadequate as the rest of it was ample. They stopped short of Alexis' wrists

by four inches and were badly stretched to accommodate his wide and powerful shoulders. It had a polo-neck collar which was clearly too tight, and above it Alexis' face, unspectacled, appeared distressed. Natasha began to laugh.

'My glasses,' Alexis said, with dignity and urgency. 'Where the hell did I put my glasses?'

'Alexis!' Natasha made an attempt to smother her laughter. 'What on earth are you wearing?'

'It's a present.' Alexis regarded her shortsightedly and mournfully. 'From one of my post-graduates. She knitted it for me as a surprise and guessed all the measurements. The neck is so tight it nearly strangled me getting it on ...'

'Perhaps that was her intention,' Natasha said drily. Alexis appeared injured by this suggestion.

'I hope not. I don't think so.' He paused. 'She said it matched the colour of my eyes.'

'She did?' Natasha looked at him more closely. It was true that he did have the most extraordinary eyes, although normally she never noticed them behind his spectacles. She had always vaguely thought that they were hazel. Now, looking at him more closely she saw that the student had been right; they were a clear dark green, like emeralds. And they were now regarding her coldly.

'So, if you've finished laughing at me, perhaps you could help me find the glasses. I think they must be in my bedroom ...'

'Okay, okay. I'll look—hang on ...'

She darted across the room and into the bedroom beyond, pausing for a moment on the threshold. She had never been in this room before, and it surprised her. It was both beautiful and tidy; it was very plain. The walls were panelled, and hung with some of Alexis' collection of eighteenth century watercolours. By the bed was a table piled with the inevitable books, on top of which were the missing spectacles. But the bed ... Natasha stared. It was a double bed, and placed neatly beside it on the floor was a pair of women's high heeled shoes. She stared open-mouthed, since it had never occurred to her before that Alexis might have other reasons than work for the nights he chose to spend in college. Then, with a grin, she quickly bent and picked up one of the shoes. What a God-given opportunity! If she could embarrass Alexis sufficiently she might escape the Serious Talk altogether. She went back into the next room, the shoe in one hand, the spectacles in the other.

'Is this yours, Alexis?' She managed to keep her voice quite serious.

'Is what mine?' Alexis peered in the general direction of the bedroom door. Natasha advanced upon him.

'This shoe. The other's in your bedroom . . .'

Alexis bent over the shoe and then straightened up.

'I don't think so, do you? It would hardly fit, even if I had transvestite tendencies, and I haven't.'

'Then whose is it?'

'One of my student's, I should imagine.' To Natasha's irritation he appeared totally unembarrassed.

'The same one that knitted that sweater?'

'Since you ask, the very same. She needed somewhere to change and didn't want to go back to Girton, so I said she could borrow my room. I expect her other things are in the wardrobe. You can look if you like. Now, do you think you could give me my glasses?'

Somewhat sulkily Natasha handed them over. She knew that her temporary advantage would vanish, frail as it was, the second Alexis could see properly again, and she was right. Once the spectacles were on, Alexis' eyes focused on her face with a cold alertness that did not bode well. Natasha felt her nerve quail. Without another word she returned the shoe to the bedroom, and came back. Alexis watched her, and Natasha felt awkward. She folded her hands together and regarded him meekly, her earlier idea returning to her. Obedience, compliance, and the quicker they got this over the better.

'Sit down,' he said abruptly, gesturing to one of the sofas. Natasha sat.

Alexis hesitated, and then finally sat down opposite her.

'I've ordered lunch,' he said. 'It should be up in a minute.'

'Lunch?' Natasha could not prevent the dismay from creeping into her voice.

'Yes, lunch. This may take some time. I thought we might eat while we talked. Unless you have some other pressing engagement.'

'Oh, no. Nothing. Not at all. That is . . .'

'Good.' Alexis was now fully in command. He leaned back lazily, his arms behind his head, and stretched his longs legs out before him. Natasha looked at him resentfully. This was probably how he looked when he conducted a seminar, she thought: when he tore someone's work to shreds. A passing sympathy for the blonde girl lit in her heart. He paused, and Natasha looked at him under her lashes. She was used to Alexis' odd and abrupt silences, which at least gave one time to gather one's wits, and it gave her a chance to look at him.

If he hadn't been her cousin, if she hadn't known him so long, she supposed she too might have thought him handsome. His face betrayed his cleverness, though also his tendency to arrogance. It was narrow, tanned, he looked younger than his years. How old *was* Alexis? She couldn't even remember. She had always thought of him as middle-aged, although when he first became her guardian he could only have been in his twenties. Now he was, what? Thirty-five? No, younger, surely. Anne was thirty-four, and he was a year younger, that was right.

He resembled Anne very little, one would never have taken them for brother and sister. Where Anne was small and beginning to be plump, her brother was tall and rangy, his athleticism proclaimed by his build. His face was less gentle than his sister's, his movements quicker, more impatient. Though Alexis too could look dreamy and distracted, just as Anne often did. But whereas Anne was usually thinking about her painting or her children on such occasions, it was unwise to assume Alexis was abstracted when he looked vague. All too often it meant he was about to pounce on some ill-considered statement, some action Natasha hoped had escaped his notice. He looked vague now; she tensed.

'It's time we had a serious talk,' he said suddenly.

It was on the top of Natasha's tongue to tell him not to sound so Victorian when she remembered her resolve to eat humble pie. She sighed and lowered her gaze. She knew what was coming. Why didn't she find a proper job? How long did she intend to stay on the dole? Why didn't she sit her exams again?

Alexis stood up abruptly and turned his back to her.

'What I should like to know is,' he began, 'are you intending to get married?'

CHAPTER TWO

NATASHA stared at Alexis' back in stupefied astonishment. When he received no answer he turned, and to Natasha's surprise she saw that dark colour stained his cheekbones. Alexis was embarrassed!

'Well?'

'No.'

'Is that all you have to say?'

Natasha glared at him resentfully. 'Yes, it is. Why do you ask?'

Alexis sat down again and regarded her coldly.

'I ask because I have been racking my brains to try and think of an explanation for your behaviour. It was the only one I could find. After all, you're not stupid, you're not lazy. I don't think you're unambitious. So. Unless you have decided to devote the rest of your life to the needs of some member of the opposite sex, unless you have decided to dwindle into a wife, I find your behaviour inexplicable.'

'Dwindle into a wife? That's an odd phrase, isn't it? Some people might think quite the opposite. They might think you could aspire to being a wife . . .'

Alexis cut her off with a wave of the hand. 'It's a quotation. Never mind that now. And don't try and divert the discussion into a generalised one about women and marriage. I know your tactics of old.' His green eyes glinted at her, and Natasha swallowed nervously. He paused. 'Did you sign on this morning?'

Natasha nodded.

'And how long is it since you worked?'

'Three months.' She hesitated. 'Well, nearly four.' She leaned forward pleadingly. 'Honestly, Alexis, I have tried, really I have! But you know what my typing's like, and all the stupid jobs are for secretaries, and I never wanted to be a secretary anyway, you know that. I . . .'

'I'm perfectly well aware of that. I never suggested you should be a secretary. If you remember, I suggested that you stay on at school, sit your exams again, and take university entrance.'

16

Natasha opened her mouth and then shut it again. With difficulty she suppressed the desire to argue.

'Yes, Alexis,' she said at last. 'I know you did. You were probably right . . .'

Alexis was warming to his theme, however, and her unusual meekness failed to register. He ran both his hands through his hair, a habitual sign of agitation with him. The hair stood up in little spikes; Natasha looked away.

'It was pure perversity on your part, failing those exams in the first place. You set out to mess them up because you were terrified that if you did your best it might not prove good enough. You couldn't bear to be compared with the rest of the family, so instead you failed dramatically. That got you off the hook . . .'

'Goodness! Maybe you're right, Alexis. I never thought of that . . .'

'And since then, what have you done? You've spent the last three and a half years drifting aimlessly, complaining about the jobs you're offered, and making no effort whatsoever to acquire proper qualifications. You say you want to write, yet you don't even answer letters, let alone attempt anything else. It's feeble, defeatist behaviour, and since you're neither feeble nor defeatist, I can only assume you must have some other plan at the back of your head.' He looked at her suspiciously. 'You say it's not marriage. So, what is it?'

'Well,' she stalled. 'I have various ideas, Alexis, but they need firming up a bit. And you might not like them of course . . .'

'Try me.' Alexis folded his arms.

Natasha had a strong suspicion he knew perfectly well that she had virtually no ideas for her future at all, and foresaw trouble. Alexis was not tolerant of others' indecision.

'Suppose they—my ideas—suppose they involved my leaving Cambridge? Going somewhere else . . .'

'Going somewhere else?' Alexis looked genuinely astonished. He stood up, picked up a book, put it down again, and then began to pace up and down the room. 'What on earth would you want to do that for?'

Natasha stood up quickly.

'Oh Alexis,' she said quickly, keeping her voice low. 'Don't grill me, please. I know it must seem weak and stupid to you, and I am trying to sort myself out, really I am. But I just don't feel I can talk about it now, do you see? If you could give me a little more time, not much longer, a week or so. I want to get my ideas into shape you see, because otherwise I know you'll just tear them to shreds and . . .'

'Tear them to shreds?' Alexis came to an abrupt halt in his pacing. He looked hurt. 'I hope I wouldn't do that. I wouldn't mean to do that . . .'

Natasha looked at the ground. She had discovered years before, at school, that if she focused her eyes with intense concentration on one spot in front of her and thought fixedly of the pain of life in general and the unhappiness of her own lot in particular, she could cry with surprising ease. To her relief, the device was working yet again; she lifted her eyes slowly to Alexis' face, confident in the knowledge that they brimmed decoratively with tears.

'Oh, Alexis,' she said softly.

Alexis stared. He shifted his weight awkwardly from one foot to another.

'Natasha.'

Somewhat to her surprise he came and sat down beside her on the sofa, and with extreme tentativeness, put an arm around her shoulders.

They sat like that, stiffly side by side, for some moments while Alexis stared into space. Then he removed his arm.

'You mustn't cry,' he said finally. 'I don't want you to be unhappy.'

For some extraordinary reason, the unexpected kindness of his tone acted as a trigger upon Natasha's feelings. Now she burst into genuine tears, flung herself with abandon into Alexis' arms, and wept against the prickly green wool sweater. He took it surprisingly well. He put his arm around her again and made generalised soothing noises and eventually produced a crumpled white handkerchief so Natasha could wipe her eyes. She sobbed a little longer, and finally stopped. Alexis smiled at her kindly.

'There!' he said. 'I'm sorry. We won't discuss it anymore just now. I hadn't realised you were so . . .' he hesitated. 'Overwrought.'

'Neither had I,' said Natasha.

There was a knock at the door, and Alexis removed his encircling arm and leapt to his feet.

'Ah,' he said. 'Lunch.'

The old college servant was carrying an enormous butler's tray. With considerable ceremony, he set it up and began to remove large silver lids from a great many dishes. Natasha looked at them with dismay. They looked delicious—the Trinity kitchens were justly famous for the meals they provided for dons, and equally infamous for those they produced for undergraduates. Natasha was now hungry, and crying had increased her appetite, but it did not look as if it would be a quick lunch.

When the servant withdrew she looked at Alexis.

'I don't feel terribly hungry, Alexis,' she began.

'Nonsense,' he said brusquely. 'You don't eat enough. You're looking thin. I ordered this specially. It's years since we had lunch together.'

Clearly there was to be no escape, so Natasha resigned herself to eating. Alexis produced a bottle of excellent claret, they balanced their plates on their knees, and after a while Natasha forgot about the time and began to enjoy herself.

When she had finished every scrap of a superb *boeuf bourguignon*, and spooned up the last of the *crème brûlée* with its delicious crunchy caramel top, she sighed and leaned back comfortably.

'What a feast! Do they always feed you as well at high table, Alexis?'

'Better, sometimes.' He regarded her with amusement.

'I wonder you ever come home then.' She looked at him teasingly under her lashes. 'After all, what could be a better life for a confirmed bachelor like you? Wonderful rooms, servants to take care of everything. Superb food. One of the best cellars in Europe. Witty, erudite conversation on all sides . . .'

'It's obvious you've never dined at high table. There's remarkably little wit, and the erudition is generally confined to mutterings into the soup. Besides.' He paused. 'I'm not a confirmed bachelor. Whatever makes you think so?'

Natasha smiled. 'You, of course. You treat women so oddly. Half the time you never even notice they're there, and if you do, you look at them as if they were an exotic insect. Of course, I realise you don't *need* a wife, in the way some men do. I mean you don't need a household slave, do you? You can always come into college and at home there's Anne and I, fluttering around, looking after your every need, cooking for you and washing your socks and . . .'

'What a shamefully inexact description.' Alexis looked cheerful. He always enjoyed an argument, no matter how trivial. 'In the first place, neither you nor Anne is given to fluttering, thank God, and in the second you've never had to wash my socks. I do it myself. And my shirts. Then I hang them on wire-hangers over the bath and . . .'

'Don't try and dodge the issue,' Natasha looked at him sternly. 'You know exactly what I mean. And besides, the main point is you have absolutely no . . .' She broke off. She had been about to say 'sex drive', but she knew Alexis would be deeply offended by the vulgarism. She had also just remembered the shoes on Alexis' bedroom floor. It occurred to her for the first time in her life that she had possibly misjudged Alexis in this respect. Maybe he led a secret life? She regarded him with new interest.

'Absolutely no what?' Alexis prompted. There was a steely glint in his eyes which made Natasha think he knew perfectly well what she had intended to say.

'Absolutely no interest in women,' she finished lamely. Alexis sighed. 'You . . . you live like a monk.'

'I do?' Alexis was looking at her fixedly.

'Yes, you do.' There was a dangerous little silence. Natasha spread her hands; better not to back down now, it was too late.

'Well,' she said defiantly, 'what do you say to that?'

Alexis rose to his feet. He was very tall and now towered over her. He looked down into her upturned face.

'I say you don't know me very well,' he said. He paused, and removed his spectacles. 'I also say that, with respect, you are a young and inexperienced girl and you should mind your own business. Now.' He lifted his arms over his head. 'Perhaps you would be so good as to help me off with this ridiculous sweater, which I shall take to Oxfam this afternoon, and then you should go home. You have your bicycle?'

Natasha decided to ignore the slight. She rose to her feet, and, giggling, began to help Alexis remove the offending sweater. It was extremely difficult. It traversed his chest easily enough, then stuck at the shoulders.

'Bend forward a bit, I'll have to sort of ease it off.' Natasha slipped her hand under the wool. Through the thin cotton shirt he was wearing, she could feel the warmth of Alexis' skin. It felt extraordinarily pleasant. She sighed. She was beginning to feel somnolent, lassitude crept through her own limbs. It must be the after-effects of the claret, she thought. Alexis twitched.

'Get on with it . . .'

Obediently Natasha began to push and pull at the shoulders; they remained obstinately stuck.

'Honestly, Alexis, it won't budge. I think you're in it for life. It's your shoulders—they're so muscley. How did they get like that? Is it the cricket?'

Alexis flexed irritably.

'No, not especially. It's the way God made me. Get on with it, woman, for heaven's sake. This is getting damned uncomfortable. The wool's prickly . . .'

'Hang on. . . . Bend forward a bit more, that's it . . .'

Natasha slid her hands around Alexis' chest, and began to pull from the front. She could feel his heart thudding under her hands. A look of angry exasperation masked his features.

'Maybe you're not so fit,' she said unsympathetically, giving the sweater a vicious tug. 'Your heart's beating like mad. Surely it shouldn't do that?'

'Just pay attention to what you're doing. It's probably a metabolic condition. It always beats like that. Pull!'

'Honestly! You are ignorant, Alexis. You should stick to the modern novel. Your metabolism has nothing whatever to do with your heart-rate. . . Just relax. Stop fighting me. . . There!'

With a final hefty pull she managed to extricate Alexis' arms. He stood, looking at her forlornly, the sweater now gathered in folds around his neck.

'Nearly there—just the last bit . . .'

'Christ! Mind my ears . . .'

'Relax! Your hair's too thick. Keep *still* . . .'

As gently as she could she reached up her arms, encircled his neck, and from underneath the wool began to ease the sweater upwards. She had to stand on tiptoe to do it, and she swayed against him. Alexis put out an arm to steady her and gave a muffled groan from the depths of the wool. Very carefully, her hands pressed to either side of his face, Natasha worked the sweater upwards and off. As it freed him, Alexis caught it deftly and then let it fall to the floor. They were standing very close, Natasha still with her arms upraised, he with one arm around her waist. There was a moment's silence. Alexis' ears were very red, and Natasha expected agonised complaints. None came.

The sun beat into the room; her eyes met those of Alexis. The silence lengthened, then Alexis stepped back, bent and picked up the sweater.

'Thank you very much.'

'I'd better go now.'

'Fine.'

They looked at each other, then, remembering the fish, Natasha turned away. She picked up the carrier bag.

'Anne's fish. For tonight.' She indicated the bag.

'What an odd place to put it.'

'Yes, well, I thought it was out of the sun.'

'Of course.'

'Goodbye then, Alexis.' She hesitated in the doorway. 'Are you really going to take that sweater to Oxfam?'

Alexis looked down at the sweater as if he had forgotten its existence.

'The sweater? I was going to, yes.'

'You'll hurt your student's feelings.'

Alexis shrugged. 'Too bad. And she's not my student. Not in the vulgar manner you seem to be implying.'

'Goodness, Alexis, you can be ruthless,' Natasha said, and skipped smartly out of the room. The somnolence had passed, the evening lay ahead. She felt extraordinarily re-vivified.

Anne and William were seated at the long deal table in the kitchen. Anne was peeling tiny onions at one end of it, so her eyes ran, and William was chopping up angelica and arranging crystallised violets at the other. From the Aga stove delicious smells drifted; Anne was an excellent cook.

'If you eat any more of those violets, William,' she said companionably after a lengthy silence, 'there will be none to put on the top of the soufflé. And I'm sure they rot your teeth.'

'Sorry.' Abstractedly William put another into his mouth.

'Natasha's a long time.'

'Yes, well, Alexis thought she needed a Serious Talk.'

William chopped reflectively. He was extremely fond of Natasha. For a girl she was not bad. No good on computers of course, too old, but not bad.

'Do you think she'll leave?' he said eventually.

Anne raised her head briefly from the onions, and gave him a vague look.

'Leave? Leave where? Well, I suppose she might do. She doesn't like Cambridge very much. Naturally, at her age, she must want to see the world a bit. London, for instance. I think she'd like to go to London. I can't think why. I think it's a horrid place. But no doubt Natasha would see it differently.'

'Would you mind if she went?'

'Mind?' Anne laid down her knife and considered. William waited patiently. 'Yes, I suppose I should miss her. But she'd come back, wouldn't she—for weekends, and so on.'

'Would Alexis miss her?'

'Alexis?' Anne came as near as she ever did to registering surprise. 'I suppose he might. On the other hand, he might not notice very much. One never knows with Alexis. He wouldn't want to stand in her way, I'm sure, so if she'd set her heart on it he wouldn't oppose her, of course.' She sighed and returned to the onions. 'Although with Alexis it's so difficult to predict. I'm his sister and I never know what he's thinking.'

'I do,' said William.

'Do you, darling? How clever of you. If you've finished the angelica, would you like to go and pick me some parsley? I need it for the fish.'

William stood up.

'I'll pick the parsley,' he said. 'In a minute. I might just tidy all that computer stuff up first.'

Anne raised her face fondly.

'Oh, thank you darling. I ought to straighten that room up a bit, but Mrs Hodge dusted it yesterday so I expect it looks all right. I think if they eat well no one will mind a bit of a muddle, will they? But they might trip over the computer, so . . .'

Her voice trailed away. She began to hum contentedly.

William mooched out to the drawing room, put away the computer, and surveyed the room gloomily. It was a mess. When he was grown up, he thought, he would live in a super-efficient module, like a space capsule, with everything made of stainless steel. The untidiness of his home, famous for its air of pleasant chaos, depressed him. It also depressed him that Anne thought Natasha might leave. He took a proprietorial interest in Natasha, whom he regarded as a sister, and he liked her to be there. Probably she didn't even realise that anyone cared either way, he thought crossly. Everyone in this household was so vague and so endlessly accommodating of everyone else and their vagaries, that you could be gone six months before anyone else really noticed.

Absently he climbed the stairs to the top floor and looked into Natasha's room. He wrinkled his nose with distaste. God, what a horrible mess! Records and clothes and make-up everywhere, the bed not made. He pulled the duvet back into place and sat down.

Of course, one of the things that stopped people leaving was getting married. 'Settling down', as Mrs Hodge called it. William had a deep interest in the members of Mrs Hodge's large family, none of whom he had ever met; Mrs Hodge liked to pause in her dusting or Hoovering and light a cigarette and tell him all about them. Mrs Hodge had a daughter, Tracy, who was, Mrs Hodge said, a bit of a goer. William wasn't sure what that entailed, but gathered it meant Tracy liked going to parties and having holidays in Corfu. Tracy had been all set to go out to Canada. Then, lo and behold, Tracy had met a very nice boy, and got engaged, and any minute now was going to get married in a white satin frock and a pearl-drop headdress and settle down two streets away. William thought Natasha would look very beautiful in a white frock and a pearl-drop headdress. If such things could make Tracy forget about going off to Canada, why shouldn't they have the same effect upon Natasha?

The difficulty was finding the right marital candidate for Natasha. William had a highly developed critical sense where grown-ups were concerned, and clearly not just anyone would do. They had to be suitable, they had to be around and likely to remain around, and they had—presumably—to have the right inclinations. This idea, which had been at the back of William's mind for some months, had recently been sharpened by certain observations of his own, and he was almost certain that he might have the perfect candidate. All that remained was for this candidate to make a move.

Thoughtfully he reached under Natasha's bed and drew out the pile of magazines she kept there. There was one *Vogue*—it had a picture of Paul Vansittart in it—and a larger collection of magazines aimed at a more youthful readership. William had settled down to scan them contentedly when one particular item attracted his attention. It was the agony page. A picture of a forceful young woman who looked as if she had never experienced any agonies whatsoever adorned the top of it. She was called Gloria Chatham, and she was answering a letter from Miss M.W. of Bromley, Kent, who had just experienced the pangs of jealousy for the first time and was worried about it.

'Do not fret,' ran Gloria Chatham's soothing italicised

reply. 'This is quite natural. We all go through it, believe me! Just remember, jealousy can be a catalyst. It can be useful! Of course, taken to extremes it can be a very destructive emotion—we must all beware of the little green god. But to look at the problem positively, it can also be a help. Sometimes jealousy can clarify our feelings. Maybe we hadn't realised before just how much we cared. Maybe we'd been taking the person we loved for granted. Maybe we hadn't even realised how much we loved them! It can happen! That's where jealousy comes in. We're hurt. We realise how much we care. Believe me, Miss M.W. . . .'

Slowly William put down the magazine. He thought for a while. Then, replacing the pile carefully first, he went downstairs to look up 'catalyst' in the *Oxford English Dictionary*.

CHAPTER THREE

THE Lydiard house had—and this was typical of Alexis—been bought in a hurry. When Anne's husband had died, suddenly, leaving her with very little money, and two sons to support, Alexis had insisted at once that they should set up home together, with Natasha—who had previously spent most of her holidays either with Anne or with Sophie—joining them to make the new Lydiard house her permanent home. Faced with the problem of finding a house for three children and two adults, Alexis, who had previously lived in college, had bought the first place he saw, which belonged to a friend of his who was in need of money and anxious for a quick sale. He paid, inevitably, too much for it; the friend promptly disappeared to America, leaving Alexis to cope with a house which proved, on closer examination, to have numerous disadvantages. It was leaky, it was draughty, the plumbing made noises in the night, and the lights constantly fused.

In the seven years they had lived there the house had, undoubtedly, improved. It remained impractical, but it had acquired charm; it was a house in which people instantly relaxed, and generally enjoyed themselves. It was not, however, in spite of its size, a house which facilitated privacy, which Natasha minded very much. The bathroom, cold, draughty, unmodernised, and with an insecure lock, was the bane of her existence. For Natasha, who liked rituals, liked—if she had an important date—to prepare for it at length.

That night, she planned her campaign carefully. She got to the bathroom first, so she had prior claim, before Anne, before Alexis, and above all before her two younger cousins. As usual, she attempted to bolt the door, and as usual, failed. She switched on her transistor radio full blast, so no one could be in any doubt as to her occupation of the room, and then ran off the entire evening's supply of hot water. Into the water she poured a lot of sticky bath oil, which smelled pungent and left a ring round the bath, then she mixed some henna powder and applied it to her long dark hair. She had never used henna before, but looked forward to the mahogany highlights promised by the packet. The mixture,

26

when finished, was gritty, greenish, and distinctly smelly—it reminded her of a compost heap. But she was not easily discouraged, and rubbed it into her hair energetically. Then she leapt into the bath, leaned back luxuriantly, propped her copy of *Couplings* on the soap tray and prepared to read. She stayed there quite a long time, her eyes growing rounder and wider as she read on, the bath water cooling. Once or twice the handle of the door was rattled, and Natasha shouted, 'Go *away*,' and whoever it was did.

Finally, having read three chapters, she set down the book, scrubbed herself energetically, rinsed her hair—which was difficult, the gritty henna stuck—and jumped out of the bath. She dried herself, stuffed the clothes she had been wearing into the overflowing laundry basket, and then realised she had entered the bathroom without her dressing gown.

She hesitated; then she turned off the radio and listened. Not a sound, the coast was clear. If she made a dash for it, wrapped in a towel, she reckoned she could just make it to her bedroom without encountering a chorus of mocking young male cousins. She had just managed to tie a skimpy towel fairly decorously round her middle, and had picked up her copy of *Couplings* when the door was thrown back.

'At last . . .' said a harassed male voice. 'My damned shaving things are . . .'

The voice broke off; Alexis, framed in the doorway, came to a dead halt. He stared at Natasha and she stared at him. Neither spoke. Alexis went crimson. He stood for a moment, as if paralysed, and then, muttering wild and incoherent apologies, withdrew abruptly.

Natasha counted ten for safety, then fled back down the empty corridor to her room. There, with shaking hands, she began the long and complicated procedure of making up her face. She could not concentrate; the encounter with Alexis had left her shaken; even as she recalled it she saw herself blush to the roots of her hair. Yet it was not just embarrassment she felt, but something more.

She stared at her reflection uncertainly. Alexis had never even seen her in a swimming costume; he had just confronted her, stark naked, well, nearly naked, for the towel was very small, and his reaction had simply been—embarrassment. Was she so unattractive? Surely, most men in such circumstances would have behaved differently? She wasn't at all sure how she would have preferred Alexis to have behaved, but she felt obscurely injured, slighted. She swabbed sadly at her eye-shadow and began to apply it with a shaking hand to her eyelids. Damn Alexis, she thought, as she applied blusher to her cheeks; she wished he would notice she was a woman, not a child.

Along the corridor, having retrieved his shaving things, which had been borrowed by Julian who believed, mistakenly but hopefully, that he now had a beard, Alexis was attempting to shave at the wash basin in his room. His hand was unsteady; he cut himself and swore. Fumbling for cotton wool, and putting his spectacles back on in order to find it, he observed that his youngest nephew, William, had come into the room and was sitting composedly on his bed watching this performance. Alexis glowered at him.

'Out,' he said tersely.

William did not budge. 'I knocked,' he said, in a reasonable tone. 'I thought you might feel like a little chat. I haven't seen you since breakfast.'

Alexis raised his eyes to the heavens. 'This is my room,' he said. 'It is supposed to be my room. I am in it because there is no hot water, so I cannot bathe. I am attempting to shave and wash. Then I shall change. I do not want a little chat. Go away.'

William crossed his legs comfortably. 'What are you going to wear tonight?' he remarked conversationally.

Alexis stared at him. 'Wear? Tonight? Clothes, I suppose. Why?'

'Which clothes?' William persisted. 'Not that awful old tweed jacket, I hope.' He indicated a jacket laid out on the bed. 'I think you ought to wear those black trousers and that black cotton sweater Anne gave you last Christmas. The one with the polo-neck. You look terrific in that, I heard Natasha say so.'

Alexis hesitated. 'I don't think I could face another polo-neck today,' he said. William trotted over to the chest of drawers, rummaged around, and then laid the sweater in question on the bed.

Alexis shrugged. 'Oh well, I suppose I might as well,' he said. 'It might please Anne.' He glanced at William suspiciously. 'What are you playing at? What's made you decide to act the valet?'

When William didn't reply, Alexis returned to his shaving. William was watching him with an intent gaze.

'How's the computer?' Alexis asked at last, because William was clearly immovable.

'All right.' William sighed. 'I was trying to re-programme it, but Natasha kept interrupting. She was in and out all morning. Rabbiting away about that awful writer—the one who's coming to dinner. What's his name? Paul Vansittart, that's it. It nearly drove me mad. If you ask me she's potty about him. Absolutely potty.'

'Don't be ridiculous.' Alexis' voice was crisp. 'She's never even met the man . . .'

'*That* doesn't make any difference,' William said scornfully. 'I told you, she saw him on the box. Every time he's on, she watches it. *And* she's read all his books. She's got a picture of him too, stuck on the inside of her wardrobe door . . .'

'Calf-love.' Alexis snorted. 'A typical teenage crush . . .'

'Natasha's not a teenager. She's a woman.' William paused to let that one sink in. When he judged it had he decided to press on. In the circumstances, he thought he might risk the lie direct.

'She says she had a sort of presentiment about him. You know, that they were going to meet. As if it was inevitable. Fated. In the stars.' William gestured vaguely in the direction of the window. 'When she heard he was coming tonight, she said her heart . . .'

'William. Go away. Now. This minute. I am not interested in Natasha's idiocies, or your indiscretions. Go away.'

Alexis' eyes glinted. William withdrew to the comparative safety of the doorway.

'You will wear that sweater, won't you, Alexis?' he said anxiously.

'Go away!' Alexis roared. William went away.

He went downstairs, and there he discovered that the gods were with him. The guests had been vaguely invited for seven-thirty. Most of them, familiar with the Lydiard household, had interpreted this as meaning eight; Paul Vansittart, who had not been to the house before, had not. As William came downstairs he saw Anne, still in her apron, wandering back and forth in the drawing-room, talking wildly about the weather, and a tall, dark extremely handsome man, standing in the room smoking a cigarette and looking awkward. Anne, spying William, seized him with relief.

'Ah darling. I wonder if you could look after Paul for a moment. I must just . . . that is, I won't be a . . .' She disappeared.

William approached Paul Vansittart in a man-to-man manner and held out his hand.

'Good evening,' he said politely. 'I'm William. Anne is my mother. Alexis is my uncle. You must be Paul Vansittart, the famous novelist. How do you do?'

'How do you do?' The famous novelist took his hand warily.

Anne's head reappeared round the door.

'I expect you'd like some . . . wine or something,' she said. 'William, will you . . .' She disappeared again.

'Whisky,' said Paul Vansittart firmly. 'With water.'

William poured out an extremely stiff measure, added a small quantity of water and handed it over. Paul Vansittart lit another cigarette and sat down on the sofa. William sat down opposite him and regarded him intently. The novelist took a large swallow from his glass and did not even splutter. William was grudgingly impressed. He decided to come straight to the point.

'You'll be meeting my cousin, Natasha, tonight. She admires your books very much.'

'I'm flattered to hear it.'

'Of course, she's not supposed to read them. Alexis would be furious if he knew.' William paused. There was a flicker of response from the watchful face across the room.

'How old is your cousin?'

'Twenty-two. Just,' said William. 'But she's led a very cloistered life. She's just beginning to rebel.'

'Is she now?'

'I expect that's why she likes your books, don't you think?' William put his hand behind his back and crossed his fingers. 'Because there's such a powerful sense of rebellion in them.'

'Yes, well.' Paul Vansittart smiled for the first time. 'I am a bit of a rebel, I suppose. I had to make it the hard way. I grew up in the north. No money. My mother couldn't afford to send me to university, so I had to be a wage-earner. I expect that's difficult for you to understand. I had to fight to get published at all. I wasn't born into the literary establishment . . .'

'Alexis reviews novels for the Sunday papers,' said William innocently.

'So I've observed.'

'He's never reviewed your novels though.'

'I wouldn't know. I never bother with the notices.'

•

'Natasha would like to escape from all that academic stuff.' William paused. 'She hates it. She'd like to break out. But Alexis is very protective, and when you're that young and beautiful . . .'

'Twenty-two's not that young now. I know girls younger than that who've been through a husband, had kids. As a matter of fact, I find myself drawn to the female consciousness. You won't have read my novels of course, but in *Heartblows*—that was my second book by the way—I spent a lot of time with women from one of those refuges for battered wives. In Stepney. Now some of those women—once they'd learned to trust me, of course, which took a bit of time . . .'

He was warming to his theme, and William who had experience of talking to novelists, recognised the warning signs. But luckily at that moment Natasha came into the room. Even William could see that she looked amazingly beautiful. Paul Vansittart rose to his feet with alacrity; his eyes raked Natasha from her slender legs to her delicate face. Natasha's eyes were shining; her hands trembled a little. William knew when to exit.

'This is my cousin, Natasha,' he said, and backed out of the room. From the nursery kitchen upstairs he could smell the welcome scent of sausages frying. He went up to supper, confident that his work that day had been done, and done well.

Paul Vansittart advanced across the room to Natasha. He took her hand between his, raised it in the direction of his lips, but was not so unsubtle as to kiss it. His eyes met hers.

'Natasha,' he said. 'I feel as if I know you already. Your cousin William's been telling me all about you . . .' He released her hand. 'What an extraordinary little boy.'

'Er, yes,' said Natasha guardedly, wondering what the hell William might have been saying, and observing that, close to, Paul Vansittart's eyes were, like Heathcliff's, black.

'Let me get you a drink.' Paul Vansittart moved in the direction of the cupboard. 'You'll have a whisky?'

'Oh yes,' said Natasha, who hated the stuff.

As he put the glass in her hand Alexis came into the room. Natasha nearly dropped the glass.

'Alexis!'

'Paul!'

The two men greeted each other. They shook hands. Alexis,

who was not gifted at social deception, promptly wiped his hand absent-mindedly on his black corduroy trousers. A silence fell. Above Natasha's head the eyes of the two men met; they were equally tall. The air seemed to crackle with their mutual antagonism. Natasha sat down. Alexis immediately sat next to her. Paul Vansittart sat opposite, and lit another cigarette.

'Well,' he said after a lengthy pause. 'How's life in the citadel then, Alexis?'

'The citadel?'

'Academia. The ivory tower. Cambridge . . .'

'Ah. Much as usual.'

'You do surprise me . . .'

Dinner at the Lydiards' was a disorganised informal affair, with everyone seated at a long pine refectory table off the kitchen. Everyone sat where they liked, and Natasha was sitting next to Paul Vansittart. Most of the other people she knew—there was a painter friend of Anne's, several colleagues of Alexis', two Polish writers whom Alexis had befriended, a literary critic from Venezuela, a playwright once famous, whose work was fashionable no longer, two younger women who were probably Alexis' students, and the young man who mowed their lawns who wanted to be a potter. To Natasha they were a blur, a background: she saw only Alexis at the head of the table, and Paul Vansittart, darkly attentive at her side. He kept re-filling her glass with wine.

They had finished the trout, which were excellent. People were now having second helpings of *coq au vin*. Anne hopped up and down to the stove, helped by her painter friend, and Alexis constantly replenished the bottles on the table. The candles, some in blackened silver candelabra, some in egg-cups, were beginning to burn low; the whole room seemed to her to be lit with a glorious hazy radiance. For once, everything she said seemed to the point. When she had risked a teasing joke, Paul Vansittart had laughed, and Alexis had glowered, and her own courage had flowered. Before dinner Alexis had seemed reluctant to leave her side, but when forced to go and greet the other guests, he had done so, and since then Paul Vansittart had monopolised her. He was a writer; to Natasha, writers were only a little lower than the gods. She had expected, therefore, that this monopolising would not last, that he would quickly find her provincial, boring and naïve. Yet, so far, she thought, sighing, he did not seem to. His attentions were marked, marked by Alexis anyway, and Natasha felt both flattered and curiously triumphant. Now Paul was telling her about his writing, and Natasha turned her gaze intensely upon him, simultaneously overwhelmed that this man should take her into his confidence, and pleased too that Alexis should witness their conversation.

'And so,' he was saying now, 'I just took a flat in Stepney for three months. That's always been my approach. You have to live it, you see. It's no good looking at things from the outside. I research it, of course. You might say it was almost a journalistic technique. Except it's more than that. I live it. By the time I start writing I can feel it all, it's under my skin. I'm as close to it as I am to you now . . .' He reached out a hand and placed it deliberately on Natasha's arm. She sighed.

'I envy you,' she said simply. 'Being able to do that. Just deciding that's what you want to do and then doing it. Moving around the world. A free agent. Writing. It must be wonderful.' She paused, wondering if she dared mention her own writing ambitions after all.

Paul Vansittart smiled. 'There's nothing magical about it. You just have to do it. Just decide where you want to be——' he paused, 'and with whom if necessary, and then do it. You could do the same.'

Natasha sighed. 'I couldn't,' she said. 'I'm not brave enough. I'd like to make a break now. Leave Cambridge. But it's so difficult.'

She looked up as she spoke, to meet Alexis' eyes, regarding her coldly from the other end of the table. She looked away quickly.

'It's not that I'm not happy here,' she added a little guiltily. 'I am. I have a family, they couldn't be kinder to me, or more patient, but . . .'

'But it's not enough, is it, Natasha?' Paul Vansittart leaned closer towards her. 'You don't need to tell me what you feel. I know. I've felt it. Out there the world, the real world, is waiting. You can't turn your back on it, not when you're as young and beautiful as you are . . .'

'But how?' she asked wistfully, meeting his gaze.

'Just go, make the break. You won't regret it.' He paused. 'You could go to London. What is it, after all? An hour on the train. Get a single, Natasha. Never a return. A ticket to life . . .'

'Let me take your plate, Natasha.' Alexis had appeared from nowhere and was hovering at her elbow. He looked down at the top of Paul Vansittart's head.

'How's the book going, Paul?'

The novelist stretched easily. 'Oh, pretty well. You know how it is. It's Book Society Choice, of course, which helps. And the advance word from America is pretty good . . .'

Alexis disappeared. Natasha blushed prettily.

'I've started reading it,' she said. 'Your latest book.' Even now she couldn't quite bring herself to pronounce its title.

'Ahh,' he gave a little smile. 'Now that particular one I didn't have to research . . .'

'You didn't?'

'Not consciously.'

'I expect you're working on something else now.' She hesitated. 'Maybe you're going abroad? You must have to travel a lot.'

'Right in the first place, but wrong in the second. My new book's set in London. I've moved to Soho now and . . .' He pulled himself up short. 'But you mustn't make me say any more. I hate talking about my work.'

'But this cannot be true . . .' Natasha jumped. It was the Venezuelan literary critic, who was sitting opposite them, and who had, clearly, been listening to their conversation.

'I beg your pardon?'

'I say, this cannot be true. It is impossible. In my experience, the literary process is a mysterious one, a private one, that goes without saying. But one which needs to be aired. It is fascinating, I feel, the artist's desire for privacy, and his simultaneous need for—what is the word?—feedback . . .'

The Venezuelan was launched. He fixed Paul Vansittart with an intense gaze.

'I am over here to write a series of articles on the modern European novel, and of course, your name . . .'

Paul Vansittart leaned forward; Natasha leaned back. He was lost to her for the moment. It was only to be expected. She let her eyes wander dreamily towards the head of the table. A snatch of conversation intruded into her ears.

'But it was wonderful,' she heard. 'I read it straight through, then I took it to bed with me and read it again. You're too modest, Alexis. It's the best thing you've written so far. I mean, when I came up I thought I should go mad.

That dry Cambridge understatement—no fire, all ice. Criticism needn't be dry, don't you think? It ought to be impassioned, and when I first went to your lectures, I found . . .'

Natasha stared. The room focused from its vague golden haze and became sharp. The last speaker was a woman, of about twenty-five. She was sitting next to Alexis, and leaning forward to him, her face intent and serious. She had a tip-tilted nose, a gamine face, and very short hair. She was extremely pretty. Not English, Natasha thought. Greek perhaps. Or Italian. Her voice had a slight lilting accent and a warmth that made it attractive; Natasha looked at her with dislike. Not for the first time in her life she reflected on the unfairness of accents; with a foreign voice it was possible to say all sorts of things that would have sounded perfectly ridiculous in clipped English tones. One of the girl's thin tanned arms was adorned with heavy gold and ivory bracelets; Alexis's eyes were fixed on these. His face wore the closed look that Natasha recognised was one of concentration. To Natasha's intense surprise she felt a sudden pain, physical and mental, grip her, an awful rising agitation she did not understand and could not suppress. She stared at Alexis. He appeared to have forgotten her existence.

'Tell me about yourself.'

The Venezuelan had disappeared in the direction of the lavatory, and seeing the would-be potter about to make conversational overtures, Paul Vansittart turned back to Natasha at once.

'Go on,' he prompted. 'I know it's a cliché. I like cliché. I want to know. Everything. You interest me, Natasha . . .'

'There's not much to tell,' Natasha turned back to him blankly.

'Of course there is. There always is. There's always a story.' He paused. 'Have you always lived here?'

'With Anne and Alexis? No.' She shook her head, forcing her attention back to him. 'My parents were killed in a plane crash, when I was very young—about eight.'

'An orphan. Mmmm . . .'

His gentle tone encouraged her. 'I never knew them very well,' she went on more strongly. 'They were very social. You know, parties and things all the time. I was parked with nannies mostly.' She paused. 'Then Alexis became my guardian. But I lived mostly with Anne, and Sophie—that's the eldest sister—until Anne was widowed. Then we came here. That was seven years ago. I was sent to boarding school . . .'

'What did your father do?'

'Not much.' Natasha managed a smile. 'All the brains went to Alexis' side of the family. Daddy dealt in antiques for a while. Mostly it was just an excuse to sell off some of the old family things when he needed money . . .'

'Was he rich?' Vansittart looked censorious.

'No, no,' said Natasha hastily. 'I mean, they had been once, I suppose. But it got spent somehow. I don't know really.' She hesitated, glancing along the table. 'I saw very little of them, you see. So I don't . . .'

'Still, you had old Alexis to step into the breach, didn't you? He's not exactly hard-up, from what I hear. What relation is he to you, anyway? Uncle?' He paused, and gave her a wicked glance. 'Grandfather?'

Natasha blushed crimson. 'Don't tease,' she said. 'My father was his cousin, so that makes me—I never know what. Second cousin, or first once removed or something.'

'Kissing cousins maybe?' He stroked her arm. 'No, don't look like that, I'm teasing because I like to see you blush. I thought women had forgotten how to do it . . .'

'I'm his ward,' Natasha said in a small voice. She was beginning to feel suddenly out of her depth. 'Except not even that any more. I'm—of age.'

'Of age.' He smiled. 'A ward. It sounds like one of those dreadful Victorian books Alexis is always banging on about. Very out of date for a spirited young woman. I can quite see why you might want to make a break, to rebel . . .' He paused thoughtfully. 'After all, Alexis isn't exactly living in the modern world, is he?'

Natasha looked at her plate. 'He's very kind . . .' she began.

Paul pressed her arm again softly.

'Natasha,' he said, leaning towards her, so his dark hair almost brushed her skin. 'Never let yourself be trapped. That's all I have to say . . .'

In fact it looked as if he had a good deal more to say, but just at that moment Alexis' voice cut through the babble of conversation.

'Coffee!' he announced.

Anne was already advancing into the room, carrying an enormous tray. Behind her Alexis was fiddling with the percolator. Anne allowed him to make the coffee because he thought it helped. With machines Alexis was not to be relied upon: the result was unpredictable.

'We'll have it next door, maybe,' Anne said.

'I think it's perking. It's doing something,' Alexis said in a hopeful manner. He stared at the machine in puzzlement. It made guttural noises. Anne sighed. Her eyes made signals at Natasha.

'Natasha, you help him, darling.' She smiled at the company benignly. 'The machine's a bit eccentric,' she said loyally.

Natasha rose; gradually the room cleared. She and Alexis were left alone. The percolator spluttered. Alexis stared into space.

'He's an idiot,' he said at last, with some passion. 'An utter idiot. I can't stand him.'

'Who, Alexis?'

'Don't look at me like that. You know perfectly well, Vansittart. That twit. That fourth rate, devious, conceited, patronising, snobbish ... William could write a better novel than he could.'

Natasha stared at her cousin. She was used to Alexis' vehemence, but it was usually directed against ideas rather than people. Alexis, who preached charity, was oddly given to practising it.

'I don't agree at all,' she said coldly at last. 'As it happens, I've looked at some of his books, and ...'

'I know that,' Alexis growled.

'And I think they're very good. His characterisation of women, for instance ...'

'His *what*?' Alexis had gone white. He adjusted his spectacles angrily. 'Vansittart hasn't a clue about women. Not a clue. As far as he's concerned, women are there for one reason and one reason only, and that's ...' He broke off.

'That's what?' said Natasha boldly.

'Never mind. You wouldn't understand.'

'Yes, I would!' Natasha felt suddenly furious. She banged the table and Alexis jumped. 'Stop treating me like a child! I know what you mean. You mean he ... he just wants to make them.'

'Make them? Make them?' Alexis was now seriously agitated. He moved sharply and nearly knocked over the percolator. 'What a disgusting phrase, I don't know how you

can use a phrase like that. Jargon. Awful cheap jargon. I
thought you . . .'

'What's wrong with it?' Natasha glared at him. 'It's honest,
isn't it? As a matter of fact, I don't think it's true, but even if
it was . . .'

'Were.'

'Were. Even if it were, so what? It's natural enough. He's a
man, after all and . . .'

'Oh my God.' Alexis gave a cry of despair. The percolator
had boiled over. By the time Natasha had helped him to clear
up the mess, and the percolator was re-filled, both of them
had calmed down. Silence fell; they looked at each other
ruefully.

'Sorry, Alexis,' Natasha said at last. She reached for his hand.

Alexis held hers in an odd manner as if he didn't quite
know what to do with it. Eventually he patted it. To
Natasha's surprise, the pain which had been lodged
somewhere near her heart for the last fifteen minutes suddenly
disappeared.

'Natasha,' Alexis began, in a most peculiar voice, which
sounded throttled. He cleared his throat. 'I don't want to
seem boring about all this. But—er—maybe you ought to talk
to Anne, or . . .'

'Oh, Alexis, you are a fool!' Impetuously, unable to stop
herself, Natasha gave him a warm hug, from which he
recoiled. 'When will you realise? I'm a woman now, not a
schoolgirl. I can take care of myself. . . . Now come *on*, and
stop looking so paternalistic. They must be dying for that
coffee . . .'

When they returned to the drawing room Paul Vansittart
was talking to the intense young woman who had been seated
next to Alexis. Her bracelets jangled. Alexis directed a look of
such venom in their direction that Natasha was shaken.

Paul rose at that moment and crossed to Natasha. He
began to steer her in the direction of the windows, where no
one else was sitting.

'Christ,' he said under his breath. 'God preserve me from
intellectual women. Dead from the neck down. Can't stand
them.'

Natasha felt more cheerful; for the first time in her life, her
lack of intellectual distinction seemed a positive asset. She
smiled at him. Alexis hovered in the background. Anne
looked up brightly.

'Alexis, darling,' she said. 'Isn't it wonderful? Paul plays cricket. He says he'd love to join in the game tomorrow. You said the village team was a man short—didn't you? Isn't that lucky?'

Alexis looked in the direction of the windows.

'I shouldn't think we'll get a game,' he said gloomily. 'It's going to rain, I think. I expect we'll have to call it off.'

'Nonsense, it's as fine as can be. Don't be such a Jonah, Alexis . . .'

Paul Vansittart turned to Natasha; he pulled a wry face.

'Can't stand the game,' he said. 'But it's only a scratch team, isn't it?'

Natasha looked doubtful, but he pressed on.

'After all—it's an excuse, isn't it? Meet me tomorrow, Natasha.' He gave her a dark mocking glance. 'Over the cucumber sandwiches. Eh?'

'We don't have cucumber sandwiches, damn it,' Alexis said loudly, but no one was listening.

CHAPTER FOUR

THE next day was glorious. Natasha woke early; sunlight streamed into her room. She lay in bed for a while, looking at the ceiling, and thinking. She felt odd, she decided, happy and yet curiously nervous and keyed up. She felt as she had done when she was a child, when term had ended and she had come home for the holidays. The day felt momentous; my life is about to change, she said to herself, and when she asked herself why, could think of only one possible answer. Why, it was meeting Paul Vansittart, of course, what else could it be? She jumped out of bed; of course, that was it. She sang as she dressed, and went down to breakfast with a light heart.

Julian, William and Alexis were already seated at the table, eating bacon and eggs. Their faces wore conspiratorial expressions; they conversed in lowered tones.

''Morning,' said Natasha, smiling upon them benignly. As she passed behind Alexis' chair she bent quickly and dropped a kiss on his hair. Alexis dropped his knife. Natasha, humming, went into the kitchen with Anne to make some more toast.

'I think I might wear my flowery dress,' she said dreamily, 'the drifty one that Alexis likes. And maybe that big straw hat. Do you think that would be too much, Anne?'

Anne closed the kitchen door. She was not listening.

'You missed the Scene.' She sighed. 'Paul Vansittart hasn't any flannels, naturally, so I said he could borrow some old ones of Alexis'. They're almost the same size, after all . . .'

'Alexis is taller . . .'

'Alexis was not pleased.'

'How odd.' Natasha turned back to her in surprise. 'Alexis is usually so generous . . .'

'I know. Men are funny sometimes, aren't they?'

Anne began to put slices of wholemeal bread in the toaster; there was a little silence.

'I hope it will be all right,' Anne continued at last. 'You see, Paul says he hasn't played since school, and I don't think he was very keen then. I think I may have given him the wrong impression. I said it was just village cricket, because Alexis says one mustn't be pompous about it. And so I think Paul rather dismissed it all. Whereas, of course . . .'

'Oh dear.'

'I know. Precisely.'

The two women looked at each other.

The village games were an important fixture in the Lydiard summers, no match more so than the annual one in which the village took on an university team captained by Alexis. Both teams, though very different, were formidable. Alexis had been Captain of cricket at Winchester, and had a cricketing Blue from Cambridge. His team was composed mainly of ex-Blues like himself, together with the best of the undergraduate players—one of whom, this year, was exceptionally good, destined, it was rumoured, to bat for England. The village team was less classical, and more aggressive. It contained a number of men who played the ground since they were children, and three county players, now retired, whose age had not diminished their skills. Both sides took their matches with profound seriousness.

Natasha smiled to herself. Really, how seriously they all took it, what did it matter, after all? She took her toast back into the dining room, and surveyed William and Alexis provocatively. Both now appeared in high good humour.

'Don't tell me,' she said, sitting down, and directing her remarks to Alexis. 'You're going to thrash them. Someone says that every year. It's too pathetic. I suppose you realise the whole thing is just re-directed aggression?'

Alexis gave her a dazzling smile. 'Spare me,' he said. 'Please, Natasha. I can do without diluted Freud at breakfast.' He paused. 'Cricket is a game of tactics and skill . . .'

'Brain and brawn,' put in William.

'Capable of dull moments, I admit. That's the essence of its greatness if you like. Just when it *seems* dull, given the right circumstances . . .'

'Oh, shut up,' said Natasha, suddenly cross. 'You're boring me already. And you don't believe a word you're saying. You're just teasing. Trying to provoke me.' She paused. 'That's the trouble with this household,' she finished cuttingly. 'You never know when anyone's serious. One of these days something *really* serious will happen, and everyone will make a joke of it, and laugh themselves silly, and then they'll wake up and realise there's been a disaster. You wait. I can see it coming.'

There was a little silence. Alexis gave her a sharp glance. William composedly helped himself to some more Sugar Frosties.

The match—of two innings only—was due to start at one-thirty. William arrived early and took up his position near the pavilion. From inside it came the sound of hearty male laughter. He waited patiently, sniffing the air appreciatively. It was balmy and soft; the scent of newly cut grass reached him. He sat happily, riffling the pages of his score book. The players came out; William watched them.

In one corner, slightly apart from the others, was Paul Vansittart. He was wearing whites—Alexis' old ones, which were slightly too tight for him—and gazing at his own reflection in one of the pavilion windows.

'Hi.' William approached.

'Oh, it's you. Hello.' He glanced up into the sun and grimaced. 'Bloody glare. It's giving me a headache already.'

'Maybe you have a hangover,' William said helpfully.

'I don't get hangovers.'

'Alexis has fielded a good team today,' William said at length.

'Oh, really?'

'One of his best ever, I'd say.' William gestured at various players. 'That's John Middleton, the spin-bowler. He's terrific, but I shouldn't think he'll be able to do much on this wicket. Alexis will probably do most of the bowling. And that's Edmund Fiennes, you might have heard of him. He'll make the England eleven one day, they say. He's the star bat.'

Paul Vansittart stared in the direction of a small fair-haired man talking to Alexis.

'Fiennes.... Isn't he a Lord or something?' His lips compressed.

'Is he?' William looked vague. 'He might be. Or a Viscount maybe. Or is it an Earl? I can never remember. Anyway, he's in love with Natasha. Has been, ever since he came up. It isn't reciprocated.'

'I should think not.'

'He and Alexis will hold the batting together. Alexis will go in first, of course, because he's like a rock. Then Eddy will probably go in third, when we really need to start scoring . . .' He paused. 'Have you ever seen Alexis play? He's brilliant.'

'I don't follow cricket.' Paul Vansittart turned away.

'Especially amateur cricket, riddled with snobbery. My idea of a good game is snooker.'

'Alexis plays snooker very well too,' said William sweetly.

'Is there anything Alexis isn't good at?' Paul Vansittart enquired nastily.

William gave the question long and irritating consideration.

'It's hard to think of anything,' he said finally. 'He's not much good on computers which is a shame, because I'm very interested in them. Did you know there's a computer now that can write novels?'

'They should get Alexis to review its next book then,' said Paul Vansittart. 'That should be just his drop.'

He moved off, and William jumped down with agility and trotted off across the field. In the distance he could discern a blur of billowing white. Natasha was approaching.

The audience for the match was beginning to grow. Most people, anxious for shade, had made for the ground near the trees, which gave a good view of the wicket. Anne was there, with her painter friend. The small knot of spectators was growing fast. Natasha sank down into a deckchair with relief. Julian and William, as if by pre-arranged signal, took up their places on either side of her, crouched on the grass at her feet.

'This is an unaccustomed honour.' She looked at them both suspiciously. 'Are you staying?'

Julian grinned. 'Yes. We've decided. We're going to educate you.'

'Explain the finer points,' William put in.

'Must you?'

'Yes,' they chorused. Natasha decided to give in gracefully.

She sat there, fanning herself, gazing out across the field, watching the ebb and flow of people.

'Fifteen,' said Julian eventually.

'Fifteen what?'

'That's the fifteenth undergraduate who's seen you, recognised you, and turned away reluctantly. Blushing . . .'

'A visible tremor shaking his manly shoulders,' William added.

'Hard-hearted Natasha. How can you be so cruel?'

'Shut up, both of you.'

La belle dame sans merci.

'She scorns all men . . .'

'She scorns *young* men . . .'

'I'll bang your heads together, you beasts . . .'

'Oh look, there's Paul Vansittart.'

'*Where?*' Natasha nearly fell off her deck-chair. Both boys dissolved in a loud chorus of raucous chucklings and gigglings.

Just as Natasha had decided to get up with dignity and leave them, it stopped as suddenly as it had begun. She relaxed again, staring dreamily in the direction of the pavilion. She could just see Alexis, tall and elegant in his whites, talking to Ben Jarvis, captain of the village team. She sighed, fanning herself. She had spent the morning writing her diary, which she did religiously every day, and the latest entry had been a long one. Alexis' lecture about her future and Paul Vansittart's remarks at dinner had found themselves side by side on the same page, and now she was glad to have time to think. They were both right, she decided. She had marked time too long, drifted, just as Alexis said, and she must do so no longer. By the end of today, she resolved to herself, I shall decide. Either I shall stay, or I shall go. Cambridge or London: it shall be one or the other.

But although that was a neat way of summing up her dilemma, it did not go to the root of the problem, and Natasha knew it. Stay or go, what should she do, where could she find work? The problem revolved and revolved in her mind, and the more she tried to think it out the hotter and more confused she felt. It was as if she were looking at some terrible puzzle, and could not solve it because one of the key pieces was missing. There was something which she had not taken into account, some key factor, she knew it.

'And Bernard said . . .' she heard.

'Who's Bernard?' she asked, her mind still far away. Both boys groaned.

'Bernard. Anne's Bernard. The painter. Over there.'

'I think she'll marry him, don't you, Julian?'

'I should think so. She ought to. He's jolly nice. Just what she needs.'

'What are you talking about?' Natasha stared at them both.

'Mother. And Bernard. If you weren't so blind, so self-absorbed, you might have noticed. Anne's in love.'

'Rubbish,' said Natasha crisply. The suggestion made her uncomfortable.

'Of course, things would be very different then,' added William. 'I mean, we'd go to live with Bernard, wouldn't we? And then what would Alexis do? And Natasha?'

There was a little silence.

'Alexis might marry, of course,' said William reflectively. 'It could be on the cards. Ariana. . . . Oh, talk of the devil . . .'

He turned; Natasha followed his gaze. Across the field, leaving the pavilion area was the dark, shorthaired girl who had been at dinner the previous evening. She was wearing very brief white shorts, a loose white tee-shirt and tennis shoes. Natasha instantly felt overdressed. She took off her hat.

'Ariana?'

'That one over there.' Julian pointed helpfully. 'She's post-graduate now. Alexis was her director of studies. Now he's helping her with her thesis.'

Natasha sniffed. 'What a pretentious name. Ariana. It's stupid.'

'Not if you're Greek, it isn't,' Julian said reasonably.

'And heiress to the Papenglou shipping millions,' added William.

'How do you know all this?'

'Alexis told us,' the boys chorused, and started laughing again.

As predicted, Alexis was the first in to bat. The village team sent in their fast bowler. He was built like a bus, and the ball hurtled out of his enormous fist, pelting down the wicket at what seemed to Natasha an alarming speed.

'As I said this morning,' William pronounced. 'Brawn. In this case, brawn versus brain . . .'

For the next fifteen minutes few runs were scored. The bowler pounded and hurled. Then there was a satisfying thwack as willow met leather, then the ball seemed to Natasha just to dribble away. She sighed.

'Why doesn't Alexis slash at it a bit more? It seems so unadventurous,' she complained eventually. Both boys raised their eyes to the heavens.

'Because he's a great stroke player. He could be clean bowled. Or caught. Look how short the ball's pitching, for God's sake, woman. There! You see!'

The other batsman, as if overhearing Natasha's complaint, had taken a somewhat wild swipe, off balance. The ball smashed through his wicket.

'Howzat!' came a banshee scream from the bowler.

'You see?' said William. 'Thirty-five. Not bad. Now the fun should start. Eddy's coming in.'

Certainly, from Natasha's point of view, things began to liven up with the partnership of Eddy Fiennes and Alexis. The village put on their most feared bowler, a tall lanky man who took a terrifyingly long run up to the wicket, and from whose hands the ball hurtled so fast her eyes could scarcely follow it. The two batsmen, however, far from being intimidated, seemed to rise to the challenge. The rhythm of their partnership established itself almost at once; stroke after stroke sent the ball to the boundary. Natasha grew attentive. Her gaze, which had been resting on Paul Vansittart, in mid-field on the leg side, happily placed almost opposite where she was sitting, now wandered from his tall figure, and concentrated on the two batsmen.

Alexis *was* graceful, even her untrained eye could appreciate that, and very strong. His movements were contained; they seemed minimal. Just a shifting of the weight, a swift re-alignment of his body, and his bat met the ball with unhesitating accuracy, sending it winging past the fielding. At her feet William and Julian smiled at one another smugly.

'Terrific. He's really on form today. Look at *that*!'

'He knows Ariana's watching, of course . . .'

'Wow!'

A particularly fast ball, pitched long, broke close to Alexis' feet on the leg-side, curving in towards the wicket. Natasha gasped; Alexis seemed to shift his weight to his back foot; he hardly lifted his bat, but seemed just to turn the face of it. The ball sped fast and low over the grass to the boundary, for four. There was a ripple of applause.

Natasha leaned forward; a feeling of benevolence began to possess her. She was glad the match was going well, glad Alexis should distinguish himself. A sense of pride—family pride, she told herself—lit in her heart. Paul Vansittart's comments on Alexis, though veiled, had indicated a certain contempt for her cousin that had left her uneasy. Now she felt glad that the novelist should see Alexis perform well: Alexis was so modest, so tolerant of mockery from others. Natasha enjoyed mocking him herself, but—she realised now—she hated to see him mocked by outsiders, who didn't understand how gifted he was, and how good. Anxiously, protectively, she watched Alexis, hoping that Paul Vansittart would alter his measure of the man.

As she watched another Victorian tag sprang into her mind—*grace under pressure*—yes, that was a good description of Alexis, who in spite of his fierceness and his occasional rages, could be depended upon always, in extreme circumstances, to be both calm and wise. And beautiful; yes, Alexis was beautiful, she could see that now, watching him as a spectator across the field. If she went to London, she would sever her ties with Alexis—with all the family. Perhaps it was that that made the decision so hard . . .

Alexis hit the ball through cover for two, taking the somewhat chancy runs easily with his long graceful stride. Natasha jumped to her feet impulsively and clapped. Alexis, back in his crease, glanced across in her direction. Though he probably did not see her, it seemed to Natasha that he slightly inclined his head. She blushed; she should stay, perhaps, she thought suddenly. Going to London, that purposeful act, seemed suddenly less purposeful. Perhaps it was a little like running away.

She sat down again. It was the end of the over. With the first ball of the next over, Eddy Fiennes was caught in the slips. William and Julian groaned.

'Oh God, and we were doing so well . . .'

'It'll probably be all right. Alexis will hold them together . . .'

But Julian spoke too soon. The next batsman was out LBW for three; the one who succeeded him was clean-bowled for a duck. William and Julian's faces assumed expressions of doom.

'Clowns,' Julian said contemptuously. 'Now Alexis will have to farm the bowling . . .'

'It means taking chances,' William explained helplessly. 'Snatching quick runs if necessary, so Alexis is always facing the bowler, not the other man. Jack's okay—he'll have a bash. He'll probably hit a few sixes and then he'll be caught. They can't afford that now. Watch—there, you see what I mean?'

As he spoke Jack Middleton, a useful spin-bowler, but not an all-rounder, poked the ball somewhat awkwardly past the slips and began to pound down the wicket. Alexis reached his crease before his partner, puffing and sweating, was three quarters of the way down. Alexis frowned, bent forward, took up his stance. He put the next ball away for four, the one after for a glorious six.

'Right on the meat of the bat! Wow!' William cried ecstatically.

'Just missed Vansittart's ear,' Julian added caustically.

'What's happened to him? There could have been a catch there. Maybe he's gone to sleep.'

'Don't be ridiculous,' Natasha said defensively. 'No one could have caught that . . .'

She glanced across at Vansittart as she spoke. The ball had indeed been close; perhaps he had felt it whistle past his ear, for he was now rubbing it thoughtfully, and looking at Alexis with an expression that was not, even at this distance, interpretable as one of admiration. He bent forward in an attitude of pugnacious concentration. Even before the next ball left the bowler's hand he was already moving in towards the wicket. The next ball, pitched long, struck a bump, rose fast on the off-side, and hit Alexis on the thigh.

Paul flung himself into the air, both hands above his head, his face contorted with triumph.

'Howzat!' he screeched ferociously, in tones that echoed around the outfield.

There was a silence. Alexis straightened up, then resumed his batting stance without even glancing in Vansittart's direction. Neither umpire moved. Ben Jarvis coughed and looked up at the sky.

It was from that moment, the boys judged afterwards, that Alexis began to play with a brilliance which electrified everyone. That he was on form had already been apparent. Now he began to hit the ball all over the field with an accuracy and a strength that made his opponents seem pigmies in comparison. If there was the tiniest gap in the fielding he found it, though Ben Jarvis brought the field in as tight as he dared. In vain the village brought on a succession of different bowlers. Relentlessly the score mounted. When Alexis took it past one hundred and fifty, the applause was long, and enthusiastic. It was becoming apparent to everyone, even to Natasha, that the holes Alexis was finding in the village's fielding, were almost all in mid-field on the leg side, to the right, to the left, over the head of—and on one ignominious occasion between the feet of—Paul Vansittart. His handsome face was flushed with the exertion. Now, while Alexis waited in his crease, in an attitude of insolent indolence, the novelist glanced towards him, his face wearing a discernible scowl.

Natasha looked away; she was beginning to scent trouble. Nearby, Anne and Bernard were sitting side by side, engrossed in the game; they held hands, Natasha saw. A horrible suspicion that William and Julian might be right

about their mother came to her. Instantly she checked herself;
the suspicion was not horrible; that was foolish. She loved
Anne; if Bernard brought Anne happiness, wanted to marry
her, why then she would be delighted, of course. And yet . . .

The two boys had risen to their feet. They were regarding
her with an air of polite solicitude.

'Where are you two going?'

'Oh, just to get some lemonade. Won't be long . . .'

They bolted. Two minutes later a shadow fell across
Natasha's lap and a pair of ragged gym shoes and long tanned
legs appeared before her. The owner of the legs sat down next
to her, and stretched decoratively. She squinted up into
Natasha's face.

'Hi,' she said. 'I'm Ariana.'

Natasha regarded her coldly. 'Yes?' she said. The girl's
assumption that Natasha should know who she was on the
basis of this brief announcement annoyed her considerably.
She was even more annoyed when the girl made no attempt to
elaborate on it, but merely settled herself more comfortably
on the grass, unzipped the large canvas bag she was holding,
and took out some knitting. Natasha dropped her hat. She
picked it up again, and stared moodily back at the wicket.
Alexis had just sneaked another, dangerous, single.

'Alexis is having to farm the bowling,' she said at last, with
sweet patronage.

The other girl grinned.

'I know. I play cricket.'

'Really?' Natasha examined her hatband with attention; her
mind was moving rapidly. 'For Girton?' she hazarded. Ariana
laughed.

'Oh my God, no! I am at Girton, but that might be too
hearty, don't you think?' She turned her smiling and
exceedingly attractive face up to Natasha. She had perfect,
even white teeth, and her nose was deliciously freckled. 'I play
in Corfu. Since I was a child. We have a house there—in the
summer, you know. The English brought cricket to Corfu. We
take it very seriously.'

As she spoke the ball nicked the edge of Alexis' bat and
rose alarmingly. The fielding had been re-arranged, and Paul
Vansittart, now in the slips, leapt forward, his hands cupped.
The ball sailed into them and fell through them on to the toe
of his boots. Both girls tensed, then relaxed as the ball fell.
Ariana turned with a smile of relief.

'A near thing. He is lucky your uncle, as well as everything else.'

'My cousin, actually.'

'You don't say.' She had dropped a stitch and was now attempting to pick it up.

'You find you can knit and watch?' said Natasha.

'But of course.' The girl nodded tranquilly. 'I am a very restless kind of person, you know? I must be fully occupied always. Alexis says I must learn to relax, and I tell him, this is my relaxation. To be busy.'

Natasha regarded her sourly. She herself could not knit, indeed detested it, but Ariana didn't seem to be doing that well either, she noted. The few inches of knitting were tatty looking and uneven.

'What are you making?'

Ariana laughed again. 'It is a sweater. For Alexis, by the way. The second one I have made for him. The first was very bad, all the wrong size. So last night I measured him, very carefully, and now I am beginning again.' She shrugged. 'I told him, I do not give up easily. And besides, he is so sweet-natured, don't you think? He will keep the first one, even though it fits so badly. As a memento, he said.'

'Was it green?' Natasha said. 'A very strong, virulent sort of green? If it was, I saw it. I thought he was going to give it to Oxfam.'

She blushed at her own rudeness even as she spoke, and felt instantly ashamed, but Ariana seemed not to mind in the least.

'It was the colour of his eyes,' she said imperturbably. 'Dark emerald. And he is not giving to Oxfam. But certainly not.'

She did not look at Natasha as she spoke, but put down her knitting and clapped. Alexis had just hit a cover drive for four. She has no sense of humour, Natasha judged, and hoped she was right.

'You're post-graduate, aren't you?' Natasha said at last, curiosity getting the better of her determination not to let Ariana know she had the slightest idea who she was.

'Yes. I am working on my thesis now. Alexis mentioned it perhaps?' She looked up at Natasha hopefully.

'Not that I recall.'

'It is most rewarding. Very interesting. Alexis has been of the greatest assistance to me. Do you take an interest in English Literature?'

'It would be rather difficult not to,' Natasha answered. 'Living with Alexis as I do.'

'But of course. I had forgotten. You are part of the *ménage*...' Ariana smiled her wide pearly smile again. Natasha seethed.

'What's your thesis on?' she asked eventually, as Ariana seemed to feel no compulsion to continue the conversation.

'Ah...' The girl sighed and laid down her knitting. 'It is to be entitled, *Eros and Thanatos: An Analysis of Allegory and Image in the Poems of John Donne*.' She paused. Natasha was silent. 'Eros and Thanatos—love and death, you know?'

'Yes, I did, actually.'

'I have read his poems first when I was a child, of course. But it was Alexis, when I first came up, who made me see them truly.'

'Really?'

'They are so sexual, you know, those poems. Don't you think?' She turned her gaze intently on Natasha. 'I find it fascinating, the metaphysical sensibility. The entanglement of sex and death. The little death, the swoon of sexual pleasure. It is such a fierce image, is it not? I like it very much. I think it is apt, don't you?'

'Er—yes,' Natasha said cautiously, not having the least idea and determined not to proclaim that fact.

'Alexis understands such things, of course. That is his paradox. It is what makes him so fascinating. Today...' she gestured to the cricket field, 'he seems the epitome of Englishness, does he not? At other times I find him very un-English. He has a passion in him, I find. Like Donne. You do not notice this perhaps? You are too close to him. Like a sister.'

Natasha opened her mouth to reply, and then closed it again. She had been about to say that she certainly did not regard Alexis as a brother, when an unpleasant suspicion dawned on her. She might not feel like that, but very probably Alexis did. He might even have said so to Ariana, for the girl made her diagnosis with great confidence. *Ménage*; sister: so that was how Alexis saw her, indistinguishable from her other cousins, just part of his large household. Part of the family—part of the furniture. A wave of desolation passed over her; mumbling some excuse she turned, stood up, abruptly, and walked away.

She moved off from the crowd, standing apart in the cool

of the trees, her eyes fixed sightlessly on the field in front of her. Her head had begun to ache; the still air felt suffocating. She wished passionately then that the game was over, that she could talk to Alexis. Her mouth tightened; William and Julian were coming back; she had no wish for them to see she was upset.

'What's the score?' she said casually as they reached her side. 'I lost track . . .'

William and Julian exchanged glances. 'A hundred and seventy,' William said. 'I should think Alexis is hanging on for the two hundred, then he'll declare. They can't get him out. Ben's tried every trick in the book . . . Hello . . .'

Julian followed his brother's gaze. 'Well, there's a turn up for the books,' he said. 'It looks as if Vansittart's going to bowl . . .'

Paul had been having a protracted huddled conversation with Ben Jarvis, accompanied by much vehemence on his part and non-committal silence from Ben. Now he had the ball, and was energetically polishing it on his trousers. The other batsman was now facing the bowling; at the bowling end Alexis had his bat in his crease, and was poised for the first opportunity to snatch another single. As he passed him, walking back for his run up, Paul Vansittart gave him a smile and said something inaudible. It was presumably some kind of jokey greeting; but its humour, if so, was wasted on her cousin. His face darkened palpably. Paul Vansittart strolled on, turned, polished the ball once more, took a very long run up, and bowled wide.

William guffawed.

Alexis, who had been half-way up the wicket, looking for his run, the second Vansittart bowled, returned to his crease. This time, as the novelist passed him, they studiously ignored one another.

The second ball was fast and on wicket. The batsman took a swipe at it, which, if the stroke lacked grace, was well-timed. The ball sped on to the boundary for four. Still Alexis was not facing the bowling.

What happened next took place so fast that Natasha hardly saw it. Paul began his long run-up once more. His right arm swung down, and back. As it came over, Alexis started to move forward out of his crease like a greyhound let off the leash. But the ball was never bowled. Instead, Paul swung his arm over and down, and, still holding the ball, crashed it through Alexis' wicket, knocking the bales high into the air.

There was a moment's stunned silence.

'What's happened? I don't understand . . .' Natasha stood up, craning her neck. All was confusion. Ben Jarvis was running forward, blocking her view. Paul had leapt into the air, his cries of triumph sending the rooks scattering from the nearby trees. Alexis, half-way down the wicket, out of his crease, had come to a dead halt.

'I don't *believe* it . . . I just don't believe it.' Julian was shaking his head.

'What's *happened*? Is Alexis out?'

'Yes, he's out. Run out.'

'How can he be run out? Paul hadn't bowled. Oh, I don't understand! What's going on?'

William fixed her with a basilisk stare.

'Alexis was trying to farm the bowling. So he needed a single. He was starting to run a little early—it often happens. Especially when some clod-pole who wouldn't know a cricket bat from a tennis racquet takes a three mile run-up. So, technically, if he's out of his crease, he can be run out . . .'

'But it's not done!' Julian interrupted furiously. 'It's absolutely not done. Not without a warning—no one ever does that . . .'

'I thought you said cricket was about winning . . .' Natasha's voice had taken on a plaintive note, she herself could hear it. Suddenly she felt hot and tired and curiously close to tears. As she stared at the field, and before either umpire could make any ruling, the matter was decided by Alexis. Only a few seconds had passed, though they felt to Natasha like hours; now Alexis lifted his bat, tucked it under his arm, and, pulling off his gloves, began to stride back towards the pavilion. The knot of players around the umpires parted to let him pass. Across the field people rose to their feet to applaud. Alexis passed within inches of Paul Vansittart and never glanced in his direction. He simply walked off the field with every appearance of perfect good humour. William watched him go; he was almost in tears.

'Oh, it's not fair. After such a wonderful innings. To go out like that . . . Why does Alexis have to be so gentlemanly about it? If I were him I'd punch that idiot on the nose . . .'

Natasha watched the tall white-clad figure of Alexis until he disappeared into the pavilion. As the next batsman came out, and the village fielders turned from Paul Vansittart as one man, her cheeks flamed with colour. Leaving the two boys glowering and arguing, she began to run, across the grass, around the edge of the outfield, towards the pavilion. In a patch of shade from the beech trees she paused.

After a little while, as she had known he would, Alexis came out. He had taken off his pads; his cotton shirt, damp with sweat, clung to his body. Not seeing her, he paused, then took off his glasses and wiped his brow with his handkerchief. He sat down, his back to her; then, with an abrupt angry movement he lay back in the grass, staring up at the laced branches of the trees above his head. He lay like that for some moments, perfectly still, then he sat up again.

Hesitantly Natasha moved to his side, and stood looking down at him.

'I'm so sorry,' she burst out, before she had time to think. 'I'm so sorry, Alexis. But he doesn't play cricket much. I'm sure he didn't realise . . . William says it's very bad form, and if he had known that, I think . . .'

'Natasha . . .' Alexis looked up at her short-sightedly. Then, reaching up his hand, he drew her down beside him on the grass. Positioning her so that he could see her face, he surveyed her solemnly, his expression softening.

'You are het up,' he said at last. 'Don't be. I'm not. And don't take any notice of William. It's only a game.'

'But you'd batted so well. Even I could see that. It was beautiful, Alexis—daring and graceful and—I enjoyed watching you,' she finished lamely.

Alexis smiled. 'You mean we might have converted you a little? Then it was certainly worth while.'

'Oh Alexis, don't be generous about it. Please. It was awful. It was such a horrid way to go out. If you'd been clean-bowled or . . .'

'Don't be silly. I was out, that's all. Now stop looking so mournful. It's not a tragedy. This isn't like you, Natasha.'

'No, it isn't.' Natasha met his eyes. For a moment they held her, with their curious deep green depths, then she looked away. She sighed. 'I don't feel like myself at all today, you're right. I feel—oh, I don't know. All jangled and odd. Like someone else. I don't know what's wrong with me.'

There was a little silence. Gently Alexis put his arm around her shoulder and let it remain there. His eyes rested on her face, then turned back to the cricket field, where they followed the players' movements abstractedly, as if he hardly saw them.

'You're probably—tired,' he said at last, his voice a little sad, as if he did not believe his own diagnosis. 'And bored.' He smiled at her. 'It's not been a very good year for you, I know that. We were very late last night, and now all this cricket ...' He shrugged. 'You ought to—I don't know. Forget your problems for a while. Forget about jobs. Have some fun. Go out somewhere ...' He gestured vaguely across the field. 'There's any number of young men there pining to take you out—Eddy for instance. Yet you hardly ever go. Why not?'

Natasha swallowed. 'I don't know,' she said sadly at last. 'As friends—but they never want to be just friends. Not even Eddy. And so ... They bore me.'

'They bore you, or Cambridge does?' He looked at her sharply.

'Oh, I don't know. I wish I did.' She paused, turning to him. 'Oh Alexis, I feel so odd sometimes. So muddled. As if ...' She hesitated. 'As if something were about to happen, something important, and it was very close but I couldn't quite see it, or reach it ...' She broke off. He was regarding her intently. 'Do you ever feel like that, Alexis?'

'Sometimes,' he said. 'Yes, I think I do.'

'And what do you do about it?'

'What do I do?' He paused, then glanced at her wickedly. 'Why precisely what you were describing at breakfast. I sublimate my emotions. I go out and play cricket ...'

In spite of herself, Natasha laughed. 'Don't tease,' she said, giving him a little push. 'I'm serious.'

'But so am I.' He caught her hand, and held it for a second. An odd awkward little silence fell between them. Natasha looked down at the ground.

'*You* could take me out,' she said at last in a small voice. 'I'd like that. Then we could—oh, I don't know. Talk. I'd feel better if I talked to you.'

Alexis smiled wryly. 'We talked yesterday,' he said. 'At lunch. I rather had the impression you couldn't wait to get away.'

'That was different. That was yesterday.'

She waited a little, staring at the ground, watching an ant crawl between the blades of grass, but Alexis said nothing more, and no invitation was forthcoming. Eventually Natasha drew her hand away. Her heart seemed to be beating very fast, and her throat felt hot and tight. She stood up, and brushed down her dress. Alexis watched her; his clever greenish cat's eyes glittered in the sunlight. Natasha set her mouth.

'I've been talking to your friend, Ariana,' she said deliberately. 'She's knitting you another sweater, you'll be glad to know.'

'Oh, really?' His tone was neutral; not a flicker of expression passed across his face. To her own dismay Natasha felt an ugly painful anger knot and tighten in her heart.

'She told me about the sweater,' she went on, hearing her own voice sound high and forced. 'And about her thesis. And how much you had helped her. And about Donne. And about the metaphysicals and sex . . .'

'That must have been instructive.' Alexis' voice was totally bland. If he noticed the taunt in her voice he gave no sign of it.

'No, it wasn't. It was very boring. It gave me a headache.'

Alexis rose to his feet in one swift easy movement. He looked down into her face, and Natasha wondered miserably if she must look as ugly as she knew she sounded. He looked searchingly into her face, his expression puzzled.

'You're being unkind,' he said at last. 'Why? It's not like you.'

Natasha turned her face away.

'I don't know,' she said at last, for he clearly intended an answer. 'I told you—I don't feel like myself at all. It's as if I were a stranger. I . . .'

There was a shout from the field; Jack Middleton had been bowled. Alexis turned, then glanced at his watch.

'I should declare,' he said. 'Natasha . . .'

'You'd better go back. I'm interrupting you . . .'

'Perhaps I had.' He hesitated, then turned. Natasha watched him go.

'I'm sorry, Alexis,' she called after him, but if he heard her, he did not turn round.

CHAPTER FIVE

THE score was two hundred and three when Alexis declared. At four o'clock everyone adjourned to the pavilion, where trestle tables had been set up and Anne, installed behind a huge urn, was dispensing cups of tea. Her sons passed round plates of scones and sticky buns; the small room was hot and overcrowded; people were already spilling out of it on to the wooden verandah when Natasha arrived.

She could sense at once that the atmosphere was uncomfortable. The conversation was more muted than usual; players were huddled in groups; they glanced over their shoulders and lowered their voices when they spoke. Natasha hesitated in the doorway. In the far corner was Alexis; he had his back to her, and was talking to Eddy Fiennes. To his left stood Ariana; as Natasha watched she glanced over her shoulder, then took Alexis' arm, and, reaching up on tiptoe, said something into his ear. She had glanced towards the trestle table; there, apparently ostracised, Paul Vansittart stood alone, smoking a cigarette and surveying the room around him with an expression of savage contempt. As Natasha watched, Alexis turned and crossed the room. A little silence fell; heads turned.

He went straight to Paul Vansittart, and took him by the arm in a friendly fashion.

'Paul,' he said. 'You haven't any tea. Let me get you some . . .'

Next to Natasha, William stared, open-mouthed. Someone in the corner of the room tittered nervously; Alexis shot them a cold glance.

'You haven't had a chance to meet half the opposing team,' he said gently. 'Let me introduce you to Eddy Fiennes. He's in his second year at Magdalen, and . . .' Eddy Fiennes, blushing scarlet, turned as Alexis spoke, and held out his hand.

Paul did not take it.

'Don't you bloody patronise me, Lydiard,' he said crisply. He looked around him at the embarrassed faces, hesitated, and then, as his eyes fell on Natasha, abruptly pushed through the throng.

57

'Let's get out of here. I need some fresh air . . .' He gripped
her arm painfully, and began to pull her out of the doorway
in the direction of the field.

For a moment Natasha hung back. Across the room she
saw Alexis start towards her, his face pale with anger. Her lip
trembled; the grip on her arm hurt her.

'Are you coming, or not?'

Her eyes met those of Alexis. She stood for a moment,
poised, knowing everyone was staring at her, but caring only
for the expression she saw on one face. Alexis stopped.

'Yes or no?'

Very carefully she released Paul's hand from her arm. His
fingers had left red marks that stood out against the pallor of
her skin. In the silence that had fallen, she heard noise; her
mind seemed filled with a sudden tumult, a cacophany of
emotion and indecision. She stared at Alexis, willing him to
speak, to move, to do something, anything, to break the chaos
that had sprung up in her mind. Alexis stood still; his fist
clenched. From behind him Ariana moved to his side and put
her hand on his arm.

Paul brushed past her, and out; still she stood looking
across the tiny room. The events, which were happening so
fast, seemed to her infinitely slow, moving at a dream pace.
She stared at Alexis, and at Ariana, at the tanned fingers
resting so possessively on Alexis' arm, and a terrible wild and
painful anger which she could not begin to understand rose
up in her heart. She saw her own hand give an odd little
gesture, as if warding something off, then, abruptly, not
looking back, she turned and ran out of the pavilion.

Paul had reached the bottom of the steps; blindly, not
thinking, she ran after him.

'Paul, wait, please,' she called after him, as he strode ahead
of her. 'Don't be angry, you don't understand . . . Alexis
didn't mean . . .'

She caught up with him, plucking at his sleeve; he did not
slow his pace, but caught her hand, drawing her after him,
through the trees at the edge of the field, and into a narrow
lane that led down to the church.

His face was dark with anger, his breath came quickly;
Natasha stumbled to keep up with him.

'Paul, please . . .' she said.

'Shut up. You don't understand,' he said, and his grip on
her arm tightened. Only in the lane, out of sight of the field

did he slacken his pace. He let her go then, and Natasha, her mind whirling, uncertain what to do or what to say, feeling as if her whole world had suddenly tilted on its base, followed him.

Their surroundings could not have been more peaceful. Late afternoon sun filtered through the trees. The ditches on either side were thick with cow parsley; at the end of the lane Natasha could just see the churchyard, with its tilted gravestones, thick sweet grass and buttercups. She saw all this with a mad precision; her mind, incapable of thought, registered impressions only—the shape of a leaf, the fall of a shadow, the glint of the stones beneath her feet.

There was a bend in the lane where there was a five-barred gate that led into the fields beyond. There, abruptly, Paul stopped. Natasha, hard on his heels, trying to keep up with him, almost fell against him. Before she knew what was happening his arms came roughly around her, she felt the heat of his body against hers.

Then he kissed her.

He did so without preamble or gentleness, forcing her head back and her lips apart, crushing her against him. Natasha, taken completely by surprise, had no time to do anything— she could not push him away, she could not speak, she could not even think. The turmoil of her mind had now been overtaken by another turmoil; her hands were imprisoned against his chest, his mouth was suffocating her, she felt imprisoned by the anger that made his body rigid against hers, his mouth punishing as he kissed her.

Then, as suddenly as it had begun, it ended. He broke off the kiss, and drew back a little, holding her still, looking down into her face.

'I hate them,' he said. 'Do you understand that? All of them. Alexis, that supercilious Greek bitch, all of them. Except you.'

Then, before Natasha could speak, or draw away, he pulled her to him again, forcing his mouth down on hers, his hand tightening around her waist and moving up to the swell of her breast.

'I want you,' he said, against her mouth, and Natasha, her heart lurching with panic, realised it was true. Not thinking, acting on instinct only, she pushed at him sharply, and wrenched her head away. He let her go and she stepped back; they stood looking at each other for a moment, their breath coming quickly. Natasha was shaking; brilliant colour flamed in her cheeks; she could not speak.

Paul looked at her, and then seemed to relax. The anger left his face; he shrugged, and leaned back against the gate.

'I rushed you,' he said at last. 'I was forgetting how—young—you are. I apologise.'

His tone was not apologetic, but Natasha was too confused to say so. She stared at him transfixed, seeing an aspect of men she had read of, but never experienced, bewildered that he could move so quickly from anger to desire, astonished that she seemed to have provoked that desire. She knew she ought to say something, but the words that flew about in her head choked in her throat.

'Well?' He looked at her, his eyes very black in his tanned face. He now appeared completely composed. 'Are you going to stay here or not?'

'Stay here?'

'In Cambridge.' He gave an impatient gesture. 'Well, are you? What do you want to do with your life?'

'I . . . I wanted to write,' Natasha heard herself say, and flinched, waiting for him to laugh, to sneer. He did neither. There was a long silence. Looking up at last to meet his eyes she saw something there, a momentary intentness, a sharpening, then he smiled.

'Then write,' he said, and turned away from her, leaning over the gate and looking out over the fields. Natasha stared at his back.

'You realise you'll never do it here, do you?' His voice was quiet and even. 'You'll never do anything here. That's obvious. You'll get swallowed up. By Cambridge. By your—family. By your nice safe tasteful ordered life . . .'

'Do you think so?' Natasha said, uncertainly, and some part of her mind began to argue, that her life wasn't like that, that no one could describe it as ordered, that he was wrong, that it didn't feel safe either, but precarious, full of shifts and tilts that she did not begin to understand. But then, in the silence, as his words hung in the air, another part of her mind argued back. Perhaps he was right, he must know, he was a writer . . .

'Do you mean . . .' She looked at his back. 'Do you mean that I might, well, see things more clearly if I went away. See them in perspective?'

'You might.' He shrugged.

'So then, if I tried to write . . .'

'Who knows? Some people have to write. They just know it—they just know, from childhood, that that's what they are . . .'

'Do they?' Natasha said humbly.

'But I expect there are other ways. For people who haven't that . . .' He hesitated.

'Vocation?' Natasha prompted nervously.

'Let's say gift,' he said, turning around and giving her a modest smile. Natasha felt dwarfed by him; his self confidence then, his maleness, his casual acceptance of his own role—all these intimidated her. She hung her head, wishing heartily that she had kept silent. He cleared his throat.

'I've been thinking,' he began. 'If you liked—if you wanted. I could help you.'

'You could?'

'If you want.' He paused. 'My new book—I mentioned that? Well, I need an assistant, in London. There's a lot of ground work, a lot of research involved. I cover most of it myself, of course, but my publishers are pressing me, I'm up against a deadline, and it might be . . .' He paused, and Natasha looked up. 'I'd be willing to give you a try. You might find it useful. I can get you somewhere to stay—you wouldn't have to worry about that. I can't pay that much, of course, but . . .'

'You would do that?' Natasha stared at him. He laughed.

'Why not? But you have to make up your mind quickly. I need someone now—in fact I had a couple of candidates lined up already, one was rather bright, just down from Oxford, actually, but I haven't said anything definite to her yet and so . . .' He paused, looking her up and down. 'In any case, in some ways, you fit the bill rather better than she does.'

Natasha looked at him uncertainly; a whisper of doubt surfaced at the back of her mind.

'And no strings,' he said, as if he read her thoughts. 'I don't operate that way with women.'

Natasha felt chastened. She swallowed. Her heart was beating very fast.

'I don't know if I'd be much help to you,' she began. 'I've never done any formal research, and I'm not sure that . . .'

'This isn't formal research. Don't worry. I won't be burying you in the British Museum reading room. I'm not Alexis . . .'

'Oh . . .' Natasha's eyes widened.

'You're worried about Alexis. Don't be. If he gives any trouble I'll take care of him . . .'

'No, it's not that. It's just that . . .' She hesitated. An image of her cousin swam before her gaze, cool, green-eyed, slightly mocking. She tried to wrench the image from her thoughts. She couldn't go through life depending on Alexis' judgment, she knew that, yet sometimes it felt as if she were fated always to imagine him and imagine his response, to a person, to a conversation, to a suggestion. He rose before her now, his mouth twisted with his wry, slightly mocking smile, and for a second she saw Paul Vansittart as Alexis might see him, then the image fled, the moment of disassociation passed.

'If it makes you feel better, don't tell him. Say you're going up to find work, that you're staying with a friend . . .'

'Oh, I couldn't lie. Not to Alexis.' She rounded on him, suddenly alarmed.

'I'll have to get back,' he said, his manner suddenly losing its sympathy. 'You'll have to make up your own mind on this, I'm afraid. There's no point in my trying to persuade you.'

He turned away as he spoke, and began to stride back down the lane. Natasha ran after him.

'No, please,' she said. 'You're very kind. But everything's happened so fast. I can't think.'

'I'm leaving after the match,' he said. 'Think then. I'll phone you—Wednesday—Friday, sometime next week. I can't say exactly. I'll be pretty tied up . . .'

Natasha's face fell. Seeing it, he paused, and put an arm around her shoulders. His hand brushed—accidentally, she was sure—against her breast.

'Come,' he said. 'You should. And don't worry. I'll phone you. I shan't forget.'

They had reached the edge of the cricket field; through the trees Natasha caught glimpses of white, a ripple of applause.

'Maybe we'd better go back separately,' he said. 'It might be more discreet—don't you think? At this stage?' He bent and brushed a kiss lightly against her forehead. 'Goodbye, Natasha,' he said softly. 'You're very beautiful—do you know that?'

Then he was gone.

A little later Natasha went back to the field. The light was fading fast; the game was nearly over. Alexis was bowling; she watched as one by one the tail-end wickets fell. She sat on the grass, away from the other spectators absorbed, silent, thinking. She could go, or she could stay; which?

When Paul came out to bat it was late, and it was clear that Alexis' team had already won. Natasha watched his tall dark figure stride out from the pavilion, and she clasped her hands tightly around her knees. If Alexis bowls him out I shall stay; if he doesn't I shall go, she said to herself, suddenly, knowing it was silly, knowing it was arbitrary, but feeling relief that— this way—the decision need not be hers.

She was thwarted in her plan. Alexis, as the novelist came out, glanced towards the figure of Natasha in the distance. He appeared to hesitate, then he tossed the ball to John Middleton, and retired to the field.

Later, when the game was over, when Paul Vansittart had returned to London, William pronounced his decision to stop bowling incomprehensible.

'He'd taken three wickets in three overs,' he said crossly. 'Why stop then? Especially when the you-know-who was going to bat.'

'He robbed Paul of the confrontation he wanted,' Anne answered with a smile, and a glance in Natasha's direction.

'But Vansittart would have been the loser,' said Bernard, puzzled.

'Exactly. It's very typical of Alexis, don't you think?'

Wednesday was reached, and went past; Paul Vansittart did not telephone. Natasha, who had spent Monday and Tuesday convinced he would not ring, yet terrified that he might, had still not made up her mind as to her answer. When she went to bed on Wednesday she could not sleep, but paced up and down her room. He had not rung, probably that meant he never would. It seemed likely; in spite of what he said, why should he bother with her? Probably he had hired the Oxford graduate he had mentioned, she told herself, and instantly pictured a woman who was a mirror-image of Ariana— beautiful, efficient, intelligent, energetic. She felt a moment's relief, and then pain. Part of her wanted to stay in Cambridge—but she felt that was the coward's part. And another part said that at least if she were offered the job it would prove something—that someone valued her at least. If she did go away, she told herself, then perhaps this feeling of unease and unhappiness would go too. She needed to work, so her mind did not go off at the odd and perturbing tangents which it seemed to have been taking lately. And if she found such a job, even if it were working for a man he loathed, then perhaps Alexis might feel more respect for her.

Alexis she had hardly seen since the day of the cricket match. He had begun a new book, Anne said; he had a heavy programme of lectures and seminars. He had spent the two previous nights in college, and seemed to be spending this night there too, for he still had not returned, and it was three in the morning. Did he spend these nights alone, working, or did he spend them with Ariana? And if he did, why did that possibility make her feel so miserable? She felt protective to Alexis, of course, that was probably why. Alexis out of kindness and his own peculiar kind of innocence could make such disastrous mistakes. What if he were to marry the wrong woman? A woman who would cause him unhappiness and pain? Natasha's heart contracted at the thought. It would be horrible; dreadful. And Ariana was certainly the wrong kind of woman, she was sure of it. In fact, when she came to consider it, she couldn't think of anyone she knew who was suitable. Alexis deserved someone so splendid, so good, so . . . She turned away impatiently from the window, where she had been watching for Alexis' car. It was no good thinking like this. Alexis, determined and definite when it came to the important matters in life, would make his own choice. Ariana was very clever, after all. And beautiful. Natasha lay back on her bed, and groaned.

The next day passed very slowly. Alexis was out; Paul did not telephone. As her hopes of being offered an escape diminished, her desire that it should be offered increased. What else was she to do? It was horrible being here, unable to find work, despising herself, worrying about Alexis. At lunchtime she went up to her room, locked the door and spent the whole afternoon trying to write. She began another novel, putting from her mind the memory of the other one and a half efforts hidden in her underwear drawer. She wrote furiously. She introduced a hero possessed of green eyes. At tea-time she read what she had written with mounting embarrassment, and then tore it all up. The telephone rang three times, each time for Alexis, and by six o'clock Natasha felt that with very little prompting she would jump out of the window.

At six-thirty Alexis came home. He was dropped at the gate by a silver Porsche, and came up the driveway whistling.

William looked up from his homework.

'What a car,' he said, as Alexis entered the room. 'Has it got five gears? Whose is it?'

Alexis looked vague, as if he had never heard of gears.

'The Morris wouldn't start,' he said evasively.

'It's Ariana's, isn't it?' Natasha gave him a cold glance. 'I caught sight of her.'

William coughed sepulchrally; Alexis leaned over his shoulder and examined his mathematics with what Natasha felt was exaggerated interest. Silence fell. Natasha prayed that the telephone would ring, and her prayers remained unanswered.

Soon afterwards Alexis and William began to play chess. Natasha sat on the windowseat, a book on her lap, and watched them. Alexis had his back to her. She stared miserably at the back of his neck, where his thick dark hair curled over his collar. Both he and William were absorbed in the game; the clock in the corner ticked; as far as they were concerned she was invisible; she simply did not exist. She watched them; it became apparent that Alexis was letting William win, and that fact—for some reason—lit a wild irrational irritation in her heart. Alexis was the kindest person she knew, but he was so blind.

'Would you like a game, Natasha?' he said suddenly, laying his king on its side in resignation. Natasha jumped.

'No, I wouldn't,' she snapped. 'I hate chess. What's the point? You always win when we play.'

'He mightn't, Nat,' William said encouragingly. He was pleased with himself, re-arranging the pieces neatly on the board, the way he liked them, so that all the knights' heads pointed forwards.

'Yes, he would. Unless he let me win, the way he does you . . . and don't call me Nat. I've told you a thousand times.'

William looked up slowly from the board, his face clouded.

'Alexis doesn't let me win,' he said.

'Yes he does! He's just done it—I was watching——'

She broke off. To her horror William had grown very red in the face; the corners of his mouth trembled.

'I won,' he said tremulously. 'It was my new strategy, and I won—didn't I, Alexis?'

'Yes, you did. Fair and square,' Alexis said, but his face was troubled, and something in his expression must have betrayed him, for quite suddenly, William's face crumpled. Tears spilled from his eyes and obscured his glasses. Without another word he put down the knight he had been holding and ran out of the room. From upstairs a door slammed. There was silence; Alexis stood up. Natasha felt deeply ashamed; she could not meet his eyes, and would have dodged out of the room had she had the chance, but Alexis gripped her arm and swung her round to face him. He was pale, as angry as she had ever seen him.

'What the hell's the matter with you?' he said furiously. 'What do you mean by that? How could you be so unkind?'

'Is it unkind to tell the truth?' Natasha countered, trying to shake him off and failing. 'Why lie?'

'For God's sake. He's eight years old. He's a child. I was trying to encourage him, that's all. You had no right to interfere, do you hear me? No right at all. And certainly not like that. It was bullying—cruel. You ought to be ashamed of yourself.'

'Well I'm not!' Natasha lied, raising her voice defiantly. 'I'm not ashamed and I'm not sorry. William's old enough—he can learn. The object of the game is winning—I've heard you say that often enough. *Winning*—whether it's chess or cricket or . . . anything else. That's what you say, but it isn't what you do. Because basically, you don't care—it doesn't matter to you. Win or lose, you just shrug it off . . .'

'I was playing with a *child*, for God's sake. What on earth are you talking about?'

'You, I'm talking about you.' Natasha rounded on him, suddenly furiously angry. 'Alexis, the all-time graceful loser, who goes out with a gentlemanly bow. Alexis, who never had to fight for anything in his life, and wouldn't bother if he had to . . .'

She broke off; Alexis had let go of her arm. The coldness of his expression terrified her.

'You're being a little wild,' he said, his voice perfectly level. 'Perhaps you'd like to be more specific. Is there something you think I ought to be fighting for other than victory in a game of chess with an eight-year-old child?'

'Yes, as it happens, there is!' Natasha shouted. 'Not that you'd notice, of course, but there is.'

'What?' Alexis folded his arms.

'Don't *look* at me like that!' Now almost beside herself with anger, she gave him a violent push. 'Why should I tell you? You wouldn't understand. You're so cold, so dried up. Stuck there in your study surrounded by books. Books—that's all you think about. They make me sick. I can't bear to look at them any more. When I leave here I never want to see another book as long as I live. You can't learn about life from books.'

Alexis' face had taken on a closed expression.

'You're becoming stupid,' he said coldly. 'And hysterical. I suggest you apologise to William and then go to bed.'

'Don't *talk* to me like that!' Natasha gave him another push. 'You treat me like a child.'

'Calm down, Natasha.'

'*Calm down, Natasha,*' she mimicked him bitterly. 'You would say that. You don't care. You don't care about anything and anyone—just your books. That stupid Ariana said . . .'

'Leave Ariana out of this.'

'No, I won't. Why should I?' Natasha advanced on him. 'Ariana thinks you're a man of passions, which just shows what she knows. I told her how wrong she was. You wouldn't recognise passion if it was standing three feet in front of you, you're so goddamn myopic.'

'Were. Were standing. Do passions walk about rooms like that? How odd.' Alexis smiled, and Natasha lost her temper totally.

'Don't laugh at me, damn it, Alexis, don't do that.'

Before she knew what was happening, she had lifted her hand, and struck him hard across the face. The blow had such force that it knocked his glasses off and sent them spinning half way across the room. Alexis grabbed her hand; but not before it had left a long scarlet weal down his cheek.

They stood there for a moment, neither moving, and although he gripped her wrist painfully hard, Natasha was not conscious of that, only of his eyes which met her own, and seemed to look down into her very being, beyond the anger and shame and confusion she felt to some place where she was herself.

He looked neither angry, nor hurt, nor cold, but very alert, as if her torrent of wild abuse had suddenly made something clear to him. He looked severe and yet beautiful, and before the candour of his gaze, Natasha felt herself shrivel up, crumple with shame and self-hatred.

Very deliberately he reached up with his other hand and lifted her face back to his as she turned it away. They stood like that, quite still, not moving, then Alexis bent towards her. The telephone rang.

Natasha twisted away from him, hastened across the room, picked up the receiver. It was Paul Vansittart.

She looked up at Alexis, keeping her face cold.

'It's for me,' she said pointedly.

Alexis hesitated, and then abruptly left the room.

She would go, then, to London.

Paul Vansittart had asked her and she had said yes, straight away, incautiously, hardly asking any questions, just yes. She knew why she had done it too; to prove something to Alexis, that was why, and because she hated herself, hated what she was becoming, here in Cambridge, and the only way out she could see was to leave. She had been unkind to William, whom she loved, and though he had forgiven her when she apologised to him that night—like Alexis, he never bore a grudge—she could not forgive herself. That night too, she stayed awake late, examining herself and her behaviour, contrasting it with the behaviour of others, and appalled by what she saw.

When Alexis had been her age he had taken on the responsibility of a little girl, the daughter of a cousin whom— she gathered, though her parents were not often discussed— Alexis had hardly known. When Anne had been widowed he had added, to that responsibility, another far greater one—his sister and her two sons. For the first time in her life Natasha thought seriously about what that must have meant for Alexis. How it must have confined him, narrowed his life. Apart from the expense, which must have been considerable, for her father, she knew, had left nothing, and Anne had little money of her own, Alexis' whole life had been dominated by his ready-made family. All the fantasies she had spun about Alexis at school—how callow and stupid they seemed now! How could Alexis have had a private life—how could he have married, had he wanted to, when he alone was responsible for supporting his sister and three young children?

And now, when it seemed possible that—if William and Julian were correct about their mother—some of that burden of responsibility might be lifted, how had she herself reacted? Meanly. Selfishly. Jealously—yes, that was it, she saw it now; she was jealous and possessive of Alexis, and she had no right to be.

She had one consolation only. She had found a job. She would be going away, so Alexis' life need not be trammeled or complicated by her existence any more. Yes, that was a consolation. It made her weep bitterly.

*   *   *

The next day she felt a little better; her mind at least felt clear. She packed, so she would be ready to leave early the next day. Into her suitcase she put some drawings of William's, the photograph of Alexis from school, and the small leather frame that held the only photograph she possessed of her father and mother. She folded it away, then took it out again, curiously, trying to remember. She had seen them so little; it was a photograph of strangers. What had they been like, her mother and her father? She studied their faces—her mother's beautiful, fashionable; her father's handsome, the mouth a little weak. Was it from him that she had inherited her own selfishness? she wondered, and then put that thought aside. Unworthy, to blame the dead for her own failings. If she was as she saw herself it was her fault, no one else's, and she would have to cure herself.

She told no one her plans; she would have to, of course, but she wanted to tell Alexis first, and he had left early for lectures. So, methodically, she made her arrangements. She collected her dole money, bought her ticket to London—a single—and then, still trying to assuage her guilt, spent almost all of the rest on a model aeroplane for William, a A10A Fairchild that he had coveted, she knew, for ages.

She gave it to him that afternoon, when he came home from school, with more apologies, and an excess of emotion that she knew he found curious.

'I don't know why I was so horrid,' she said contritely. 'I'm sorry, William.'

'That's all right. You're on edge.' He smiled at her complacently. 'It's only to be expected.'

'Why?' Natasha stared at him.

'You're in love, of course. It's obvious.'

Natasha blushed crimson; William began to unwrap a great number of tiny plastic aeroplane parts; his tone was casual.

'It's a bit soppy, I suppose,' he went on. 'But then you're a girl. You can't help it.'

'Not just girls fall in love, you know, William.'

'That's true. Alexis is in love right now, for instance.'

Natasha sat down abruptly and stared at him.

'Alexis?' she said faintly. 'Are you sure?'

'No question. You must have noticed.'

'Well, I did think that . . .' Natasha pulled herself up short. 'Nonsense,' she said, looking at William pleadingly. 'I'm sure you're wrong. You've got love on the brain at the moment . . .'

'It's the best place to have it, in my opinion.' William regarded her solemnly. 'Alexis thinks so too, I heard him say so. He said love—you know, romantic love, between a man and a woman -was responsible for most of the mischief in this world. He said it was a most troublesome emotion, and the more it was confined to the mind the more likelihood there was of controlling it. It was when it sort of sneaked out, into the heart and—er—other places, that the problems started.'

'Who did he say that to?'

'Ariana. He was very het up about it. He was waving his arms about, the way he does, you know. I rather got the impression that in his case it had started sneaking out already.'

Natasha stood up. 'You have a fevered imagination,' she said as firmly as she could. 'It's very unhealthy in an eight-year-old boy, even a precocious one.'

'If you say so.' William grinned. Natasha dropped a kiss on his hair.

As she drew back, William regarded her unblinkingly and earnestly through his spectacles.

'Are you going to London then?' he said.

'What?'

'Well, you've packed your case and hidden it under your bed, so I thought you might be.'

Natasha sighed, and sat down.

'Yes,' she said at last. 'I am. Tomorrow.'

William shrugged. 'Okay,' he said. 'It's your funeral.'

He returned to his plane and his glue; Natasha felt dismissed. But when she went to the door, to her great surprise, for William scorned demonstrations of affection, he ran after her, clasped her tightly, and planted a wet kiss on her cheek.

'I shall miss you, Nat,' he said. 'You will come back, won't you?'

CHAPTER SIX

DOWNSTAIRS Alexis was pacing the hall. his car keys in his hand.

'Oh good,' he said, when he saw Natasha. 'Come on, I'm taking you out to dinner.'

Natasha came to a stop at the bottom of the stairs; colour swept up her neck to her cheeks; she stared at him. Alexis had never taken her out to dinner on her own before.

'I've apologised to William,' she said stiffly. 'I wanted to apologise to you, too.'

'Oh good, fine,' Alexis said vaguely.

'Are you going to give me a Serious Talk?' She tried to keep her voice light and scanned his face. There had to be a reason for this. Could it just be the result of her behaviour the previous night, or had Alexis discovered her plans?

'A serious talk? No, why? Should I?'

Natasha felt relief flood through her veins.

'Well, you've never taken me out to dinner before.'

'Haven't I? I must have done, surely? No? Then it's time I did, don't you think? Are you ready? You don't need to change or anything?'

'Yes, I do—I feel tatty. I'll just change my shirt. You start the car—I won't be five seconds . . .'

Not giving him a chance to argue, Natasha raced back up the stairs to her room. All her unhappiness had fled. Her heart sang with extraordinary joy. She would still have to tell Alexis, of course, but she needn't tell him immediately, and the sudden invitation thrilled her. At top speed she tore off her blouse and pulled on a tight black tee-shirt which clung to the outlines of her slender fighre dramatically. Her black trousers were equally tight; she changed into her new black suede boots. Then she brushed her hair energetically, tipped rather too much *Rive Gauche* on to the back of her neck, and surveyed herself in the glass. The whole affair took more like five minutes than five seconds, but Alexis, when she came running out and leapt into the car, did not seem inclined to complain.

It was a lovely evening, warm and still sunny: Natasha

banged the car door. Alexis stared at the tee-shirt and stalled the car. Natasha turned to him, summoning up her nerve.

'Alexis,' she said. 'Darling Alexis, I'm sorry I was so foul last night. And I'm sorry I hit you. There!'

She leaned across and kissed his cheek where she had hit him the night before.

'Am I forgiven? Please.'

Alexis rubbed his cheek thoughtfully. 'That was really rather pleasant,' he said. 'I think you might do it again.'

'Kiss you, you mean?'

'Well, I don't mean hit me, certainly.'

Natasha laughed, leaned across, and kissed him again. His skin beneath her lips felt warm, slightly rough to the touch. This time she made the kiss more lingering, and it was Alexis who drew away.

'Thank you very much,' he said. 'You're certainly for-given.'

He started the car again, and reversed it into the garden wall. This was not such an unusual occurrence, for Alexis' driving was eccentric to say the least, and it appeared not to dismay him. Whistling cheerfully, he slammed the car forward, performed a surprisingly accomplished U-turn, and sped out of the driveway into the middle of the road. Straddling the central line he proceeded fast in the direction of Cambridge.

Natasha looked at him sideways.

'You're looking remarkably debonair and cheerful,' she said eventually. 'What's happened?'

'Nothing's happened. I always look this way when I'm taking a beautiful young woman out to dinner.'

Natasha digested this remark in silence. It was extremely uncharacteristic, and she would have suspected him of mockery, but his face was perfectly serious.

'Where are we going?'

'I haven't decided. I'm not very good at this sort of thing. Where do you think we ought to go?'

'You mean you haven't booked?'

Alexis looked as if he'd never heard of such a custom. His face fell.

'Oh dear,' he said. 'No, I didn't think of that.' He paused. 'Where would you like to go?'

Natasha smiled to herself. She knew Alexis' tastes.

'I'd love an Indian meal.'

'Would you?' Alexis brightened up again. 'Oh good. That's all right then.'

They drove on for a few more miles in silence, until they reached Cambridge. There Alexis drove three times round the one-way system. He was just about to go round for a fourth time when Natasha stopped him.

'What are you doing, Alexis?' she said gently.

Alexis slammed on the brakes. A cyclist behind him narrowly avoided death.

'This is all wrong,' he said gloomily. 'You don't really want an Indian meal. You're just saying that. I ought to have thought this out. I ought to be taking you to—I don't know—one of those country places. In Granchester or something. With wine. And a long menu. And candles. That sort of thing.'

'I don't want candles and a long menu. I don't want that God-awful pretentious place at Granchester either—I can't stand it. I want—oh, egg biryani or something like that. And a chapati. And poppadums. Somewhere with red flock wallpaper . . . really, Alexis.'

'Are you sure?'

'Yes, I am. Now park in the market place, for God's sake. We've gone round in a circle so many times I'm giddy.'

Alexis did as he was bid. He parked the aged Morris, leapt out and opened Natasha's door for her. Then, taking her arm in a very gallant fashion, he led her down a side turning past shoe shops and a supermarket and then into a small alley. Across the alley two Indian restaurants faced one another. One was called the *Taj Mahal* and was empty; the other was called the *Café India* and was crowded. Alexis hesitated.

'The thing is,' he said, 'I rather like the *Taj Mahal*, but no one goes there any more.'

'Then let's go to the *Taj Mahal*.'

Purposefully Natasha pushed open the door. It clanged and rattled against a heavy beaded curtain. The inside of the restaurant was murky. She could just make out red flock wallpaper, and several little niches contrived from hard-board cut into the shape of Islamic doorways. There was a bar at the far end, where a man stood polishing glasses, and about twenty tables, all deserted. There were speakers on the wall from which issued, faintly, the wailing singing of an Indian pop star. The place was very Alexis; Natasha liked it.

When he saw Alexis, the owner greeted him like a brother.

Alexis asked if they might sit in a table near the window; then he ordered a bottle of wine.

When the man withdrew he leaned across the table to Natasha.

'The thing is,' he said, 'it seems so awfully unfair. The food here is really very good, and it used always to be full. Then that place opened up—and suddenly . . .' He gestured around him. 'So I make a point of coming here, and I always sit in the window. I think if they see people inside it might encourage others to come in. Don't you?'

Natasha smiled. 'I think it's lovely, Alexis,' she said. 'Why don't you order?'

He seemed oddly unrelaxed, she thought, but he cheered up when the wine arrived, and spent a considerable time with the owner discussing the menu.

Natasha felt suddenly irradiated with a warm affection for her surroundings and for Alexis, who had brought her here. She thought how kind he was, and how handsome he looked, and how lucky she was to have him. If everything went wrong in London, she could come back to Cambridge, certain at least of a welcome from her family, certain that no matter what else happened, Alexis would be there—loyal, kind, capable of sternness certainly, but clever, more than that—wise—and good. The thought comforted her; she realised she did not want to think about London, much less discuss it with Alexis.

The owner of the restaurant had left them; Alexis re-filled her glass. He was staring at her, she realised. She hesitated, wondering how to begin, whether it would be best to make her confession quickly.

'Do you realise, Alexis,' she said carefully at last, leaning towards him, 'how provincial and narrow I am? I've hardly been anywhere. France, once, and that ski-ing holiday from school. Apart from that—nothing. It's awful.'

'Well, I haven't been anywhere much either.' Alexis smiled. 'We're a pair of provincials.'

'Yes, you have. You were at Harvard—you went all over America. You used to go to Europe all the time when I was little. You did that lecture tour in Eastern Europe . . .' She sighed; there was a picture of the Taj Mahal over Alexis's head. 'I'd love to go to India.'

'I've never been to India either.'

'I think it would be lovely. The Taj Mahal by moonlight . .'

'There are beggars as well as temples, Natasha . . .'

'I'd still like to go.'

'Then let's go. Why not?' He paused. 'We could go in the summer vacation.'

'What, you and I?' She stared at him, and Alexis laughed.

'Well, don't look so shocked. Why not? We could.' He hesitated, and began to draw lines on the white tablecloth with his knife. 'I thought about what you said,' he went on finally. 'Last night . . .'

'You shouldn't have. I was angry. I was being stupid . . .'

'No.' He looked up to meet her eyes. 'You weren't, not altogether. I do tend to—bury myself in my work, forget to come up for air. Cambridge does that to people. It's one of the dangers of the place. All those beautiful courts, facing inwards, shutting out the world.' He shrugged. 'So—you're right. Why not? Let's go to India.'

Natasha drained her glass; her heart lifted. *I could,* she thought. *I could. I don't have to go to London.* She stared into Alexis' eyes and felt suddenly as if the world were boundless with possibility. An enormous heady optimism surged through her veins; she felt a little light-headed from the wine, it was true—but also light-hearted.

'A houseboat in Kashmir—on the lakes?'

'If you like . . .'

'Going to the bazaar at dawn?'

'If it's open.'

'Beaches with palm trees, and ruined temples with monkeys?'

'But certainly.'

'A journey to Bombay, on a steam train? I've always wanted to do that—I love trains.'

'So do I. We'll book it.'

'Oh Alexis!' Natasha said, reaching impulsively for his hand.

'*Sag prawn,* sir?' said the waiter.

'Thank you,' said Alexis. He let go of her hand only because the waiter was having difficulty finding space on the table.

By the time he withdrew, Natasha felt embarrassed. She looked at Alexis ruefully.

'We're day-dreaming,' she said. 'You should stop me. It's wrong.'

'No, it isn't, and no, I shouldn't.' Alexis helped her to the food.

'Yes, it is.' Natasha hesitated. 'It's—impossible. How could we go? It would cost the earth. Besides, we can't just take off like that. What about the others—Anne, the boys.' She hesitated. 'Your *ménage*.'

Alexis gave her a sharp glance. 'My *what*?'

'Your *ménage*. There's four of us—it wouldn't be fair just to take me.'

'For once in my life . . .' Alexis paused, holding the spoon aloft, 'I wasn't thinking about being fair. And in any case, as it happens, I don't think that would be a problem.'

Something in his tone alarmed her.

'Why not, Alexis?'

Alexis had lifted his fork; he put it down again, and looked at her.

'I'm not sure if you've realised,' he said. 'But Anne——'

'She's going to marry Bernard?'

Alexis lowered his gaze. 'Yes,' he said. 'I think she is. I also think she ought to.'

'Ought to?'

He shrugged and looked away. His colour had risen, and Natasha saw that he was embarrassed.

'They love each other. Bernard has been pressing her to marry for some time. Anne wasn't sure . . .'

Natasha cleared her throat. A little cold shiver of fear ran down her spine. 'She should marry him,' she said carefully. 'It would be lovely for her. The boys approve. They told me.'

'I think she was worried. Not about the boys. About us.'

'Us?' Natasha's voice came out in an odd absurd kind of croak.

'Try the prawns. They're usually delicious.'

Dutifully Natasha tasted them; they were delicious, just as he said, but they might as well have been cardboard. Suddenly all her appetite had gone; the anxiety she had tried to set aside now returned full blown. She felt her nerves stretched taut as wires; her mind buzzed with the incomprehensible refrain of the Indian song from the loudspeakers. Suddenly she cared for nothing except what Alexis should say next; she felt as if her life depended upon it.

'Us?' she prompted again, when Alexis did not speak.

Again he laid down his fork.

'Anne would like to marry Bernard. She—er—well, she loves him.' Alexis seemed to find speech extraordinarily difficult; Natasha began to suspect that what he was going to say was rehearsed, was, indeed, the reason for this invitation.

'But were they to marry . . .'

'Are they going to marry?'

'Yes. I think they are. Yes.'

'And live together?'

'It is customary.'

There was a heavy silence. Alexis pushed most of his prawns aside, uneaten. Natasha followed his example. She swallowed an entire glass of wine with great rapidity and took a deep breath. Whatever he had planned to say, she doubted Alexis' ability to come out with it.

'You mean we'd be left alone? Is that the problem?'

He evaded her eyes.

'Well, is it?'

'Yes.'

Natasha swallowed. Now, quite clearly, was the moment for her to confess. All she needed to say was that there was no problem, that she would be going to London, would be finding work there, beginning a new life. She shaped the necessary sentences in her mind, opened her lips and then closed them again. Somehow the words refused to come out. She looked miserably down at her plate, feeling herself grow hot with nerves and embarrassment. If she didn't speak now, the obvious moment to do so, it would become harder and harder.

'Anne has said that of course you must stay on there with them, if you want to,' he said abruptly.

'What about you?'

'I could stay too, of course, if I wanted to. But I don't.'

'You could always move back into college, though, couldn't you?'

Natasha was aware that her own voice sounded oddly choked. Alexis raised his head and looked her directly in the eyes.

'I don't want to do that either,' he said.

The sudden determination in his voice, something in the way he said this, filled Natasha with the deepest alarm. She felt the blood rush to her cheeks; to her dismay she felt all the symptoms she knew were preparatory to tears. Her mind, which had seemed frozen, began all at once to accelerate rapidly. Suddenly everything fell into place, the hints dropped by the boys, Ariana's proprietorial manner at the cricket match, Alexis' own behaviour—the very fact that he had brought her here this evening. Now, with total clarity, she understood. William and Julian *were* right about Alexis, as they had been right about their mother. He *was* planning a new life: Alexis, who had found it so funny when she dubbed him a confirmed batchelor. He meant to marry.

'Natasha,' he said. He leaned forward, and she knew her face had betrayed her sentiments, for his was filled with gentle concern.

Quickly she interrupted him.

'It's all right, Alexis,' she said. 'You don't need to say anything else. I see now why you brought me here. I see the problem—Anne has her life to lead, you have yours. There's just one problem: me.'

'Natasha, please . . .'

'Stop. Before you say anything else. I just want you to know it's not a problem. You don't need to worry, any of you.' She paused. 'I'm going to London. I was going to tell you tonight in any case. What you've just said has made it easier.'

Her words came out in a rush, tumbling over one another. Their effect on Alexis, who could guard his feelings very well when he chose to, was not easy to interpret. His eyes did not leave her face; he might have grown a little paler; he did not speak.

At this moment the restaurant owner brought their second course. He took some time, arranging the dishes on the table with care, fussing over them both, as if he sensed something had gone wrong between them and wished in some way to ease the moment. Natasha watched his hands fixedly as they moved plates, arranged cutlery; she could have screamed from tension. When he went, finally, Alexis said,

'When are you going?'

'Tomorrow,' she answered.

That reply did startle him. She waited for the outburst that must surely come, the questions, the criticism. There was a long silence.

'I see,' he said finally. His face set in cold hard lines. He picked up the spoon in front of him to serve the food, and then set it down again.

'You have somewhere to stay?'

Natasha looked away. 'Yes,' she said quietly.

There was an ominous pause.

'You have work to go to?'

'I'm not sure. I think so. I don't know if it will work out.'

'Do you intend to remain there—in London?'

'I'm not sure. I can't say. Yes, probably. The point is, I'm going, so the rest of the family can go ahead with all their plans. They—you—don't have to worry about me.' She hesitated, knowing she said too little, feeling she ought to say more, but not daring, then, to tell him the whole truth. But as she opened her mouth to speak, he lifted his hand with a little gesture and cut her off.

'Please, Natasha,' he said. 'You don't need to say anymore. You clearly don't want to. And I'd prefer it if you didn't lie.'

'You mean I can go? Just like that?'

He smiled sadly. 'But of course you may go. You don't need my permission. You're a free agent.'

Natasha felt the tears fill her eyes, and she blinked them back angrily. She had not expected this, she realised it now. Somewhere at the back of her mind, even as she made her preparations, she had expected Alexis to act. Not to stop her leaving, no, she had not expected that. But she had thought he would question her, examine her, query the wisdom of her actions, show at least some concern. And now—nothing. Obviously the news was a relief to him—so much so that the details did not even concern him. She swallowed. The temptation to tell him about Paul Vansittart was very great: that surely would provoke some reaction. But she fought the temptation off. If she told him that, Alexis might feel he had to forbid her to leave, and that wouldn't be fair. As far as he was concerned, the sooner she left, the better.

'I ... I expect it will all work out,' she said eventually.

Alexis seemed to be making an effort to appear cheerful. He agreed over-quickly.

'Oh, I'm sure it will. You've wanted to leave Cambridge for some time, I know, and ...' He broke off. 'You're sure you wouldn't like to stay at Sophie's? You could, you know. I could arrange it.'

Natasha looked at her plate. 'No, thank you, Alexis. I'll ... I'll be fine.'

He paused. 'You don't want to tell me where you'll be staying? What you'll be doing?'

Natasha, at that moment, wanted nothing more passionately, but she shook her head.

'Not yet, Alexis,' she said quietly. 'I'd just like to see first—how it works out. But I'll phone. Write ...'

She looked up at him pleadingly as she spoke, and seeing

that he *was* worried and was trying to hide it, she smiled gently.

'Oh, Alexis,' she said. 'Don't look like that. You know what you're like. You fuss, and then, the moment I've gone, you'll forget all about me. Three months from now you'll suddenly look up at breakfast and say, "Oh, where's Natasha?"' Her voice trailed away; his dark green eyes glinted dangerously.

'Is that what you think? You think I don't care? Well, as it happens, I do. Would you like me to tell you exactly why?'

'No,' said Natasha, very fast, interrupting him, because she knew he would talk about the family, and how much he cared for them, and how he looked on her as a younger sister, and—just then—she felt she could not bear it. There was a little silence. Natasha, frightened of the silence, suddenly seeing a vision of herself, returning from London and being met by Alexis, a changed Alexis, a married Alexis, began desperately to talk, saying the first things that sprang into her head. Amid the torrent of quite meaningless remarks, Alexis leaned forward abruptly and took her hand.

'I shall miss you,' he said. 'Very much.'

'Will you, Alexis?'

'Yes.'

Natasha stared into his eyes; his hands held hers tightly. A thousand things, all unsaid, crowded and confused her mind; the one clarity was the touch of her hand in his. She felt at once that she knew him better than she would ever know anyone in her life, and that she knew him not at all. His familiarity and his mystery drew her, and yet also frightened her. Something held her, then faltered. She lowered her gaze.

'What time is your train?'

'Ten-thirty.'

'Then I shall take you to the station.'

It was all he said; then he changed the subject. He humoured her, teased her, drew her out. He talked with his own kind of dry understated wit, which she loved, and though she knew he set out deliberately to change her mood, to cheer her, gradually she succumbed. Alexis, when he chose, had great charm. He manipulated her, she knew it, but she began to relax once more. She fought it briefly, but her unhappiness did fall away.

When they left the restaurant, she told him she wanted to go for a walk.

'Please, Alexis,' she said. 'I want to. Look, the moon is shining. Let's go somewhere silly, somewhere impossibly romantic. Just this once. So I can say my farewells. To—Cambridge.'

'Very well,' he said, and took her arm.

He led her across the market place, down a narrow street, through a college, which admitted her—though it was late—because she was with Alexis, and then out on to the Backs. They stopped, at last, on one of the bridges over the river. Under its arches the water flowed darkly; to their left were the crenellations of King's College Chapel, to their right other bridges, shadowed buildings, isolated windows still vivid with light. They were quite alone. It was silent, and on the other side of the water the trees shifted their leaves against the moon. They stood in the middle of the bridge. Natasha rested her bare arms on its stone balustrade and looked down into the water.

'Will this do?' Alexis said at last. 'For a valediction?'

'Yes.' She turned to him, impulsively. 'Alexis, say goodbye to me now, here, won't you do that? I hate station goodbyes. Take me to the station if you want, but say goodbye to me now.'

She was afraid he might think her absurd, that he would mock her, but his face was quite serious.

'Please, Alexis.' She touched his arm. 'It's—important. I want to remember this afterwards. For ever and ever. When I think of Cambridge, I want to think of this.'

His face was shadowed from her; in the moonlight he looked so dark, so tall, so strange to her, that she almost faltered. Her throat felt dry and as she lifted her hands and rested them against his chest, she trembled a little. She lifted her lips to his cheek. Very deliberately, he turned her face to his, so he could look down into her eyes. His arms came around her strongly. Then he bent and kissed her on the mouth.

When they broke apart at last, Natasha was shaking. She bent her head; the sound of the river rushed in her ears. She thought: now, everything is changed; now he will not let me go to London.

'Shall we go home, then?' said Alexis.

The image of Alexis tormented her throughout a sleepless night. At ten she crept downstairs telling herself that he had been waiting for the morning, waiting to see if she meant to go through with it, giving himself time to think. He had not spoken last night; now, this morning, he would.

Alexis was waiting for her; fresh, washed, shaved, his car keys in his hand. He looked up from *The Times* as she came in.

'Good,' he said. 'All ready? We'd better be off then.'

He drove to the station fast, with none of his usual eccentricity; he was silent. Politely, a little abstractedly, he saw her on to the platform and bought her magazines. He pressed her hand briefly, wished her luck, and then just turned and melted away into the crowd. Natasha, straining to catch a last glimpse of him, saw he did not look back, but left with an unhurried composure, just as he had left the cricket field nearly a week before. She watched his tall dark figure until he was out of sight. Then she climbed on to the train, locked herself in the lavatory and cried. When she had finished crying, she looked at herself in the glass.

You are beginning a new life, she told her reflection silently, seriously. *You are. Stop being childish.*

It was as good a word as any. The exhortation worked. She washed her face, went to a carriage, opened a book, forced all thoughts of Cambridge, of home, of Alexis, from her mind. It's pathetic, this dependency, she said to herself, turning an unread page, growing calmer.

By the time she reached Liverpool Street it seemed to have worked. As she found her way to the tube, worked out her route, bought her ticket, she felt composed; quite composed. And ready for anything.

CHAPTER SEVEN

'Is *this* the club?' Natasha came to an abrupt halt. They were half-way down Greek Street. She had had no breakfast and no lunch, and was still lugging her suitcase.

Paul Vansittart tossed his cigarette end into the gutter.

'This is it,' he said cheerfully.

'But it's a strip club.'

'Not exactly. It's a drinking club.'

'Then why does it say, "Girls, Girls, Girls" outside in neon letters? And why is there that photograph of a woman with large . . .' She swallowed. 'Almost nothing on.'

'That's Brenda.' Paul Vansittart smiled. 'You'll love her. She's forty-five if she's a day, but she's terrific.'

Natasha put her case down with a bang on the pavement.

'I am not working in a strip club,' she said. 'Not for you, not for your book, not for anyone. That's flat.'

He shrugged. 'Go back to Cambridge then.'

'I would never have come! If you'd said, if you'd explained . . .' She rounded on him accusingly. 'That's why you were so mysterious about it all, wasn't it? At the cricket match, and on the phone. Because you knew quite well that if you told me the truth I wouldn't come . . .' Her voice had risen; Paul began to look embarrassed.

'Oh, come on, Natasha,' he said, his manner more conciliatory. 'Can you blame me? I wanted you to come—you know I did . . . Listen . . .' He drew her aside a little, and put his arm around her shoulders. 'Let me explain. Forget about the stripping for a minute, will you? You're not going to have to do anything like that.'

'Then what do I do? You've been very vague so far.'

'You serve behind the bar. That's it. That's all.' He paused. 'You'll wear a costume, of course, Gentleman George insists on that. The costume's okay—really. It's sexy, of course, but nothing outrageous. It won't offend even your maidenly sensibilities . . .'

'I serve behind the bar. In a costume. What else?'

Paul Vansittart spread his hands wide. '*Nothing* else. Would I lie to you? That's it. You serve behind the bar, and you get to know the clientele—and the girls. And you report back to me. That's all.'

'Report what back to you?'

'Look, I explained, I told you. It's *research*. The book's set in Soho, in the clubs, the private cinemas, the shops ... You just get to know them, the people you're working with, the guys who come into the club. You get friendly with them. What you find out you pass on to me. Everything of interest—their backgrounds. Then I take what you give me, and if it's any good I work it in, weave it into the fabric of the book ...'

'Spy on them, you mean. Why can't you talk to them yourself?'

'I will be talking to them. I have been talking to them. For God's sake, I've been living here two months. But there's a limit. For a man—can't you see? These girls, they're very suspicious, they don't open up easily ...'

'Why not? You said the women from that battered wives place did. You said they all came to trust you. They all told you their life stories. You were like a father confessor to them, you said.'

'That was *different*. *They* were different. Look——' He dropped his arm from her shoulders and turned away. 'I thought you'd be able to help me with this—I thought you'd want to. If you don't, well then stop wasting my time. Go back to Cambridge.'

'It just doesn't seem very nice, that's all,' Natasha said. 'Trying to get people's confidence, and then telling it all to someone else.'

'Nice? *Nice*?' He groaned. 'We're talking about a book now, *my* book. When it comes out it's going to cause a major scandal—I suppose you realise that? It's going to blow this whole thing wide open. This whole stinking set-up. And you talk to me about *nice*? Do you *know* what kind of interest there is in this book already? My agent's having to fend them off. It'll go to auction for the rights and she's not going to take a penny under half a million. *That's* the kind of interest I'm talking about.'

Natasha suddenly felt quite extraordinarily tired. Her head was spinning from lack of sleep; Cambridge seemed a million miles away. She looked at him uncertainly.

'You mean you want to expose it all—the rackets and so on?'

'Keep your voice down.' He looked over his shoulder, and then stepped a little closer to her. 'Look, Natasha, I'm sorry. I see now that I've gone about this all the wrong way. Maybe I made a mistake, maybe I allowed my personal feelings to get the better of my judgment. I don't want you getting upset—maybe it might be better if I soldiered on alone.'

'No—no really.' Natasha tried to sound decisive. 'I'll try Paul. And then . . .'

'All right.' He placed a light kiss on her cheek. 'Good girl. Come and meet George. He's certainly not a gentleman, and I doubt if his real name is George, but come and meet him all the same.'

He bent then, and picked up her case for her, and ushered her inside a narrow unmarked door to the side of the club.

From the door a flight of steps, dimly lit, led sharply downwards.

On the wall was a large notice which read, *'Club Members Only! Annual Subscription, £10.'*

Downstairs there was a bar, a long low-ceilinged room, lit with blueish light, and smelling sourly of cigarette smoke.

Shabby pub tables and plastic seated chairs ringed a short cat-walk which ended in a pair of red silk curtains surmounted by two large spotlights. It was empty, except for one enormously fat man, in his shirtsleeves, who was sitting at the end of the bar on a stool and studying the racing page of *The Sun.*

He looked up as they entered and surveyed them lugubriously, without great interest. Paul put down Natasha's case, and advanced upon him.

'This is Natasha, George. The girl I told you about. She could do with the work, George. She's been on the dole months now. Haven't you, Natasha?'

'Er—yes. Four months,' said Natasha.

George shrugged. 'Ever worked behind a bar?'

'No, I haven't. But I'm sure I'd learn quickly.'

George looked unimpressed. Paul cleared his throat.

'Why don't you take your mac off, Natasha?' he said brightly. 'It's warm in here.'

He made a face at her as he said this, over the top of George's head, and Natasha looked at him in confusion. Then she took her mac off; George's eyes followed her movements without great interest. Paul Vansittart pulled another face, straightened his shoulders and stuck his chest out. Slowly

Natasha began to understand. She put the mac carefully down on a chair, drew in a deep breath, stuck her chest out, and turned full profile to George. She smiled at him uncertainly: George put down his newspaper.

'She might do,' he said grudgingly. 'I say "might", mind you.'

To Natasha's surprise he slowly levered his great weight off the stool and approached her. He walked round her in a circle, looking at her intently.

'This is a clean club,' he announced, without preamble. 'No trouble with Old Bill. No trouble with nobody. I have a licence for entertainment, it's up there on the wall for all to see. Entertainment. Nice clean stuff. Nice girls, nice routines.' He ceased his circling and came to a stop in front of her. 'Measurements?'

'Sorry?'

'Thirty-six, twenty-two, thirty-four,' said Paul imaginatively.

George sighed. 'Then the costume ought to fit. That's in her favour.'

He gave her one last lugubrious glance, then returned to his bar stool.

'Forty quid a week,' he said, levering his weight back into place.

'Am I hired, then?' Natasha went quite pink with excitement. She felt as if she had passed a difficult examination.

'Be here six-forty-five. Costume's out the back. In the artistes' dressing room.'

The interview appeared to be over, because Paul, who seemed to know his way around very well, beckoned to her, and led her out a small door by the bar into a narrow stone passage.

'Well done,' he said, and squeezed her hand.

'I didn't do much.'

'You didn't need to.' He smiled, and let his hand brush gently over the tip of her breast.

Hastily Natasha shot through the nearest door, which—luckily—turned out to be the right one. She stopped on the threshold.

The room was tiny, and smelled of grease paint and sweat and hair lacquer and scent. Along one wall was a rail for hanging clothes, and on the other a long looking glass surrounded by light bulbs. There was a formica table littered with make-up, and four chairs. On one of the chairs sat a black girl in a G-string and not much else. Natasha blushed crimson; Paul pushed past her airily.

'Hello,' he said.

The girl greeted this with a silent expressive rolling of her eyes towards the ceiling: Natasha found it impossible to tell whether she was pleased to see him, or not.

'This is Natasha. Natasha, meet Myra. Natasha's going to be working behind the bar. She starts tonight.'

'Oh, yes?' Myra gave Natasha an appraising glance.

'Where's her costume, love, do you know? We just want to check it for size.'

'I'll bet.' Myra waved a hand languidly. 'It's on the end. If she can't fill it I'll lend her some Kleenex.'

'She'll fill it.' Paul Vansittart gave Natasha a wink. He found, and held up, the costume. It was of shiny black satin, heavily boned, made roughly in the shape of a scanty swimming costume. The legs were cut high, and surrounded by red taffeta frills; the neck was cut low, and similarly frilled. There were no shoulder straps. Natasha looked at it doubtfully.

'Want to slip into it now—just to check?'

'No, I don't think so . . .'

'Sure? No? Okay.' He sighed. 'You'll need some fishnet stockings, won't she, Myra? And stilettos—you've got those probably.'

'Stilettos? No, I haven't.'

Paul began to look irritated; clearly he had expected her to come better equipped.

Myra, who had been watching this interchange closely, suddenly leaned forward, reached under the table, and pulled out a pair of black patent leather shoes, with six-inch heels. She kicked them towards Natasha.

'Size fives,' she said. 'They give me corns. You can borrow them if you like.'

'Oh—may I really?' Natasha slipped one on; it fitted perfectly. 'Thank you,' she said shyly, 'Myra.'

'Don't mention it.' Myra suddenly gave her a smile of surprising warmth.

'Well, Myra,' Paul Vansittart stepped forward. 'We'll love you and leave you then . . .'

'Nothing new about that,' Myra replied waspishly. 'Not in your case, anyway.'

The insult—if it were one, it might equally have been a compliment—seemed to please Paul.

'I'll be in tonight,' he said. 'In the front row. Don't forget . . .'

His hand brushed Myra's shoulder as he moved to the door. Myra uncrewed a bottle of nail varnish; she did not look up.

They went out into Greek Street, and bought a pair of black fishnet stockings. Natasha paid. Paul kept looking at his watch.

'I ought to get back to work,' he said, as they came out of the shop. 'I like to write eight hours a day, every day. You've knocked my schedule out a bit, Natasha.'

Natasha wasn't sure if this were good or bad; she looked at him doubtfully.

'I've got you a flat,' he went on casually. 'Well, it's more of a room actually. The floor below me. It's not far from here. Twenty quid a week—it's dirt cheap. The landlord's doing it as a favour to me.' He reached in his pockets and brought out a Yale key. 'We can go round now and you can get settled in, if you like.'

The flat was in an alley-way off Berwick Street. To reach it they wove through narrow streets crowded with tiny cinemas, shops selling Indian sweetmeats and others selling exotic underwear. Then Paul Vansittart ducked past a fruit and vegetable stall, past a door with a red-lit bell-push marked, *Samantha, Intimate Massage* and *Colette, French Lessons*, and came to a halt against a green door fitted with five locks.

It occurred to Natasha to wonder if it would be exactly safe, living here, alone in a bedsitter, but not wanting to sound feeble and unadventurous, she kept quiet. Paul unlocked the five locks and led the way through a narrow hall smelling of curry and up a flight of uncarpeted stairs. On the second floor he unlocked another door, and threw it back with a flourish.

'I'm on the floor above,' he said cheerfully. 'I had my place done up a bit. I'm afraid this is still in all its original glory.'

Natasha looked round her in silence.

The room was about fourteen feet square. It had one window, obscured by greying net curtains, which overlooked a soot-blackened wall and a small yard overflowing with dustbins. There was a table, a chair, a double bed with a crimson candlewick cover, a cracked washbasin, an electric

kettle and ring, four hooks for clothes, and a girlie calendar
opened at nubile Miss April. It was two years out of date. She
sighed and put down her suitcase Paul Vansittart closed the
door.

'What do you think?'

'It's fine,' Natasha said bravely. 'Fine.'

'Like the typewriter?' He gestured to the table, and
Natasha, following the gesture, saw that the room did indeed
boast one new object. A large and expensive electric Olivetti
stood centre square, flanked by a wire tray and a new box of
A4 typing paper.

'I've got a word processor now. I don't need that. Will it be
okay?'

Natasha swallowed. 'Will there be much typing?' she said
hesitantly.

'Naturally I'll want you to type up my first drafts,' he said,
a little testily. 'I write longhand. I mentioned that surely?'

'I don't think you did. No.'

'Well, I do. That's how I work. First longhand. Then you
type that up. Then I do the second draft on the processor.
You said you typed, I remember.'

'I'm not terribly fast . . .'

'No problem. I should think it averages out to about 3000
words a day. Five if I'm really on form. But you'll have the
mornings free, won't you?'

'Oh yes,' Natasha said faintly.

'It's the best way. I want you really close to all this,
Natasha. To my work. So you see it, feel it, from the inside.
We're going to be a terrific team, you and I. And then, if it
works out on this book, who knows? We might . . .'

He had moved towards her as he made this speech; a
certain purposefulness blazed in the magnificent dark eyes.
Natasha backed off nervously.

'Yes, well . . .' she said. 'But I'm keeping you from your
work now, you said, and I mustn't do that, so . . .'

Paul Vansittart smiled; he folded his arms.

'It can wait,' he said. 'Why don't you unpack. I'll help.'

Natasha looked at him doubtfully, but he clearly had no
intention of leaving yet, so, reluctantly, she lifted the case
on to the bed, and opened it. In fact, the novelist did not help
unpack—there was no need anyway, for she had brought very
little with her. But he did watch attentively as she hung
clothes on the hooks, and, embarrassed, stuffed an armfull of

tights and panties into the desk drawer, the only one available.

'You should wrap them round the first draft,' he said dryly, eyeing a wisp of white nylon that stuck out of the drawer. 'It might bring me luck.'

'They're very ordinary panties,' Natasha said firmly. 'Marks and Spencer's. I'm sure they wouldn't.'

'You'll have to buy some new ones then,' he said. 'From one of the shops round the corner. That would be appropriate, don't you think?'

Natasha didn't risk an answer, for his tone was provocative. Flustered, she took out the photographs, and William's pictures, and banged the case shut. Paul Vansittart lifted it off the bed, stowed it underneath, smoothed the cover, and then approached the desk, where Natasha was attempting to make the photographs stand up, and pretending to take no notice of his advance. He put his arm round her waist and the pictures fell over.

He leaned over her shoulder and examined them, his breath warm against her cheek. She could smell his discreet after-shave, felt the brush of his face against hers.

'Hmmm.' He regarded the pictures intently. 'Uncle Alexis.'

'Cousin,' Natasha said stiffly. 'I told you.'

'Of course. Cousin. And who's this?'

'My parents.'

'Your parents. Ah yes.' There was a little silence. Natasha felt the atmosphere in the little room change somehow; she had a sudden instinct to turn the photograph over, to hide it from that alert gaze.

'Did he have a Russian name too, your father?' Paul said, casually enough.

'Yes.' Natasha hesitated, her hand on the frame. 'Nicolai. But he anglicised it. He was always called Nicholas. Or Nico. His friends called him that, Alexis says.'

'And your mother—what was her name?'

'She was English. Frances . . .'

'Isn't that extraordinary,' he interrupted her. 'I know someone who knew them. My publisher in fact. Ben—you'll meet him. I mentioned to him that I'd been down in Cambridge, that you were coming up to help me with . . . with the research on the book, and he said then . . . What a coincidence.'

'He knew my parents?' Natasha swung round. 'Really? Did he know them well? Shall I meet him?'

Paul Vansittart caught her hands. He laughed. 'What eagerness. Of course you will. He'd like that. And why shouldn't he have known them? Ben knows everybody.'

Natasha hesitated. 'Oh, I don't know,' she said at last. 'They lived abroad a lot. I've never met any of their friends before, not close friends, and at home, well, nobody talks about them very much and so . . .'

'Ben knew them well. Very well. He was quite definite about it. Your mother was very beautiful, he said. Exceptionally so. I said you took after her . . .'

'Oh,' said Natasha, as his arm moved around her waist. 'Did you?'

'Yes, I did.' He moved his face closer to her own, lowering his voice, his lips almost against her ear. 'I described you to him, Natasha. I told him . . . She has beautiful long slender legs, narrow flanks, a tiny waist that I could span with my hands like this. And she stands a little awkwardly, like a schoolgirl, her weight on one foot. Just like you're doing now . . .' He ran his hand gently over the curve of her bottom as he spoke, his voice low and mesmeric. Natasha hastily transferred her weight to both feet and raised her hands between his body and her own. 'And I said,' he went on confidently, before she could interrupt, 'that she has the breasts of an angel, full and firm, lifting under her dress . . .'

'Angels don't have breasts,' Natasha said desperately, her voice coming out in a squeak. 'I'm quite sure they don't. Angels are asexual, and . . .'

'Her face. She has a heart-shaped face, I said, but her hair falls forward. It's very straight and very thick and very black, and she wears it cut straight, like a little girl in picture books, and when she's shy, or embarassed, as she often is, she bends her head, and her hair falls forward and she hides behind that hair. Which is a shame, no, look up, Natasha. Which is a shame, I said, because she has beautiful eyes. Innocent eyes. Without guile. Grey eyes . . .'

'Blue,' Natasha said, 'and I . . .'

'And her mouth. Oh, that mouth. Wide and full. A little sulky sometimes. The top lip very straight, it betrays her, that mouth, because it looks bruised. Made for kisses. *My* kisses, Ben, I said, so don't get any ideas . . .'

He bent to her mouth on cue; Natasha gave him a hefty push. He recoiled, but with dignity.

'You never said any such thing,' she said. 'You . . .'

'Maybe not. But I thought it.'

He regarded her unrepentantly.

'I don't want you to kiss me,' she said, as firmly as she could. 'You said you wouldn't. No strings, you said so.'

'Then I shan't.' He grinned at her, then turned to the door. 'I'll see you at the club tonight. We can start work proper tomorrow. Okay?'

Natasha blinked. The transformation from wooer to employer was abrupt. He appeared to feel neither remorse nor disappointment.

He gave her one last dark glance.

'Till tonight, then,' he said, and then he was gone. Natasha could hear him whistle as he went up the stairs. A door slammed; a brief pause; then she heard the rhythmic tapping of keys.

Slowly she sat down on the bed; its springs sagged and squeaked beneath her. She looked around her with the calmness of extreme exhaustion. The room was horrible. The club was horrible. Gentleman George made her skin crawl. She would apparently be working morning, afternoon and evening seven days a week on behalf of a man she hardly knew and was beginning to suspect she did not greatly like, or trust. He intended her to be a secretary, which was ironic; the so-called research struck her as immoral and sneaky. She suspected that the seduction routine so quickly taken up and so cheerfully abandoned, as if it were just part of the business of the day, would be repeated. Quite clearly the obvious thing, the sensible thing, would be to pack up right now, go to the station, and get the first train back to Cambridge.

But she could not do that. To turn tail, to flee—her pride revolted at the thought. It would be weak, cowardly. And if she did go back, the old problems would be awaiting her. She would still have no job; she would still be a burden on Alexis, who had—for the first time in his adult life—the chance to be free. That thought cut her, and decided her. No, she would stick it out, stand on her own two feet, grow up.

It came to her then, as she lay back tiredly on the lumpy bed, that she might, at last, be able to repay Alexis for his years of kindness and protection. He would not realise, of course, and that made her gift the better. She could give Alexis peace of mind; freedom, and then . . .'

No, she thought, closing her eyes. She could deal with all this, but it was better not to think of Alexis.

Resolutely she put him from her mind, sleeping. Alexis, green-eyed, familiar yet strange, invaded her dreams, and when she woke, she was glad of it.

The day had been hot; the evening brought no diminution in the temperature, but Natasha, weaving her way through the alleyways to the club, felt refreshed by her sleep, felt a new energy and resolution spring in her step. At the back of her mind, somewhere, there was a little nagging aching pain. She knew she ought to confront it, face it, discover it, but she felt if she did her new purposefulness would fall away from her. No; she had made her decision; she would carry on; the pain would go away; it would weaken her, she felt that instinctively, if she examined the source of that pain too much.

In the dressing room, Myra, lethargic, acerbic, watchful, took her time sizing her up. But at some point, quite when Natasha could not have said, she obviously decided to accept her. She brought out some photographs of her two children; Natasha looked at them; she told her about her cousins, about William. There was a little pause; both women looked up; their eyes met, and across so many barriers—race, class, education, accent—Natasha felt something between them connect. She smiled, shyly; Myra smiled back.

'You want me to help you do up your costume then?' Myra said. 'You'll never manage it yourself. All of them hundreds of little hooks and eyes . . .'

She helped, then stood back and surveyed Natasha critically; professionally. She grinned.

'Here,' she said. 'You don't look bad and all. Fill it out better than I thought. Stand up straight, that's it. No point in hiding your natural advantages . . .'

Natasha did as she was bid, and looked at herself in the glass. Her own reflection astonished her. Myra smiled and put her arm round her.

'Look, love,' she said. 'It'll be all right. Just don't take any lip, don't let them get too fresh. Serve them quick and keep the change. Oh . . .' she paused. 'And watch out for the guy that got you into all this.'

'Paul, you mean?'

'Who else? Mr Sweet Talk. Him and his bleeding tape recorder. "Relax, Myra," he says to me. "Trust me. Open up a bit." "You know what you reminds me of," I said? "My bleeding dentist, that's who." He must think we was born yesterday. I mean, the lines he shoots, they were old when I was in nappies. "I can make you famous, Myra," he says. "I am famous," I says. "As famous as I want to be, thank you very much." ' She winked at Natasha in the glass.

Natasha stared at her silently. She felt she ought to defend Paul, but wasn't quite sure how to do it.

'He's a good writer,' she said eventually. 'That is. Well, he's quite famous . . .'

Myra shrugged. 'He's bad news,' she said succinctly. She seemed about to say more, and then obviously changed her mind. From beyond the door musak started up. She turned away.

'You'd better get on, love,' she said, more kindly. 'Hope you enjoy the show. Watch out for Brenda. She's an artiste, she is, old style. You know—with the twirlers . . .'

She gestured to her breasts as she said this, though her meaning did not become clear until later, when Natasha, legs aching from the strain of standing so long in such high heels, and so hot in the tight costume she felt close to fainting, had a brief respite when the customers paused in their drinking, the lights went down, and the show went up.

The men in the audience fell into silence as the lights dimmed, the spotlights came on, and Myra stepped through the red silk curtains. They looked up at her, a little greedily, a little ashamedly, and Myra ignored them, though they were inches from her legs, with a magnificent disdain. She went through her routine with a clockwork professionalism, and a total absence of any animation. Her hips undulated and jerked to the music; her legs strutted; her hands reached to the part of her garments she would adjust or remove, stayed there for exactly the amount of time required to tease, moved away, moved back, and finally exposed. As she danced her face wore a fixed expression, as if she saw no one, and heard nothing but the rhythms of the music.

Paul Vansittart, seated in the front row, leaned forward a little, frowning. The men near him left their drinks untouched. Their faces, sweaty, hot, intent, made a pale circle around the lighted catwalk like moths around a lamp.

Myra was coming to the climax of her act. Her hands moved, like a conjuror's, swiftly; in a second the last wisp of lurex was gone. Myra, naked, stood before them, quite still. A woman, a statue, an image. In an instant there was black-out and she was gone.

Natasha had thought her very beautiful, especially so in that moment of still, silent, final sad contempt. But the audience seemed to find it all routine; they clapped languidly and briefly. They shifted in their seats, began to talk again, got up to fetch more drinks. They had seen everything, and nothing, Natasha thought angrily. She jerked whisky out of the dispenser and into their glasses, took their money and slid their change back across the counter to them without a second glance.

She would ring Cambridge, she decided suddenly, as the second girl came on, and the customers moved away from the bar and back to their seats. She would ring and just tell them that she was all right, that she was safe, that she had a place to stay ... Quickly she dodged out into the corridor behind the bar where there was a pay phone. Her hands shaking, she dialled the code; the number. It rang; it went on ringing. An awful panic, a void of fear and confusion opened up within her. They must be there; someone must be there. She replaced the receiver; dialled again. No answer.

'You're paid to serve drinks, not make phone calls,' George's surly voice came from behind her. 'Get back in the bar.'

Natasha obeyed him. She served more drinks, efficiently, like an automaton, hardly seeing the men she served. Why was there no answer; why? With difficulty, she forced herself to be calm. Alexis was out, that was it. And it was the weekend, Julian was back at boarding school; Anne and William had probably gone to stay at Bernard's, that was it. There was no reason on earth to get in such a state; she should concentrate on the show.

So, making an effort, she did; the show and its permutations. There was Hazel, who was dressed like a parody of a schoolgirl, and whose props were a teddy-bear and a hair-brush. There was Star whose gear was black leather. There was Cindy, who came on in a cowgirl outfit and a ten gallon hat and made considerable play with a pair of sideshooters. There was a Japanese girl who was tiny and delicate; Jane who was blonde and big-busted. There were, in all, about sixteen girls, some plump, some thin, some pretty, some plain; every possible permutation of the female physiognomy was featured, every possible male fantasy was indulged. By the end Natasha felt nothing would shock her.

'Why don't they watch?' she said to Paul, when he came up

for a whisky. 'At the end, when the girls take everything off? I'd have thought that was the bit they were waiting for.'

He laughed. 'You are an innocent, aren't you? They look like any other woman then. Who's interested in that?'

The only performer who elicited much response from the audience was Brenda, who came on last. Brenda was enormous; her hair was a mountainous peroxided confection; the paint could not hide the lines on her face.

Brenda, it soon became clear, was the star attraction. Her appearance was greeted with roars of applause, nudges and winks from the men in the audience, many of whom were clearly familiar with her routine. For Brenda affected none of the aloofness of her co-stars, on the contrary, she was extremely familiar. She greeted her regulars, and ogled her new converts; she made cutting remarks about their appearance, their response to her act, the number of drinks they had had, their putative relationship with their wives and girlfriends, and her own extremely frank estimation of their more intimate capabilities. She was rude, and the men loved it; she was flattering, and they blushed like bashful boys. All the time the tassels twirled, hypnotically.

As soon as Brenda's act finished, Paul crossed to the bar. Natasha gave him as brave a grin as she could muster.

'That bitch, Brenda.' He regarded Natasha coldly. 'I've wasted hours on her. She spun me some line, and tonight I met some bloke who knows her. Says there wasn't a word of truth in it—not a word. She'll be sorry, I can tell you, when the book comes out . . .'

He paused, as if taking in Natasha's appearance for the first time, which, perhaps, he was, for he had ignored her all evening. His eyes fell from her face to the smooth pale curve of her breasts above the low-cut costume. He gave her his narrow-eyed smile again, and Natasha found she liked it less and less.

'So. I'll see you home then, shall I?'

'No, thanks, you needn't bother,' Natasha said quickly. 'Brenda walks through that way; she said she'd see me to the door.'

'Getting pally very quickly, aren't you?'

'I thought that was what you wanted me to do,' Natasha replied coldly.

'Well, don't overdo it.' He downed his whisky in one gulp. 'And just don't listen to anything that old cow says about me, that's all. She's got it in for me, that's obvious.'

'I'll keep an open mind,' Natasha said sweetly.

He hesitated a moment, as if suspecting she might be mocking him; then he smiled again, lifted her hand, and gave it a breathy kiss. 'I'll see you in the morning then. I might just stick around here for a bit. Have a drink with George—you know.' He lurched a little as he turned away. 'I've left some stuff in your room by the way. The opening chapters. Try and read them first thing, will you, Natasha?'

Natasha stiffened. 'In my room? But . . .'

Paul patted his pocket; he winked. 'Two keys,' he said. 'Your one and my one. In case of emergencies . . .'

When Natasha got back to her room she stared at the door angrily. It had a Yale lock, a bolt, and a chain. She slammed the bolt into place; fixed the chain, and for good measure wedged a chair-back under the door handle.

No night visitations; good. An image of Paul's face as she had last seen it, a smile of smug satisfaction on its handsome features drifted into her mind. Myra didn't like him; she suspected Brenda didn't either. She was beginning to see that they might be right.

On the desk was a large, a dauntingly large, envelope. Opening it, Natasha saw sheafs of folders; four, no five, of them, a chapter each. She flicked them open; Carrie, Anna, Beth, Lynette, Jo . . . each chapter called after a woman. She turned to the first page. *Women. I shall write about the women*, it began. Her lips curled in derision. She flicked over a few pages, turned to the next chapter, and then paused, her eye held.

Beth: she was a child; she was a woman. She wore her hair straight, cut short round the nape of her neck like a little girl in a picture book. From the back, a child you think, and then when she turns, no—a woman. Eyes like a frightened doe; mouth—a wicked orifice. Bruised full parted lips, lips fashioned for kisses not words. And breasts. Oh those breasts, full, teasing, the breasts of an angel, every man's dream woman. See her walk now, down the streets, through the alleyways. See the men watch her, watch her breasts, dream of holding them. Beth. Beth. There is mist in the streets, in the alleyways, mists and steam, the mists of our dreams, our wantings. But Beth does not see them, pretends she does not see them. She turns away her face, hides behind her hair. Her eyes are amber, liquid amber; they look in upon herself. Even when she dances, even when she strips, even then she is inviolate . . .

It went on, at length, in a similar vein. Natasha read for a minute or so, her colour mounting, and then suddenly she began to laugh. It was ridiculous, awful, the worst kind of pretention—a hideous derivative mixture, even she could see that. Alexis was right. Paul Vansittart was a phoney, and one who didn't hesitate to employ the prose of the morning for the seduction of the afternoon . . .

She shut the folder and tossed it on to the desk. She was too tired to care; she would decide what to do in the morning. She had been a fool, somehow she would have to manage to extricate herself. Meanwhile only one thing mattered; she must get through to Cambridge, talk to Alexis—not to tell him all this, but just to hear the sound of his voice, because his sanity and his honesty felt, just then, like a lifeline, the one sure thing in a mad world.

She set the alarm; she would ring at seven-thirty.

CHAPTER EIGHT

'ALEXIS isn't here, Natasha . . .' Anne's voice sounded sleepy.

'Not there? You mean he's in college? Fine. I'll ring him there.'

'No, he's not in college either . . .'

Natasha shut her eyes very tight; she dug her nails into the palm of her hand. There was a silence.

'Oh,' she said at last. 'I'm sorry, Anne. I've woken you up and . . .'

'Can I give him a message?'

'No, no message. I just wanted to let him know that I'd arrived, that I was okay. It doesn't matter . . .'

'Not that I can give him a message anyway . . .' Anne was coming to. 'He's away. When did he say he was coming back? Tuesday?'

'Where's he gone, Anne?'

'To some friends of Ariana's, I think. Yes, that's it, because they went off together in that nasty noisy car she has. They want him to do some conference or something. Now where did he say they lived? Suffolk, I think. Or Norfolk. He didn't leave a number . . .'

'Oh, never mind. I'll ring Tuesday . . . Damn . . .'

The pips were going. Natasha hastily jammed another ten pence into the slot. Through the pips she heard Anne's vague voice.

'Well, no, you can't do that either, because Tuesday he flies to Paris for that special lecture, don't you remember? That rather grand one, and I know he's going straight on because he packed his dinner jacket and . . .'

'Oh,' Natasha said dully. 'Paris. I'd forgotten.'

'He'll be back at the end of the week. Thursday, I think he said. Oh dear. You are all right, aren't you, Natasha? Are you staying at Sophie's? You oughtn't to have gone like that, you know. I've been very worried, and William said . . .'

The pips went again. Natasha swore. She slammed her last ten pence into the slot.

'I'm fine, Anne, fine,' she said, her voice rising. 'Just tell Alexis I rang and—send love and everything, won't you? I'll write. I'm not at Sophie's. I've found a room and there's no phone here, you see, and I'm not sure if I'll stay at this address, I might have to find somewhere else, and . . .'

The machine clicked; the dialling tone rang in her ears. Her ten pence did not re-appear. Natasha gave the box a hefty punch; she cut her knuckles; no money came out. Angrily she banged the receiver back, and leaned her forehead against the cool glass of the kiosk door.

She stood like that a little while, immobile. Then, slowly, she walked back through the deserted Sunday streets to her room. The sun shone; above the grey roofs the sky was clear; rubbish blew along the gutters. On the corner of Berwick Street an old woman, wrapped in rags, muttered to herself as methodically she sorted through a box full of rotting cabbages and apples left from the market.

Natasha watched her, her mind sharp with tiredness, alert with exhaustion and disappointment. Eventually the woman shuffled off, clutching one worm-eaten apple in her hand. Natasha let herself into the house, and climbed the stairs to her room. She shut the door; she sat down and thought of Alexis.

He swam, vividly alive, into the dark recesses of her mind; pain knotted around her heart. She thought of him with Ariana; the pain intensified. Very quietly she bent, and covered her face with her hands.

She sat like that a long while, hearing in the distance a church clock strike the quarter, the half. Then, forcing herself to be practical, to take action, thinking that working might fill the void that had opened in her mind and spirits, she went to the desk, to the typewriter.

First, to limber up her typing, she would write to William, and tell him where she was, and a little—not all—about her job. Then she would read the manuscript Paul Vansittart had left for her. It was her job, after all. Maybe, the previous night, she had misjudged it.

By the time she had finished it was eleven-thirty, and she felt more confused than ever. This was not the exposé Paul had spoken of, not at all. It concentrated entirely on the women he had met and interviewed; of the men of Soho, the pimps, the club owners, the purveyors of magazines and movies, the book said nothing. Facts were sparse; there was no sense of how or why these women came to be there; that apparently did not concern him. She could recognise, she thought, the characters based on Brenda and on Myra, but when those characters spoke they sounded wrong, not like the women she had met the night before. Not all the writing was as bad as the section she had read the previous night, but there was a colour to it she did not like—a malice, she thought, shutting the last folder, as if he disliked women, and sought to hide his dislike behind a wash of sentiment. Yet it was also explicit, repetitively so, obsessively so. And the closer he came to the women's bodies, the more intimate and fevered his descriptions, the hollower it all became.

She bent her head and tried to think. After all, this was only a first draft; she had no idea how he worked, how much he would change. She was not a critic, not well read, she knew if she tried to advance her arguments the novelist would find it only too easy to shoot her down in flames. And then: she was a girl, very ignorant, very inexperienced. Pushing a certain memory from her mind she told herself she knew nothing about sexual desire. So she could not judge this catalogue of breasts and thighs, of postures and gropings. How cold it all sounded!

She pushed the chapters away, searched her mind for some certainty of judgment, opened the folders again, and looked once more at the section on Myra. Her mind cleared.

I would not write it like that, she thought, and switched on the typewriter.

Four days went past: Natasha had never worked so hard in her life, never slept so little. Yet she did not feel tired, she felt charged, filled with a purpose and an energy she had never suspected she possessed. She worked out a routine, of which Paul Vansittart remained blessedly ignorant. Usually she managed to leave the club and be home by two in the morning; then she would lock and bolt her door and go straight to bed. The precautions had in fact proved unnecessary: Paul Vansittart, she discovered, was a night creature. He liked to tour the clubs, drink, pursue his research as he called it, and he liked to do that alone. Natasha suspected he returned very late; certainly he never surfaced before eleven in the morning, sometimes later, and Natasha doubted very much if his eight hours writing a day was a reality, though she said nothing.

She got up each day at six. For three hours she wrote. At first she told herself that it was an extension of her diary, nothing more, her own impressions of the people she worked with. When it became clear it was more than that, that it was a story, a novel perhaps, she had a moment of fear. She couldn't do it, she would fail, all her old sense of inadequacy returned to her. But she shut her mind to that. Alexis had said that she gave up on things because she was afraid to fail, afraid to be compared to the rest of her high-powered and successful family, and she knew in her heart he was right. So, shutting her mind to her fears she just went on writing; each day she made progress, each day she learned. She hid the typescript at the back of a drawer; each day it grew and her confidence grew with it.

She came to love those early mornings, the privacy of her room, the sounds of a waking city—milkfloats, a car starting up, footsteps outside the window, the shouts from Berwick Street as the stallholders set up the market. Each day, at nine, reluctantly, she put away her own writing and turned to Paul Vansittart's. Dutifully she typed up his pages, and the more she typed the more she knew she hated them.

Luckily, although he constantly questioned her, he seemed not to notice her reservations, he was too eager to give his own opinions of his book to observe that her view might be different. She realised too that the 'research' he had stressed was largely mythical. Occasionally, for form's sake, he asked her a few questions about the club, about Myra and Brenda and the other girls, but only occasionally, half listening to her answers. She liked Myra and she liked Brenda; she had no intention of betraying their confidences: she told him very little; he scarcely noticed.

By the third day she realised why. Paul was mean; he disliked parting with cash. He rarely even bought anyone a drink if he could avoid it. This way, she saw now, he contrived to get his typing done for free. Her wages, it was obvious, were to be the forty pounds paid for the hours at the club; she was supposed to do the typing for nothing, because he thought of it as a privilege perhaps; maybe he'd thought she would be rewarded by his continuing though oddly desultory attempts at seduction, or perhaps by his attempt, as he put it, to launch her into the literary world. This launch had so far taken the form of one party on the Sunday night, and two lunches, both paid for by the other guests. The party had been a nightmare, and Natasha had left early, alone. The lunches—in a way the lunches had been worse, for there had been no such escape. At the first she had at least met Paul's publisher, Ben Whitby, a taciturn man with shrewd eyes whom she had liked; but he had shown no particular inclination to talk to her about her parents, had indeed changed the subject as soon as they were mentioned, and that had disappointed her. Paul had become very drunk, Ben tense and irritable; Natasha had sat, feeling lonelier and lonelier, while Paul launched on a now-familiar monologue about his writing, and Ben had periodically looked at his watch.

The other lunch had been even worse, a large group, at a fashionable brasserie. The champagne and orange juice flowed; the air had been rich with scandal and malice; most of the other guests had been writers or journalists, and their favourite topic, Natasha quickly discovered, was money. Kit had sold the rights to this for so many thousand; Jimmy's last book had been an unmitigated disaster, but the Americans had lapped it up of course, and they said the paperback rights were going for . . .

Natasha had sat silent, her mind elsewhere, until Paul had suddenly pushed aside his food, and, glowering at her down the table, had launched himself on the subject of Alexis. He did not reveal her relationship to Alexis: uncurbed, the others had set to with relish: *mean, malicious, narrow-minded, devious, basically stupid, mandarin, an academic, a creep*: the epithets bounced around the table. *Someone told me . . . I heard . . . Greek shipping millions, just about his drop*. All the while Paul Vansittart sat at the top of the table, smiling down at Natasha, who sat as if paralysed, so angry she could not speak.

'Oh, don't be too hard on poor old Alexis,' Paul said at last, when it showed signs of flagging. 'Alexis had something once. Then he sold out to the literary establishment of course . . .'

Natasha stood up; she was shaking; she pressed her hands hard on the edge of the table, resisting the impulse to do something violent, to tip it over, to smack Paul's face.

'Alexis never sold out to anyone or anything in his whole life,' she said fiercely, into the sudden silence. Her voice shook with passion; a circle of pale faces stared at her in astonishment. She turned abruptly and walked out.

That had been the previous day; since then she had avoided the novelist altogether, but her anger had not abated. It had seethed in her all evening at the club; it burned in her now, the next morning, as she sat at her desk. She wanted passionately to tell Paul Vansittart what she thought of him and what he could do with this job he had conned her into. She wanted passionately to talk to Alexis, the need to do so had become a craving. But Alexis was still not to be reached.

Now she sat, stiff-backed, staring in front of her, the mad inexplicable anxiety she felt fuelling her anger and intensifying it. She heard Paul Vansittart's footsteps on the stairs; he was whistling; he stopped whistling; he opened the door.

He liked to make an entrance, Natasha knew that now. He stood, lolling decoratively against the doorjamb, in tight faded jeans, and a white cotton shirt unbuttoned just enough to display the dark hairs on his tanned chest. He gave her the old flashing smile, but his eyes were wary.

'Fancy lunch?'

'No, thank you.'

'Oh dear. Do I detect a note of antagonism?' His voice was bantering. He advanced and, before Natasha could avoid him, dropped a lingering kiss on her hair. 'You're not cross, are you, Natasha? Don't be, sweetie. It's not my fault those things they said, and anyhow, you might as well face it. People feel like that about Alexis. Here they do—maybe not in Cambridge, but you've got to learn . . .' He smiled, and put an arm round her shoulders. 'You're like a lioness, you know, defending her cub. I was touched. More than that. I found it a bit of a turn-on . . .'

He moved his hand familiarly down her arm towards her breast. Natasha pushed him away angrily, and he laughed.

'Oh, come on, Natasha,' he said, a note of impatience entering his voice. 'How much longer are you going to play this game? I mean, it has its attractions at first, but it can get a bit boring. Okay, for form's sake you want to spin it out a bit, surrender with a show of reluctance and all that, but for how long, for God's sake? You knew why I wanted you here, and you must have wanted it too or you wouldn't have come. So, let's stop messing about—yes?'

Natasha stared at him. 'You offered me a job . . .'

'Sure, sure, and you're doing it. But it wasn't just the job, was it? Let's be honest now.'

'All right.' Natasha stood up. Her hands were shaking, and she pressed them tightly together so he should not see. 'I'll be honest. I came to do a job for you—a research job. I didn't want to go to bed with you, and I don't now. I didn't want to be a typist either. However . . .' She paused, and then gestured to a typescript on the desk. 'I've typed up all the material you've given me so far. There it is. I don't want to do any more.'

There was a silence. He stepped back and regarded her coldly.

'You don't want to do any more. Do you mind telling me why?'

Natasha set her mouth. 'I'm not a typist.'

'I can see that.' He flicked the neat pages contemptuously. 'Your typing leaves a good deal to be desired.'

'Then hire a proper secretary.'

'Natasha, come on . . .' He moved back towards her. 'This is stupid. You're being defensive. Okay, so you got angry, but . . .'

'I don't like the book,' Natasha said flatly as he reached for her again.

'I see. Why?' He moved away, and sat on the corner of the desk, his voice icily polite.

'I don't think it matters why.'

'But I do. I'm interested. I'm concerned. This little girl, this frumpy little girl, straight out of boarding school, never been anywhere, done anything, or met anyone, and she doesn't like my book. God, now I really am worried. Why?'

'I think it's . . . an untruthful book.' Natasha met his eyes, and he began to laugh.

'Oh, I love it. I really love it. It's too much. Here's a girl, a not very intelligent girl, a girl who's never been to bed with a man in her life, who runs a mile if I so much as touch her, and she reads a book, a book that among many other things happens to be about sex, about men and women, and she tells me it's untruthful. She would know, of course. Still . . .' He paused. 'I do ask myself if there's anyone who could be influencing her here. Dear old Uncle Alexis for instance?'

'Leave Alexis out of this. I had enough of that yesterday.' Natasha rounded on him fiercely, her control beginning to break. 'There's no point in arguing, or making it any worse. There's the typescript, there's the money for this week's rent, and there's the keys . . . I'm leaving.'

He was smiling at her; he ignored her gesture.

'Do you know,' he began carefully, his voice suddenly losing all its sarcasm. 'Do you know I don't think we can quite leave Alexis out of this? Much as I'd like to. Much as I'd prefer to. You're so protective to him—I find that touching.

And he's protective to you. Markedly so. Oddly so. I just wonder — have you ever asked yourself why?'

Natasha stopped; she stared at him, held by something in his voice.

'At first,' he went on smoothly, 'at first I said to myself, oh dear, too Freudian. Poor old Alexis has the hots for his nubile little cousin, for his ward, his little Alice in the Cambridge Wonderland. But then I discovered I was wrong. Quite wrong. Alexis gets his kicks elsewhere, I hear, quite the Don Juan in his discreet way. But silly little girls isn't his scene. No, it turns out Alexis likes sterner stuff, older, brainier, prettier, more experienced. More of a challenge to him, I suppose . . .'

'Stop this . . .'

'So then I said to myself,' he went on without pausing, 'why so protective. What can it be?'

'Alexis isn't that protective, I don't know what you're talking about. It's nonsense. He let me come to London—it didn't worry him at all. He didn't even want to know where I was going, what I was going to do . . .'

'Maybe he had other things on his mind.' Paul smiled. 'Even the best watchdogs sometimes sleep. There's that Greek girl—when a man's just embarked on a new affair, a rather serious one in this case so I'm told, well . . .' He spread his hands expressively in the air. 'And, as you so rightly say, Alexis did not know you were coming here, that you'd be seeing me, working with me. So, perhaps, it didn't quite occur to him who you might meet . . .'

'Who I might meet?' Natasha stared at him blankly.

'Well, Ben for instance.'

'Why should he care about my meeting Ben? I don't understand.'

'Ben knew your parents.'

'But . . .' Natasha stopped. He was regarding her intently, as a snake might a rabbit, and something in his eyes, in the careful insidious way he spoke, made fear and panic tighten around her heart.

'Of course, Ben is very discreet,' he went on carefully. 'One of the discreetest men in London; you may have noticed that at lunch. Almost too discreet—a bit uptight. Polite to me, of course, but then he has to be. My books make his firm a lot of money. A hell of a lot. But, it turns out, Ben wasn't always so discreet, not when he was younger. And it also turns out,

Natasha, that you don't take after your mother at all. Not yet anyway . . .'

'I don't understand what you're getting at.' Natasha searched his face. 'Why don't you stop this—you're just talking in riddles, and . . .'

'You're so right.' He levered himself off the desk. 'It is all a great riddle, isn't it? And it's hardly my concern. But if I were you, Natasha, since—as we now know—you're so keen on the truth, I'd ask myself a few questions. Better still, ask Alexis. Ask why you know so little about your parents, ask why Alexis is so protective to you. And consider—Alexis is really the most terrible old snob, you know, especially about his family. Hates scandal, so proud of the family name . . .'

Natasha stared at him; a little chill of fear and alarm ran up her spine; she hesitated. More than anything else she wanted to press him to reveal whatever it was he thought he knew, but she could also see that that was what he wanted her to do. She didn't trust him, she thought; he was a liar, and to question him now would be demeaning. Getting a grip on herself, she tilted her chin and looked at him scornfully.

'If Alexis is proud of his family he has reason to be so,' she said coldly. 'I'm proud of them too. And as you say it's neither your concern nor your business. So why don't you just go away, and let me get on with my packing? I've better things to do than stay here and listen to your kind of cheap gossip and innuendo . . .'

'But of course.' He gave her a cold smile. 'I don't want to be late for lunch, do I? My agent's expecting me at one . . .' He glanced ostentatiously at his watch. 'But remember what I said, Natasha. Ask Alexis, why don't you? You'll be running back to Cambridge, I take it?'

Natasha turned away. 'No. It's none of your business, but since you ask, I'm not running anywhere. I'm staying in London.'

'Oh really?' He turned and gave her a long look. 'Well, never mind, there'll be other opportunities. When Alexis realises where you've been, and with whom, he'll be up here very fast I should think. Hotfoot. As I said, he hates scandal—old or new.' He smiled, seeing her blank look. 'You must have realised that people would gossip about *us*, surely? Everybody gossips about me all the time, they always assume the worst. I've told everybody you're as pure as the driven snow, that we have a business relationship—and do you

know, no one believes a word of it? Can't think why ... And
that tall thin man at lunch yesterday, the one you ignored,
remember him? Well, he's up at Cambridge at the moment on
a research fellowship. I shouldn't have invited him, I suppose,
not tactful. But there you are, I did. And after you'd left so
abruptly, everyone was very intrigued, and I may have
exaggerated, just a little bit, about you and me. Wishful
thinking, perhaps. So, word will get back to Alexis, don't you
worry ... '

'Go away!' Natasha rounded on him angrily. 'Go away. I'm
sick of listening to all this ... if I'd realised what you were
like, what your book was like, I'd never have come ... '

'But you did.' He turned to the door. 'Goodbye, Natasha.'

When he had gone, Natasha stood very still; she was
trembling with the effort it had cost her to hold her ground,
to prevent his seeing how much he had upset and alarmed her.
She shook herself, as if she could physically shake off what
she had heard, but still his voice snaked through her mind. He
was implying something about her parents, and she wanted to
ignore it, but she could not. Suddenly a hundred other
perplexing memories sprang into her mind, and began to
connect: evasions, conversations abruptly halted when, as a
child, she came into a room, Anne's vagueness, which always
intensified when her parents' names were mentioned ...

Angrily she bent and pulled out her suitcase, began to
thrust her things into it, higgledy-piggledy, anxious only to
leave this room, this house, as soon as possible. She knelt
back on her heels, and clicked the locks.

She knew what she would do, she thought. It was
Thursday—Alexis should be back. First she would ring him;
she would tell him the truth—that she had been working for
Paul Vansittart, that she was leaving, and that any rumours
he might hear about her and the novelist were lies. Then she
would go to Sophie's. She would stay at Sophie's and finish
her book. Until it was done she would not attempt to see
Alexis, or ask him about Paul's insinuations, because if she
did she knew instinctively that her fragile equilibrium would
be shattered. Paul might have lied, might have exaggerated,
but there was—something. She felt it, and feared it. No, she
must finish the book, and stay out of Alexis' way, and not
complicate his life any further. She stood up, trying to be
cold, decisive.

A terrible ache flowered in her heart; her brain pulsed with it. It all hurt—the veiled hints about her parents; the confirmation—so casually thrown out—that, this time, Alexis had embarked on a serious affair; the conviction, which grew even as she fought it, that Alexis, in whose truthfulness she had trusted implicitly all her life, had—perhaps—concealed something from her.

Alexis, her mind cried out confusedly, and the temptation then to run back to Cambridge, to lay all her worries and unhappiness at his feet, was very strong. But she resisted it. When, finally, she lifted her case and went to the door, she looked back for a moment at the sad, drab little room. She knew that everything in it, every feature, would remain sharp in her memory. The room where I grew up, she thought wryly, and closed the door upon it.

CHAPTER NINE

WILLIAM was sitting at home, reading a *Biggles* book
sporadically, and sucking blackcurrant throat lozenges which
he had persuaded Anne were extremely effective for colds. He
had positioned himself well, on the sofa, near the window.
From there he had a good view of Alexis, who had returned
looking grey and exhausted early that morning, and who was
now in the garden talking to a tall thin man William did not
recognise who had turned up unannounced, and who had, it
was clear, increased Alexis' air of agitation. William watched
them thoughtfully. His schemes seemed to him to be hanging
fire; he was dissatisfied with their progress; they had begun
promisingly, but now he was worried. Natasha had written to
him, and her letter had seemed quite calm. If London proved
too attractive to her all his plans would collapse; that was a
possibility that had not occurred to him.

He was pleased then when the telephone rang, and it
proved to be Natasha, ringing from a call-box. Through
whirrings and clickings she asked if Alexis were back and if
she might speak to him. William glanced through the window:
Alexis was now alone; he was pacing up and down the lawn
like a caged tiger.

William crossed his fingers. 'No, he isn't,' he said. 'He's not
back yet. Shall I give him a message?'

An extraordinary strangulated moan came down the line.
William heard it, and his confidence increased. When Natasha
spoke again he could hear she was fighting to remain calm.

'William, oh, William. When will he be back?'

'God knows,' William said ruthlessly. 'I expect he's
enjoying himself. Mightn't be back for days.'

There was a silence on the other end of the line. Then the
pips went, then there were more clicks and buzzings.
Natasha's voice came through on a burst of static.

'William—oh damn, this phone doesn't work properly.
Look. Tell Alexis I rang. I'll ring tomorrow. I've had to
change my plans a bit and . . .' Her voice broke.

'Are you all right?' William began to feel a quickening of
alarm. Maybe he was making a mistake—he had never heard

Natasha sound so miserable. He opened his mouth, but before he could speak the pips went again.

'William, I'll have to go. Oh God! Send everyone my love . . .'

The line went dead. Carefully William replaced the receiver just as Alexis came into the room. He was waving his hands about, and his hair was ruffled into peaks.

'Who was that? I thought I told you to call me if anyone rang?'

'It was Natasha.'

'Natasha? Oh God.' Alexis slumped down in a chair and stared gloomily into space.

'She was calling from a box. It didn't work properly. She got cut off.'

He looked at Alexis, and hesitated. 'I've had a letter,' he said eventually. 'It had an address. But she said there wasn't a phone, and she wasn't sure if she'd stay there very long . . .'

Alexis gave an alarming groan. William regarded him steadily and steeled himself. Natasha had sounded distraught; Alexis looked more miserable than he had ever seen him. Perhaps the crisis William was seeking was imminent—if so, it was no good giving way to pity. He sat down opposite Alexis, blew his nose with a Kleenex, and let the silence lengthen.

'Did you have a nice time in Suffolk?' he said eventually.

'No, I did not. I had a bloody—an awful time,' Alexis said sharply.

'Why did you go then?'

'God knows! Why did I go? I'd agreed weeks ago to discuss that conference. I wanted to get out of Cambridge. I wanted to think—I don't know. All I know is it was God-awful.'

'It doesn't seem to have done you much good. You look ghastly.'

'I feel ghastly. There's something wrong with me. I can't sleep. I've hardly slept a wink since last week, I'm exhausted. And I can't eat—I've lost my appetite totally. It's never happened to me before.' He looked at William mournfully.

'Maybe you're in love,' William said helpfully. 'There's a boy at school whose brother's in love, and he says he carries on just like that—not eating, and not sleeping, and pacing up and down all the time—it's like a madness with him, my friend said, a madness.'

Alexis stood up abruptly. 'I am not interested in your friend's brother,' he said acidly. 'Nor in your diagnosis. Why don't you get on with your book?'

'I will in a minute,' William regarded him complacently. 'And it's not just my friend's brother, it's everywhere. I mean, if you read poetry—Shakespeare—it's *there*, isn't it? *The lunatic, the lover and the poet . . .*'

Alexis gave him a baleful stare.

'My friend says that the trouble with his brother is he won't, well, *declare* himself. There he is, mooching about, irritable, irrational, making everybody's lives a complete misery, and all because he's too cowardly simply to go up to the girl and say, "Look here, I love you", or something of that sort . . .'

Alexis snorted. 'Much good that would do him,' he said bitterly.

'Well, I don't mean those exact words, of course, and I suppose he'd have to *do* something as well—you know, kiss her or something. But my friend says if only he'd get on with it, everything would be perfectly all right because *in fact*, though he doesn't know it, this girl is potty about him. Absolutely potty.'

'How does your friend know that?'

'Oh—the usual signs,' William said airily. He paused. Alexis had begun to pace up and down the room again. He stopped suddenly in front of William.

'This letter,' he said, 'the one from Natasha—does it mention me in it?'

'At the end. She sends love and everything. To you. And Anne, and me.'

'Is it a private letter? Or might I see it?'

'No, you can see it.' William had it ready in his pocket, and handed it over.

Alexis took the paper from him, and William saw that his hand was shaking. He turned away as he read it, then folded it carefully, and handed it back.

'It's a good letter,' he said, his voice tight. 'She writes very well. Just as she speaks. It brings her back—very vividly.'

William looked at Alexis for a long silent moment. Up until then he had regarded all this as a kind of game, like his puppet theatre. Now he saw in Alexis' face something which he did not understand, and which frightened him: he glimpsed, just for a second, a mystery, an adult mystery which he knew to be beyond his bounds. A few minutes before he had felt in control of the situation. Now the expression on Alexis' face, which was one of anger and deep unhappiness, frightened him. Suddenly he felt uncertain of the outcome of this game; it was one whose rules he did not understand, he saw that now. Anxiety quickened inside him.

'Why did you let Natasha go to London, Alexis?' he burst out suddenly. 'Oh, why didn't you stop her?'

'She wanted to go. I had no right to prevent her.'

'But I want her here! I love her, Alexis!'

There was a little silence; Alexis, who had his back to William, did not turn round.

'You didn't want her to go either! I know you didn't. You love her too, Alexis, don't you?'

'Of course,' Alexis said quietly. 'That's why I did not try to stop her leaving.'

William jumped to his feet, he was close to tears suddenly and knew he had gone red in the face.

'Oh, you're so stupid, Alexis! Why do you have to be so noble always? She didn't want to go—not really. She only went because she thought no one here could care either way, whether she left or stayed. That you didn't care—wouldn't notice. That's what she thought. And you just let her. You let her go off and be with that horrible man—I wouldn't have done that, I'd have put up a bit of a fight at least. Done *something*. And now she's there, and I don't think she's even happy . . .'

'Horrible man? Not happy? What makes you say that?' Alexis swung round sharply.

'That novelist—Paul Vansittart. And she sounded miserable on the phone. *Miserable* . . . she asked for you . . .'

'*What?*'

'She did! She asked for you and I said you weren't here, because I thought if she couldn't talk to you on the phone she might come home. She's been ringing and ringing, Anne said, and no one is ever in, and—where are you going, Alexis?'

Alexis was already at the door.

'London.'

The drive to London was appalling. For the first time in his life Alexis, who was not interested in cars, cursed the aged Morris, which had a top speed of fifty miles an hour, and no acceleration. He drove as fast as he could, demoniacally, his foot slamming the accelerator flat on the floor, but the traffic was heavy; the journey took over two hours. By the time he reached Soho it was mid-afternoon; the narrow streets were crowded. He careered round corners, bumped the car up on to the pavement to avoid parked vehicles, swore violently as he was trapped in a one-way system as intricate as a maze. In the end, finding his way blocked by the stalls of Berwick Street market, he simply ran the car half on to the pavement, ignoring the yellow lines, and leapt out.

He ran through the market, into the alleyway, scattering passersby and ignoring their shouted remarks. He stared in disbelief at the green door, the five locks, the overflowing dustbins. None of the bells had labels. He pressed first one, then another, then, cursing dreadfully, put his hand on all of them and kept it there. Nothing happened. Alexis stared at the green door savagely; he was about to hurl himself against it when it opened on a waft of curry smells. Paul Vansittart, immaculate in a three-piece suit, was standing in the doorway. He looked at Alexis' flushed face and bunched fists and smiled. He registered no surprise.

'Looking for Natasha?' he said pleasantly. 'She's moved out, I'm afraid.'

Alexis glared at him. At that moment, he wanted nothing more passionately than to punch the novelist on the jaw; but he needed to know where Natasha was. He hesitated. Vansittart bent, and Alexis observed for the first time that he was carrying a case.

'I'm on the move too, actually.' The novelist gestured vaguely around him. 'I'm jacking this in. Had enough. . . Bloody shame, really, I've wasted nearly three months on this dump. But there you go. You live and learn. It wasn't working out, and I saw my agent at lunchtime. She's got a really good lead for me—Italy. That drugs case—did you read about it? That guy they've arrested wants to talk, and if I get there fast enough, he'll talk to me. It really should be something—you know, it's got the lot. Drugs, politics— American connections. I'm catching the plane this afternoon . . .'

Alexis reached up a hand, and caught Paul Vansittart by the shirt collar.

'Where's Natasha?'

'No need to lose your temper.' Vansittart released Alexis' hand. 'She's perfectly okay as far as I know. We had a little falling out—she'll explain. You knew she was working with me, did you?' He managed to inflect the word 'working' in a particularly unpleasant way. 'Anyway, she took off this morning. And I don't know where she's gone, so it's no good looking like that, Alexis ...' He took a step forward; when Alexis did not move out of his way a certain nervous shiftiness could be glimpsed in his eyes. He changed his tone to one more conciliatory.

'Really, Alexis. I don't know. Ask at the club—and now I have to go—if I miss this flight ...'

'Club. What club?'

Paul Vansittart smiled. He edged towards the pavement.

'In Greek Street. Five minutes from here. A pink façade. Gentleman George's it's called ...' He took advantage of Alexis' astonishment to get past him and the dustbins. Alexis had gone very pale.

'Greek Street? But she said she was working in a bar. She wrote to William and ...'

'It is a bar. Of sorts.' He grinned. 'She serves drinks—don't worry, Alexis, no cause for alarm. If you hurry you'll probably find her there, and if not she'll be there tonight ... Now I really must rush. ... Hope you find her.'

He had managed to back off as far as the entrance to the alleyway. 'Tell her I've jacked this in, will you? She'll be pleased. Took exception to some of the things I'd written, I can't think why ...'

He lifted his hand in a cheery wave. A second later he had disappeared. Alexis hesitated; the shouts of the market filled his ears. Then he turned, and moved off, fast, in the direction of Greek Street.

Brenda, who often stopped off at the club at lunch time, came to the door of the artistes' entrance; her hair was in curlers, and her ample form was wrapped in a flowered dressing gown. A tall, extremely handsome man stood there; she surveyed him magisterially. He asked for Natasha.

'She's not here. And I don't know where she's gone, neither.'

The man in front of her took this information badly. He looked very het up, Brenda thought, white as a sheet, and also extremely angry. Maybe he'd been on the booze, except he didn't look that type. He was a handsome bloke too, no denying it, a real man, built the way she liked them built, though it was a pity about the glasses ... Her attitude softened.

'She was here, mind. Earlier ...' she began cautiously.

'Will she be here tonight?'

'No, not tonight. . . . She was feeling a bit poorly. Under the weather, you know. So she said she wouldn't be in. Dolly's going to cover for her . . .'

'She was ill?' The man now looked very alarmed. Brenda hesitated. He had a lovely voice, he was direct, didn't seem to be pulling anything . . .

'Know her, do you?' she asked curiously.

'I'm her cousin.' He hesitated. 'Her guardian. My name is Alexis Lydiard.'

'She never mentioned no guardian . . .'

'She lives with me, and my family. In Cambridge. Surely . . . Look . . .'.

He began to rummage in his pockets, and eventually brought out a dog-eared photograph. He handed it to Brenda. It showed an out-of-focus garden, the man in front of her, Natasha, and a small boy.

'It's the only one I have of us together,' the man said. 'You see, I usually take the pictures, and the camera doesn't work very well.'

Brenda's face cleared. 'That's William, is it? She told us about him. Oh well, that's all right then.'

'Please . . .' The strange man took her arm. Brenda observed that he had the most extraordinary eyes she had ever seen, and that he was not wearing a wedding ring. She looked at him thoughtfully.

'I'm afraid I can't help you much, love,' she said. 'She was round here. She come down to the dressing room, knew I'd be there I suppose. It was funny. She was trying to act normal, then all of a sudden she burst into tears. I couldn't make head nor tail of half of it. I think maybe she had a bit of a tiff, with her fella, you know . . .'

'Her what?' The green eyes darkened perceptibly. Brenda interrupted hastily.

'Maybe he was her fella. That writer bloke. Never could stand him, so good riddance to bad rubbish, I'd say. 'Course she was upset, but that'll pass, won't it. No lasting harm. Well, we hope not, anyway . . .'

'What?' The man's expression became extremely ferocious. Brenda was impressed.

'She'll be all right, you'll see,' she said encouragingly. 'If she's shot of him, it leaves the field wide open, doesn't it? I mean, you have to look on the bright side. . . . Anyway, I give her some nice sweet tea, and she calmed down. Had all her cases with her, but she had somewhere to go to, she said, so . . .'

'Sophie's!' The man stopped dead, as if struck by a vision.

'I beg your pardon?'

'Sophie's. She'll have gone to Sophie's. Of course. Oh God, what a fool I am . . .' He turned away, walked a few steps, turned back, ran his hands through his hair. Brenda resisted the urge to smooth it down in a motherly fashion.

'I don't know your name,' he said, a little wildly.

'Brenda.'

'Brenda. Thank you.' He clasped her hand warmly; Brenda's heart gave a lurch. 'I know where she's gone,' he said, incoherently. 'I'll go straight round. If she's not there, I'll come back. I'll wait here. Tell her that, will you? In case I miss her, in case she comes back here. Tell her Alexis will be back and—oh, tell her . . .' He broke off. 'Look after her, will you?' he finished lamely, looking suddenly abashed.

'I'll tell her,' said Brenda meaningfully, but the man had already gone.

When Alexis returned to the aged Morris he stared at it in stupefaction. Some vandal had plastered its windscreen and windows with large white notices; an extraordinary yellow contraption had been attached to one rear wheel. He cursed the heavens; he bent and tried to remove the contraption, which would not budge.

A stallholder from the market stopped, and regarded him with interest.

'I shouldn't do that if I was you, mate,' he said at last. 'It's an offence, that is. You've been clamped.'

'Clamped? Clamped?' Alexis straightened up, his hair in wild disarray. He stared at the man as if he were speaking an obscure and foreign tongue. The man raised his voice.

'*Clamped,*' he said with emphasis. 'Police. You'll have to pay a fine . . .' Here he made graphic and obliging money gestures with his fingers. 'Take hours. You foreign or what?'

Alexis began to swear. He swore volubly and imaginatively for some while, removing all doubts as to his nationality. He banged his fist on his car bonnet, making a sizeable dent.

'But I need it,' he ended fiercely. 'I need it urgently . . .'

'Take a taxi then, mate, you'll be here all day sorting that one out,' said the man, and strolled off.

Alexis then tried to take his advice. He tried first one street, then another; he began by waving decorously, and ended by practically flinging himself across the bonnet of every black cab that passed. None stopped. In the end, finding himself on the edge of Soho, and outside a Hertz rental office, and remembering that his pockets contained a magic piece of plastic card that Anne had once persuaded him to acquire, and which he had never used, he dived inside, and waved the card under the nose of a neatly dressed young woman.

'I need a car,' he said tersely. 'Now. Immediately. A fast car.'

'Certainly, sir.' The girl checked a clipboard. 'A performance vehicle? We could let you have a Ford Granada, a BMW 720, a Porsche . . .'

'Which is the fastest?'

'Well, the Porsche, sir, but . . .'

'Then I'll have that.'

It seemed to Alexis to take a very long time. He scribbled his name on endless forms without a second glance, aware of the bitter fact that while he did so no less than three cabs with their lights on passed the windows. He produced his card, and drummed his fingers while its credit rating was checked. At last, when he was escorted to the garage, and seated in the amazing yellow vehicle he waved all advice away impatiently. Some man was trying to tell him something about the number of gears, and Alexis cut him short.

'I know about gears.'

The man looked uncertain; the neatly dressed girl smiled professionally.

'Going on a long trip, sir?' she asked.

'Yes, yes—Wimpole Street,' Alexis cried, and let in the clutch. The result astounded him; the car shot out of the garage as if jet-propelled. Alexis wrenched the wheel, narrowly missed a bollard, and set off down the street like a starter at Le Mans. The traffic was bad—it was by then the rush hour—and for the first five minutes Alexis' thoughts were entirely taken up with the mysteries of modern engineering, and the incomprehensibility of the metropolitan traffic system. But as he grew more used to the controls, and found himself crawling along familiar streets, his thoughts began to move in other directions. They began, indeed, to collect, to shape themselves, into a hideous spiral: Natasha, living in the same building as Paul Vansittart. Vansittart's noxious smile: 'We've had a little falling-out, Natasha and I.' Vansittart's hasty departure for Italy; Brenda's worried features: 'No lasting harm. Well, we hope not, anyway. . . .'

Alexis groaned aloud. The cars in front of him were not moving; he discovered the location of the horn, and pressed it hard. To his amazement the traffic in front instantly began to move. Resisting the temptation to park on the yellow line in front of Sophie's house, he pulled into a mews, then ran back up the street.

There was a bell for Sophie's consulting room on the ground floor, and another bell for her apartment upstairs. Alexis pressed both simultaneously. Normally a buzzer would sound, and Sophie's receptionist would let him in. This time, nothing happened; the bells pealed; the house was silent.

Alexis reached for the knocker. He hammered upon the door. He pressed his ear to its panels. He imagined horrors: Natasha ill; Natasha distraught; Natasha taking an overdose; ambulances, hospitals . . .

The door suddenly opened.

Natasha stood there; her face was a little pale, her eyes a little swollen, but her manner was perfectly composed. They stared at one another. Alexis had no idea of the transformation in his own features, he was aware only of the change in Natasha's. She stared at him blankly, for a moment, as if she could not believe her eyes; then, in her gaze, something lit; faint colour mounted in her cheeks; she brushed back her hair, and smiled at him.

'Alexis . . .' she said, and drew him inside.

'And so, by then, I was becoming quite agitated. I do get agitated . . .' Alexis paused, and met her eyes, and Natasha laughed.

They were sitting at the counter of Sophie's extremely business-like kitchen, side by side, eating baked beans on toast. Through the windows there was a wonderful view of rooftops and chimneys and the trees of Regent's Park beyond. Natasha, who felt rapturously happy, thought it looked like Paris.

'So I abandoned it, and I hired a car.' Alexis paused modestly. 'A yellow Porsche.'

Natasha's eyes widened. 'A Porsche? You? Oh, Alexis, you must have been worried!'

'Not at all. But William said you'd sounded upset, and then

I met Vansittart and then Brenda, and I imagined . . . well, I imagined all sorts of things.'

He lowered his gaze, and Natasha looked at him closely.

'Tell the truth, Alexis. It wasn't just that, was it? You'd heard rumours, gossip . . .'

Alexis looked up, the light of combat in his eyes.

'Yes, I had as a matter of fact. Rather lurid gossip. I discounted it, naturally, straight away.'

'I don't believe you did any such thing. I bet you believed it. Every word.' She hesitated, and then, taking pity on him, smiled gently. 'Well, whatever you heard, it wasn't true. That's all.'

'It wasn't?' He still looked a little doubtful, and through the happiness she felt, Natasha felt a little prick of alarm.

'Would you have minded,' she said carefully, 'if it had been? Do you mind, Alexis, about—oh, scandal?'

'Certainly I do,' Alexis answered blandly. 'It might hurt you.'

There was a little silence between them while Natasha digested this, and its implications. Alexis pushed his plate aside.

'So,' he said at last. 'What are your plans now?'

'I'm going to stay here,' Natasha said. 'Sophie was just leaving when I arrived—it was very lucky really. If I'd been five minutes later I'd have missed her. But she'll be away three weeks at least, she said, maybe four—she's going to Texas and California after New York, lots of conferences and some report she's compiling. . . . Anyway, she said I could stay, and I can use her typewriter, and—well, I'll try and finish this thing I'm writing, and then I'll see.'

Alexis looked up. 'Does it make any difference to you—the fact that Vansittart's left? That he's abandoned his book,' he added quickly.

'No, not really.'

'You don't want to tell me what you're writing?'

'I can't.' Natasha reached for his hand. 'When I've finished it, but not now, Alexis. Do you mind?'

'No.' He covered her hand with his own. There was a little pause. 'It's just that I wondered . . .' He hesitated. 'Well, would you mind if I stayed here as well, for a little while? It's exams now, you see, and there's some research I need to do in London, so it would be quite useful. Provided I wasn't in your way, of course . . .'

His eyes met hers a little sheepishly, and Natasha smiled.

'God, Alexis, you are a dreadful liar,' she said. 'Your face betrays you every time. I know exactly why you want to stay here . . .'

'You do?' He looked at her quizzically.

'Yes, I do. You're guarding my reputation, that's why. You think people have been gossiping about me, and the best way to put a stop to it is for you to be here . . .'

Alexis gave her a sideways glance. 'You're very unimaginative,' he said drily. 'And rather insulting. What makes you think people wouldn't gossip about us?'

'Us?' Natasha went pink. Alexis smiled.

'Why shouldn't they, when one comes to think about it? I rather like the idea. Nobody ever gossips about me—maybe it's time they did. Maybe I should escort you everywhere, in my extremely impressive new car . . .'

'Your hired car . . .'

'My hired car. And—er—take you to the theatre, and restaurants and so on, and look, oh I don't know, threatening and jealous and possessive. Would that do the trick, do you think?'

Natasha looked at him uncertainly. His tone was teasing, but there was something in his eyes which made her uncertain. His closeness now, the quiet in the flat, the fact that he still held her hand, all these things conspired to bring singing back into her veins a memory she had sworn to herself she would bury and forget. She knew her gaze fell to his mouth, and when she looked back to his eyes she had a nasty suspicion Alexis knew just what she was thinking. He smiled, and she frowned at him crossly. Why, if she didn't know him better, she would have sworn Alexis was flirting with her.

'You would never manage it,' she said, a little ungraciously, trying to adopt his teasing tone, but letting a certain bitterness creep into her voice. Alexis raised his eyebrows.

'You don't think so? I find that very wounding. You underestimate me, Natasha. In fact,' he let go of her hand, and stood up excitedly, 'the more I think about it, the more excellent an idea it seems. You can work on your book during the day, and I'll go to the British Museum reading room, and be the acme of academic respectability, and then—in the evenings, we'll go out and—flaunt ourselves. How about that? It will be great fun, and our own private revenge on all the London gossip-mongers . . .'

Natasha looked at him, and in spite of herself, began to giggle.

'Flaunt ourselves?' she said. 'Honestly, Alexis, you're quite mad. You're not a flaunting kind of person. Not like that anyway. You wouldn't know how to begin . . .'

'Would you like to bet on that?' Alexis cut her short. He leaned forward, and with one strong arm drew her to her feet. He held her close to him, and looked down into her face with an expression on his features that made Natasha's knees feel suddenly weak.

'Alexis,' she said falteringly, her mind spinning under the suddenness and unpredictability of his change in mood. 'Stop it, this isn't like you . . .'

'I don't want to be like me. I'm sick of being like me. Sober and responsible and deathly dull. I'm going to be quite different. I shall effect a personality change. You will see a man you never suspected existed. The secret me . . .'

Natasha looked up into his face; she hesitated. She could feel Alexis' elation catch her up, draw her with him; it built on the happiness she had felt earlier, on seeing him. A mad irrepressible gaiety lifted her heart, silencing for a moment all the questions she knew she ought to ask. She looked at him under her lashes. The secret Alexis, the Alexis she had first suspected might exist the day she had gone to his rooms in Cambridge, this Alexis was a temptation indeed. But this Alexis was not her Alexis; he belonged to Ariana, and to pretend otherwise, on whatever mad impulse, would only lead to hurt. She smiled into his greenish eyes, so intent on her own. She knew, she thought sadly, how to make this new Alexis vanish as quickly as the dew.

'Alexis,' she said, very deliberately, raising her arms challengingly and putting them around his neck, waiting for him to recoil in embarrassment. 'Alexis, this is just one of your games.'

Alexis did not recoil.

'The point about games,' he said, equally deliberately, 'is that they are an imitation of life, Natasha.'

Then he bent, and gathering her in his arms, sighing deeply, he kissed her on the lips.

He kissed her for a long while, and his embrace shook Natasha to the roots of her being. It felt to her full of a sweet sadness, the kiss of two people who had been parted too long, who found one another again with joy and with anguish. But she knew it could not possibly feel like that to him, and, sure enough, when she shrank back from him at last, frightened of the knowledge that sprang up in her heart, he looked at her calmly.

'That was to seal our agreement,' he said. 'I'm not sure I should have done that. But since I did—are we agreed?'

Natasha knew only that at that point she would have agreed to anything, anything he asked. All her resolutions, to stay out of his life, to leave him free; all of them crumbled.

'Very well,' she said slowly.

'Good.' Alexis' voice had become rather husky; he now cleared his throat, pushed back his hair, and assumed a business-like manner. 'Now, you make some coffee, and we'll discuss strategy. We should go out to dinner first, I think. Somewhere very public.' He hesitated. 'Have you any suggestions?'

'Oh yes, I know just the place,' Natasha said, trying to keep her voice level. She filled the kettle with water; she wanted to laugh and she wanted to cry. Strategy! He kissed her, then he spoke of strategy! Still, she thought, an idea coming to her, Alexis wasn't the only person who could come up with a game plan . . .

Alexis had given the waiter a colossal tip. As a result, he and Natasha had been led to what was clearly the most desirable table in London's most fashionable brasserie. To reach it they had to walk the length of the restaurant; all heads had turned in their direction as they passed. The table itself was set back in a little alcove, with a banquette of soft velvet; the alcove was draped with curtains, looped back; it was lit only by candles; a silver vase containing red roses decorated the middle of the table; the candlelight winked seductively on crisp linen, silver and crystal. It was designed for, meant for, a discreet *diner à deux*; it could not have been more romantic, or—since it was the only alcove in the room—more noticeable. The fact that the other diners had slightly to crane their necks to see who was sitting there and with whom, did not seem to deter them in the least.

Alexis leaned back on the banquette, and sighed. He took her hand, lifted it on to the table, and caressed it gently, with a distinctly proprietorial air. Natasha glanced at him sideways.

He was wearing a white dinner jacket, which he claimed to have purchased for the trip to Paris. It accentuated the width of his shoulders, the tan of his skin. He looked devastating, and quite unlike the Alexis she knew. Natasha stared lingeringly at the strong lines of his profile, thinking how much more *dangerous* he looked somehow when you couldn't see the teasing gentleness of his eyes. His eyes!

'Alexis,' she said, as he glanced up and took in the room before them. 'What on earth are you doing? It's no good looking in there, I know perfectly well you can't see a thing. Where are your spectacles?'

'I wondered when you were going to notice,' he said mildly, turning to her. 'You are the most extraordinarily unobservant young woman . . .'

'I was thinking of other things,' Natasha said defensively. 'In fact, I can't think straight at all. I don't know whether I'm coming or going, and . . . well, where are they?'

'I am wearing contact lenses,' Alexis said with dignity. 'I bought them some months ago as a matter of fact, in a moment of weakness, after you had made a number of unflattering remarks about myopic men in general, and my physical and spiritual myopia in particular. Then I was too embarrassed to wear them. However, given the circumstances, they seemed like a good idea. What do you think? If you look into my eyes very closely, you can sort of see the edges of the lenses—so I'm told.'

'Told by whom?' Natasha said suspiciously, turning to him.

'Why, my oculist, of course. Who else?'

'Oh . . .' Natasha stared into his eyes as bid. She stared for a long time; she was conscious of a weakening sensation that began somewhere at the back of her neck and ran down her spine to her legs.

'Darling . . .' said Alexis very softly. Natasha jumped.

'Don't *do* that,' she said nervously.

'Do what?' Alexis looked at her innocently.

'Call me "darling". There's no need to overdo it, Alexis. Honestly, no one else can hear you and . . .'

'I'm getting into the part,' Alexis replied with maddening complacency.

'Then someone else has been rehearsing you,' Natasha said tartly, 'because it has a definitely practised air . . .'

'What an unworthy thought. Really, Natasha . . .'

Alexis summoned the waiter. The menu was a mile long, and the wine list looked to Natasha as thick as a telephone directory; Alexis would falter now, she was sure of it. But he did not. He negotiated it swiftly, succinctly, skilfully, with a man of the world air she would never have dreamed possible. She lowered her eyes, and let him get on with it; a lengthy discussion about vintages was taking place, and Natasha was relieved: at least it gave her time to think. Not that she could think clearly—not at all. Whenever she tried to focus her mind, to ask herself how this insane plot had come about and why Alexis should have provoked it, her mind went into a spin. She ought to ask him about Ariana—she knew that. After all, it was all very well to embark on some elaborate revenge on London gossips, but what if all this got back to Ariana—surely Alexis would mind that? Also, she wanted to tell him about Paul's insinuations and hints, but at the moment it was impossible. And she herself—why was she allowing this to happen? Why didn't she stand up right now, and insist on going home, and have it out with him? But no sooner did one of these thoughts dart into her head than it was replaced with another; and every time she looked at Alexis every sensible thought flew out of her head anyway. All she could think about then was Alexis kissing her, and that thought instantly set up such a tumult in her mind and in her blood, that all logic fractured. She sighed, and other, more frivolous thoughts came storming in. Alexis looked so wonderful, and she had had nothing special to wear, so she'd been forced to put on the blue dress she had worn the night of that fateful dinner party, a dress Alexis had seen a thousand times before, and . . .

'You look very beautiful, Natasha.' The waiter had gone, Alexis had lifted her hand to his lips, and was looking deeply into her eyes. Natasha swallowed.

'I am?'

'You are.'

'It's . . . it's a very old dress.'

'I'm not looking at the dress.'

Natasha blushed scarlet; then leaned back with relief. The waiter had returned and was placing two silver bowls in front of them. In the bowls was cracked ice, and in the little glass dishes set on the ice was——

'Caviar!' Natasha stared. 'Alexis, you shouldn't have.'

'Why not?' Alexis smiled. 'I'm being epicurean. Besides, I like it, and if you don't, we'll order something else.'

'But it's so expensive.'

Alexis shrugged. 'I told you,' he said. 'I've discovered this

wonderful little piece of plastic they're always advertising on
the television. It brings you all sorts of magic things—fast
yellow cars, and caviar, and—oh, restaurants like this one, I
suppose.' He gestured around them. 'Nothing important, of
course, but fun once in a while.'

The waiter poured some iced champagne into two tall fluted
glasses, and when he had withdrawn, Alexis lifted his glass.

'To you, Natasha. And the book.' He smiled. 'You look
very happy. Do you feel happier now—breaking away from
Cambridge, starting to write?'

Natasha smiled back. 'I do feel happy now,' she said
carefully. 'And I suppose it's better, isn't it, than dwindling
into a wife?'

The gleam in her own eyes was instantly answered. 'Oh, I
don't know,' Alexis said, equally carefully. 'Some people
might find that an inappropriate phrase. They might think
you could aspire to being a wife.' He paused. 'Or a husband.'

Natasha laughed; her heart lifted that he should remember
so accurately. She sipped her champagne.

'Do you know, Alexis,' she said meditatively, 'it was that
day, the day I had lunch in your rooms, that everything
started to change . . .'

'The day Paul Vansittart came to dinner?'

'Yes,' said Natasha dreamily. 'Why should that day have
been so special, do you think? It just feels as if it were,
somehow. Day one. The beginning . . .' She paused, and
looked up at him. 'Was there ever a day like that for you,
Alexis? If you look back now?'

'In my dry batchelor existence? Well now . . .' Alexis spread
a little caviar on a fragment of toast; he stared into space.

'Come on,' Natasha prompted him. 'There must be
something. Think. The day you first went to prep school—
there's an Englishman's answer for you. Or the day you knew
you'd got your First—or when your first book came out, and
there were all those wonderful reviews. A cricket match?
Something sad? Something happy? The day you lost your
virginity . . .'

'Dear God. Certainly not then. A much over-emphasised
event.'

'Well then—when you first fell in love?' Natasha, having
got over the hurdle of the first personal question decided to
risk another. She looked at him under her lashes; her heart
began to beat very fast.

Alexis appeared to take the question in his stride. His composure was complete. He broke off a piece of toast.

'Mmm,' he said seriously, as if giving the matter considerable thought. 'Then perhaps. Probably. Yes.'

'Was it—was it very long ago?'

'Quite a while ago now. Yes.'

'Oh.' Natasha stared at him. Her mouth had gone very dry, and an odd staccato pulse seemed to have started up in her throat. She very much wanted to press him further, but she did not quite dare, and she did not trust her voice. She bent her head and began to eat the caviar. There was a silence.

'This—this is delicious, Alexis,' she said at last. 'Thank you.'

'Oh good. I'm glad you like it. The thing is . . .' Alexis was staring at the tablecloth in a fixed manner. 'The thing is that falling in love is such a mysterious process. It's very difficult, I think, to mark its starting point, its staging posts. Sometimes, perhaps, the heart changes, and the mind refuses to acknowledge that change. I mean . . .' He was floundering slightly. 'There might be—er—gradations. Friendship, affection, loving someone and then being in love, all mixed up together and . . .'

'You make it sound very complicated,' Natasha said, a little sadly. 'I always thought it might be wonderfully simple, you know—flash! Just like that.'

'Like lightning, you mean?' Alexis smiled, and their eyes met, and held. Natasha felt as if she had stopped breathing; silence beat in on her; she felt blind to everything but the strange green depths of Alexis' eyes. Amusement had lit them as he turned to her; as she gazed the amusement died away, his regard became intent, serious. He was the first to look away.

'You're right, of course,' he said, a little brusquely. 'You'll find out for yourself someday.'

Natasha was stung by his tone.

'How do you know I haven't already?' she said quickly.

Alexis poured some more champagne.

'Because,' he said firmly, sounding rather as if he were trying to convince himself, 'you'd tell me.'

'No, I wouldn't. I'd be much too—shy.'

There was a pause while Alexis took this in; the information did not seem to please him greatly. The waiter removed the little silver bowls, and the wine waiter brought a bottle of claret.

'You can't be shy,' Alexis said, in more resolute tones, as he left. 'It's against the rules.'

'What rules?'

'The rules of our game.'

'Oh,' said Natasha dully. 'I'd forgotten about the game.'

'It had slipped my mind too. We were getting side-tracked. We mustn't do that. Now . . .' He leaned toward her again.

'What's the object of this game, anyway?' Natasha looked at him suspiciously.

'I haven't decided yet,' Alexis said, rather grandly.

'Oh, I see . . . you decide the rules. You decide everything. That's most unfair. What if I decide to deviate?'

'Cheat, you mean?'

'Not exactly.' Natasha paused. She darted a sideways glance at him. 'Supposing I wanted to bend the rules just a little. Make a few moves of my own . . .'

'Then I should respond, of course.'

The waiter was returning; Natasha gave Alexis a sweet smile.

'Okay,' she said. 'Supposing I asked you to put your hand on my knee, and then . . .'

'What?' Alexis began to look alarmed. 'Now? The waiter's coming. Certainly not.'

'All right. I'll put my hand on yours then . . .'

She sat up very straight, and gave the waiter a radiant smile. Underneath the tablecloth she slid her hand across the inch of space between them, and rested her hand lightly on Alexis' thigh. He coughed. The waiter bent over the table and displayed a silver dish, with lobsters. He beamed at Natasha.

'How delicious,' Natasha said. 'Alexis, how clever of you. I adore lobster . . .'

As she spoke, with the tip of one finger, she lightly traced the taut muscles of Alexis' thigh. Alexis shuddered visibly. The waiter turned to him with a worried air.

'You no like, sir? They are not to your taste?'

'No, no. They're fine. Absolutely fine . . . oh my God . . .' Alexis groaned.

'Sir?'

'Just leave them . . .' Alexis cried desperately. 'Leave them. Go. We'll serve ourselves.'

The waiter gave a polite smile. With the air of one humouring a madman he placed the silver dish on the table, arranged the serving spoons and withdrew. This took some time. While he did it Alexis sat bolt upright, staring straight in front of him. Natasha continued the chaste but extraordinarily effective stroking, just a few inches, back and forth. She wanted very much to laugh, but she kept her face straight. As a final move she shifted a little closer to Alexis and exerted a soft but definite pressure with her thigh against his. Then, slipping off her shoe, she curled her toes and rubbed one silk stockinged foot gently but insistently against Alexis' ankle.

The moment the waiter's back was turned Alexis' hand came down over hers like a vice.

'You're an exceedingly immodest young woman, do you know that?'

'Am I, Alexis?'

'Did you do biology at school?'

'No, Alexis. I did physics and chemistry.'

'Well, let me tell you—a man's chemical make-up is a very volatile thing. A woman's is too, of course, but the point is—don't *do* that, Natasha.'

Natasha withdrew her hand. 'I'm sorry,' she said meekly. She waited a beat. 'Darling,' she added.

Alexis was in the act of lifting half a lobster on to her plate. He dropped it.

CHAPTER TEN

THE meal was wonderful, the most wonderful meal she had ever had. They stayed late, sipping green chartreuse because Alexis said it was a notoriously decadent drink and so it should please her. He overtipped the waiter again, out of guilt, and escorted her from the still-crowded restaurant with his arm around her waist. Heads turned as they passed; Natasha recognised three of the people who had been at Paul Vansittart's luncheon, and noted their curious glances.

They went on to a nightclub, because Alexis said he hadn't been inside one for at least ten years, and Natasha said she hadn't for ten months, and then they danced. They danced to begin with anyway, but as Alexis said, the floor was very small and very crowded, so they had a social duty to take up as little space as possible. They ended up with their arms around one another, slowing to a shuffle, the shuffle becoming a mesmeric sway. All Natasha was conscious of was his proximity—the scent of his skin, so familiar and so dear, the firmness of his thighs against hers, the thud of his heart as she rested her face dreamily against his chest.

Late, very late, they walked home. Up Park Lane, along an almost deserted Oxford Street, past shuttered shops and dark glass windows. Their reflections followed them as they walked.

'Look Alexis, two lots of us—we're not real, we're ghosts,' Natasha cried, as she danced along ahead of him from pure mad happiness, and then danced back, and slowed, and caught his hand. They turned up through the shadows of Manchester Square, and then through to the tall Georgian houses of Harley and Wimpole streets. When they reached Sophie's house and went inside, the sky to the east was just lightening.

'Alexis, Alexis, it's dawn, we've been up all night,' she chanted happily, as they went into the hall of the apartment.

'Yes, and you are going to bed,' Alexis said firmly, and before she could argue, opened her door, pushed her inside, and shut it very quickly.

Natasha stood in the darkness of the room, pierced with a

mad unquestioning happiness. She stood very still, and listened. Alexis was sleeping in the little dressing room next door; she could hear him moving about. She hugged her arms about herself; the movements next door stopped. There was a silence.

Slowly Natasha began to undress. She slipped off her shoes, her stockings, her earrings. She reached for the zip at the back of her dress, found it, pulled. Nothing happened.

She straightened up, and tried again. It moved half an inch and then stuck. Colour mounted in her cheeks; in the silence she struggled; nothing.

She waited, then, in a very small voice, almost a whisper, she said, 'Alexis?'

'Yes?' he answered instantly.

'You're not going to believe this. I'm very sorry. But the zip on my dress has stuck.'

There was a silence, rustlings from next door; Alexis came in behind her, his bare feet almost silent on the rugs. Natasha did not dare to turn round.

'Move your arms forward. Stay still . . .'

She felt cool hands at the back of her neck, and a shiver ran down her spine. The silk of Alexis's dressing gown—she thought he must be wearing his dressing gown—brushed against her arm.

'Bend your head forward a little. That's it.'

His fingers found the zip; a sharp movement, a tug, and it moved, snaking smoothly down her back. She felt Alexis' hands against her bare skin; they rested against her back for a moment. Neither of them moved or spoke.

Alexis sighed; a long slow exhalation of breath; Natasha felt her own body go rigid with tension.

Then, very gently he moved his hands under the silk of the dress, parting the fastening, so the material slipped forward. Very slowly he slid his hands across her ribs, over the wild beating of her heart, to the soft skin under her breasts. Her breath caught in her throat. His hands cupped her breasts upwards, their fullness resting on his palms. Then, very gently, he drew his fingers across the tips of her breasts, tracing the circle of the aureole. Her nipples hardened against his hands. He drew her back towards him then, sharply, with a quick movement, so she felt the strength of his desire hard against her. His hands still held her. With a low murmur she let her head fall back against his chest, and, bending a little, he kissed, very softly, the warm skin of her offered throat. Fire shot through every vein in her body; a great drugged swell of pleasure beat up through her blood.

They stayed so for a moment, a long moment. Natasha looked across the room, into the shadows, the mixing of moonlight and daylight, insubstantial shapes. Then he released her.

'Natasha, good-night,' he said.

She heard the door shut softly behind him, then his door, then faint movement, then silence. Her body felt at white heat, her mind blinded as if by lightning. So, mind numb, senses clamouring, she slipped between the sheets.

Natasha sat at the desk in Sophie's small study, surrounded by shelves of medical textbooks, typing. She had been at work since nine that morning, and had not stopped except to re-fuel on black coffee. As she typed the last lines of the chapter, the long-case clock in the corner struck two. She pulled the piece of typing paper from the typewriter, and without looking back over it, placed it face down on the pile which had mounted beside her.

It was finished, this thing, this story. She had written it fast and concentratedly every day for the past six days, and now she felt as if she had crossed the brow of a hill and reached at last the valley beyond it. It was done then; she did not dare look back on it. She felt a little frightened.

It had helped, this being alone every day for eight hours, for each morning Alexis religiously left the flat at nine for the library. It had helped too, the knowledge that Paul Vansittart had abandoned his book, so there was no risk of her trespassing on his territory, though her own story was so different, that the small overlap of material had not worried her greatly. But most of all she had felt a sudden extraordinary freedom, an ability to use a part of herself she had believed she possessed but feared to test. She leant back now in her chair and stared out of the window, seeing nothing of the view. For a while the faces and voices of her story moved in her mind with such vitality they seemed to people the room. Then, very gradually they receded; she let them go. Other faces, other voices began to creep back into her mind.

She had come to an agreement with Gentleman George, reluctant on his part, but persuaded by the offices of Brenda. She would work only one evening at the club, Saturdays, the obliging Dolly, who was glad of the work, taking her place the other evenings. She was glad of this, because it meant she could still see Brenda and Myra, and because it meant that her other evenings were free. These she had spent, all of them, with Alexis. They had been to the theatre, to a party, out to dinner, and the memory of those evenings mixed and glittered and pulsed in her mind. They shimmered and fractured and refused to compose themselves into any sane pattern. When she tried to conjure them up in an orderly fashion, to make sense of them, they refused stubbornly to conform. One image, one memory chased another, all of them pierced through with the same intoxicating sense of happiness and excitement and fear.

She pressed her hands against the desk in front of her, trying to think. Yes, fear. She could not have said of what or why, but fear was involved, it buoyed up and supported that mad floating happiness. It was as if all this were very short, bound to end soon, so there was fear of termination. But not just that; fear of herself, of what she felt, of her inability to communicate it, her cowardly refusal to speak of it to herself, let alone Alexis. But most of all, fear of him. The closer she was to him, the more she saw him, the less she felt she knew him. All the imaginings and inventions of her schooldays now rose up to haunt and mock her; then Alexis had been a phantasm, a creature whose nature she had invented—she saw that now—because his real nature was mysterious to her. He remained mysterious still: when he smiled at her, danced with her, teased her—and yes, flirted with her, with a skill that caused her simultaneous joy and pain—still he eluded her. She did not know what he thought; she did not know what he felt. That place at his heart, where Alexis was himself, where he lived and moved and had his being—it was remote from her, as distant as an alien planet. When he kissed her, then these anxieties had faded away at once; but he had not kissed her now for—she looked at her hands—six days. Not since that first night he came to London. Perhaps he did not want to, though sometimes she suspected he did. Perhaps he felt that it was getting out of hand, this mad charade they were supposed to be engaged on. If she were truly honest with herself, she suspected that Alexis had been, still was, attracted to her, and that with another woman he would not have drawn back. With her, he had done so, not wanting to hurt her maybe, or because their former family closeness created some taboo in his mind. Maybe because of Ariana. Whatever the reason, he had not kissed her, had hardly touched her, for nearly a week, and the moment she let that fact creep back into her mind—writing kept it at bay—it instantly produced in her a mad and feverish anxiety and need.

Irritably she stood up. She paced back and forth in the room, which suddenly felt over-heated and stuffy. She opened the window and then shut it again. She went into the kitchen, felt sick at the thought of more black coffee, boiled the kettle, and then left it. In the hall she hesitated, then, abruptly, unable to resist the temptation, she opened the door and went into the little dressing room where Alexis slept. She paused in the doorway, her heart beating very fast, madly convinced that here, where he kept his things, where he slept, she might find some clue.

The room was anonymous; it had little personality, and what it had belonged to her Aunt Sophie. A small bare practical little room; she herself had been put up there in the school holidays years ago. On the chest of drawers was a bottle of after-shave; she uncapped the bottle and sniffed its sharp clear scent; instantly it conjured up Alexis, his cheek next to hers as they danced at the nightclub. She replaced the cap reluctantly and looked around her. One of Alexis' sweaters, inside out, had been flung over the back of a chair; the bed was rumpled, as if it had been made quickly; the pillow, unshaken, still bore the impress of his head. She touched it lightly with her fingers, drawing her hand over the cool linen. She opened the cupboard door, and touched the shoulders of his jackets that hung there. She peered at the titles of the books piled in the little table by his bed: nineteenth century novels in the main. She had read none of them; she shivered a little; she knew nothing, nothing. One of the books had a page torn from a notebook inserted into its pages as a marker, and she flicked it open; a series of jottings, in Alexis' distinctive, slightly old-fashioned hand; page references, a few names—of characters in the book presumably, for they meant nothing to her, with little notes and jottings beside them, enigmatic little snatches, which must telegraph something to Alexis but which made no sense to her. She closed the book impatiently, and as she did so another scrap of paper fell out and fluttered to the floor. She bent and picked it up; it was another marker presumably, but writing paper this time, and torn in half, and . . .

She stopped, looking down at it. Her hands trembled, the blood mounted up her neck and into her cheeks in a burning flush of colour. The paper was crumpled, as if someone had bunched it up to throw it away, and then flattened it out again. The tear was jagged, cutting across the sentences. It was part of a letter, brief: her eye took in its meaning at the first casual glance, then she froze, her mind fumbling after her vision.

'. . . not go on,' she read. The first word had been torn. 'I love you, that is the reality of my existence. The knowledge of it is . . .' There was another tear; the rest of the sentence had gone, so had the beginning of the next; '. . . in your bed, and in your arms,' it went on, the slope of the writing uneven, the words cramped, as if they were written at speed, under great pressure of emotion. 'Believe that. You *must* believe it . . . times, when we . . . I think that I can see in your eyes this same dark . . . Pain also. That too . . . You must understand how fierce this . . . consumes me. Since I came to London I have mis . . .'

There was nothing else; the last word was ripped by a jagged tear. Natasha stared at it. 'Missed you', said an icy cold voice in her mind. More than ever? More than I would have believed possible? More than I can say? Any of those endings were possible, but clearly the last torn word was "missed". She stared at the scrap of paper; the words on it danced before her eyes, almost blinding her with pain. It was a letter, a love letter, one Alexis had never sent to the person he had so missed since he came to London, a person he loved, whose bed and embrace he remembered and longed for now so passionately the desire consumed him. Her hand shook; the revelation was so sudden, such a cruel little trick of fate. There, in those disjointed sentences, broken thoughts, was the real Alexis, the Alexis she sensed but who always eluded her, a man of passionate feeling and intense direct sexual need. He would elude her always now; this side of him she would never, could never know.

She was ashamed to have found this now, and in this way, but it was not just shame that made her skin feel ice-cold as she opened the book, replaced the piece of paper, and put it quietly back on the pile beside the bed. Then she turned abruptly, and ran out of the room, out of the flat.

She knew where he would be: at the London Library, he had said so this morning, when he left. She hailed a taxi.

'St James's Square,' she said, and then leaned back in the seat, staring at the streets, the hurrying people, the hooting cars, and seeing nothing.

The Library was a tall narrow building, fronting the square; from the outside it looked more like a private house, or a men's club; inside it was terribly quiet. Card catalogues, indexes, shelves, a huge counter piled with books, two women, their heads bent over paperwork. A few people, consulting the indexes; calm; no sign of Alexis. Scarcely able to see she was so blinded by the force of her own emotions, she went up to the counter.

'Professor Lydiard,' she said. 'I believe he's here, and ... and I need to see him. Do you know where I might ...'

The girl raised her head briefly and gave her a curious stare. She looked doubtful for a moment, and then something in Natasha's face seemed to make her relent.

'He might be in the reading room,' she said quietly. 'Through those doors there, on the first floor. If not he might be in the stacks—you could try the literature section. There's a floorplan on the wall over there ...'

'Thank you ...' Natasha made for the doors. She took the stairs two at a time. Sepia portraits of distinguished men of letters looked down at her from the walls. The reading room was like a great Victorian drawing room; leather chairs, tables, magazines and books. Only two people were in there and neither of them was Alexis.

Her heart racing, she went back downstairs, consulted the map, retraced her steps. Within minutes she was lost; the place was like a maze. The bookstacks were in a series of rooms, above one another, to the side of one another, all on different levels and at different angles. The floors were iron-work gratings, her feet clanged and rang on them; above her head, through the gaps in the gratings, she could see other parts of the library, other rooms. Below her feet she could look down two, three floors. Vertigo caught her stomach; a lunatic panic gripped her heart.

Between the different levels were twisting iron staircases, a succession of doors and notices. It was very dark; the books, arranged in great ranks down the rooms, blocked out most of the light. To see between them you had to pull a flex, and then, sparking and flickering, hideous blueish strip lights came on, that illumined just one narrow corridor between the serried shelves, and left all the others in darkness. It was impossible to find anyone in this place; impossible. In each room there were ten, twelve tiny corridors between the books; Alexis could be in any one of them. In *History*, in *Historical Biography*, in *Natural Sciences*, *Physics*, in *English Literature*, once she located it, and when she did so it was by accident, after running up and down staircases and in and out of doors like a rat in a cage. And in *Literature*, where? Under A–E, or F–J; in one of the subsections? That floor was pitch dark, hardly any light filtered through the windows, and Natasha was reluctant to turn on the overhead lights because now she was here she was suddenly afraid, not sure why she had come, not sure she wanted Alexis to see her. She paused, and then stepping stealthily, quietly, she filed between the great flanks of books. Down one, round the far end, up the other, holding her breath. Then she stopped.

At the end of one of the stacks, tucked away in a corner near the grimy windows was a small desk. It was piled high with about thirty volumes, and walled in by them, sitting at the desk, was Alexis.

His head was bent over the desk-top; he was writing; he did not look up. Natasha was about twenty feet from him.

She stood absolutely still, just watching him, her gaze so intent, so filled with the tumult of her own emotions that she felt as if they must clamour through the silence, and he must look up. His head remained bent; his hand moved over the paper. She could hear the faint scratching of his pen. What light there was fell on the dark hair; his face was turned away from her.

'I love him,' she thought, staring, not making a sound. 'Alexis.'

Then, quickly, she turned. She could not bring herself to speak to him. She moved out of sight behind the shelves and leaned against them for a second, resting her head against the books. She shut her eyes; pain washed up through her body to her mind. She heard an abrupt movement; the closing of a book, the scraping back of a chair, and at once—foolishly terrified—she moved, adrenalin jolting her heart with an agonising stab. She could not face him now; she could not speak to him. If she did, she knew she would tell him, even without words. He would be able to read it in her face.

Alexis sighed. An impatient sigh. She moved, quickly, darting back the way she had come, up one corridor of books, across to the right, through some doors, down a tiny winding little stair-case. Her feet clattered on the steps; she hastened on, not caring where she was, anxious only not to be discovered, until at last, unexpectedly she found herself on the main stairs. She ducked out through the main hall, trying to avoid the librarian's eye, praying she would not mention to Alexis that someone had been looking for him. I love him, I love him, I love him, she thought, the phrases beating away a mad tattoo in her mind. She pushed out through the swing doors and into the square. Outside a taxi had just deposited one fare, and was starting to draw away. As he switched his light on, Natasha ran forward, and jumped inside.

The previous passenger had been a woman; Natasha could smell her scent in the cab. As the cab moved off she came into view, walking purposefully towards the entrance to the Library, swinging a large canvas bag. Natasha stared; the woman ran up the steps, pushed back a door; the taxi accelerated. It was Ariana.

'Love?' Myra said. 'Why you asking?'

Natasha bent her head. She was sitting in the dressing room with Myra and Brenda. It was their favourite time of the day, the companionable time, between five and seven, when both used George's place as a staging post. On instinct, not able to face Sophie's flat, Natasha had asked the taxi to take her there, and now, in that little room, she began to grow calmer. The dressing table lights were on; there was the familiar smell of make-up and hair lacquer; Brenda was monumental, in her flowered dressing gown, and Myra was relaxed, drawing on a cigarette, but looking at Natasha closely.

'I—I don't know,' she answered at last, hesitantly. 'I just wondered. Whether you believed in it, and . . .'

' 'Course I believe in it,' Myra said robustly. 'Can't not believe in it, can you? Not once you've had it. It's like toothache.'

'I was in love once. Really in love.' Brenda looked dreamy. 'Only nineteen I was, but I knew straight off. He come from Kidderminster, and he had this lovely black moustache. Used to bring me stockings—silk stockings. On the black market I suppose, because you couldn't get nylons then, not for love nor money. Not unless you knew a Yank, which I didn't. He'd take me for tea at the Corner House, then we'd go and sit in the one and sixpennies and see the film round twice. "Nothing's too good for you, Bren," he used to say to me. "Nothing."'

'What happened to him then?' Myra leaned forward.

'Well, he was married, wasn't he?' Brenda looked aggrieved at the interruption.

Myra cackled unsympathetically. 'How old was he?'

'Older than what I was,' Brenda said with dignity.

'That's make him about eighty now.'

'Get off.'

'Seventy at least. Still fancy him, would you, Bren?'

'Not a lot.'

Brenda began to laugh, a deep chuckle that shook her mountainous breasts. Natasha stared at her in perplexity. To lose the man you loved seemed to her then the end of the world. A few seconds before Brenda had looked sad; yet now she appeared completely restored to good humour. She winked at Myra, and then turned back to Natasha.

'What about you, then?' she asked. 'You in love? That why you're asking? Anyone we know?'

'Don't be soft, Bren.'

'Well, I'm *interested*. What's he look like, love? Tall? Dark? Handsome?' Her face took on a dreamy expression, as if she was remembering someone who fitted that description. 'I like them tall myself.'

'Carries a tape recorder maybe?' Myra said caustically. 'Drinks lemonade when he's paying?'

'Shut up, Myra. It's not him. She ain't stupid . . .'

'Well,' Natasha cleared her throat. An image of Alexis swam before her eyes. The desire to talk about him was insuperable. 'He has very black hair. And very beautiful eyes. They're sort of—dark green.'

'That's good.' Brenda looked pleased. 'Eyes is important.'

'And he wears glasses.'

'Oh well.' Myra sighed. 'Can't have everything.'

'Shut *up*, Myra.' Brenda turned back to Natasha and regarded her intently. 'Known him long, have you?'

'Years.'

'So.' It was not in Brenda's nature to beat about the bush. 'What's going to happen then? You going to get married? Settle down? Have some kiddies?'

Natasha swallowed painfully. 'No,' she said carefully. 'You see, the thing is, he doesn't feel the same way. As I do.'

Myra shrugged. Brenda began to look indignant.

'Get away,' she said firmly. ' 'Course he does. He's probably shy—that's all.'

'No, I don't think it's that.'

'Not married, is he?'

'No.' Natasha stared at the ground. She felt very close to tears. 'No. He's not married. Not yet. But—well, there's someone else.'

'He's shacked up, you mean?' Myra now began to take an interest.

'Not exactly. Not quite.'

'Then you want to get a bit of a move on.' Brenda leaned forward and pressed her arm warmly. 'If you love him and all. No good sitting moping, believe me. Men! Either you can't stop 'em or you can't start 'em. Though it's funny, mind, I'd have said . . .' She broke off.

'He has kissed me . . .' Natasha said thoughtfully. 'Once or twice.'

'Big deal!' Myra rolled her eyes heavenwards.

'And once or twice, I did think, when I looked into his eyes—you know. But I was wrong . . .'

'Listen.' Brenda's grip on her arm tightened. She gave Natasha a little shake. 'You want to get a grip on yourself, you do. Just because there's a bit of competition . . . well, there would be, wouldn't there? Stands to reason. No call to throw in the towel. That's feeble, that is.'

'Do you really think so?' Natasha looked at her appealingly. Somewhere, in the back of her mind, an obstinate spark of hope kindled.

"Course I do. You tell her, Myra.'

'Bren's right.' Myra put out her cigarette. 'You want something, you go after it. Took me a long time to work that one out, but I know now. I mean, what have you got to lose? If you fancy him, why not come right out and say so . . .'

'Give him a hint,' Brenda chimed in. 'The old green light. I expect that's what he's waiting for . . . your bloke.'

'Even if he's in love with someone else?' Natasha's eyes widened.

'In love? In love?' Brenda began to look impatient. 'How d'you know he's in love? Told you, has he?'

'Well, no, not exactly, but . . .'

'There you are then. You probably got hold of the wrong end of the stick. I'd have said, quite definite, that . . .'

'Oh, it's no good!' Natasha sank her head wearily into her hands. 'He just doesn't think of me like that. He never has and he never will. He thinks of me as a child still.'

'A child?' Brenda began to laugh. 'You? Seen you in that costume, has he?' She gestured to the costume Natasha wore in the club, which was hanging on the back of the door.

'On the other hand ...' Natasha went on meditatively, colour mounting in her cheeks as the memory came back. 'The other night, when we were together, well, he did ... It was a little more ...' She turned to Brenda and Myra pleadingly. 'Would he do that, do you think, if he was really in love with someone else?'

Brenda and Myra exchanged expressive glances. Natasha had the impression that as far as they were concerned men were capable of any duplicity, but that neither of them wanted to be the first to say so. Myra opened her mouth to speak, but before she could do so, Brenda interrupted.

'Look, love,' she turned to Natasha. 'Let's get this straight. This fella—is it the one that come here? The one I met?'

Natasha nodded silently; Myra's eyes widened.

Brenda heaved a sigh of relief. 'Oh well then, *that's* all right,' she pronounced magisterially. 'He's crazy about you, he is. I could spot it a mile off, and ...'

'Crazy about me?' Natasha stared at her.

''Course he was. In a terrible state, he was, when he couldn't find you. And he had this picture of you, all crumpled up, like he looked at it a lot, and he took it out of a pocket right over his heart, lovely it was, I thought. And his eyes! What eyes! Made my knees go quite weak when he looked at me. I thought to myself then, this man is head over heels, head over heels. Doesn't know whether he's coming or going ...'

'Did you really? Oh Brenda, are you sure?' Natasha's eyes shone.

''Course I'm sure. And what's more, he's shy—no, more cautious, that's the word. Nearly come straight out with it to me, what he felt, and then, at the last minute ... well, that's your Englishman for you, isn't it? Has its advantages and its drawbacks. But once they're roused, believe me ... he's waiting for a hint, that's all, from you. A nice clear one, so there's no mistakes. I mean, he *respects* you, doesn't he, and maybe he thinks you're not inclined, so ...' She paused for breath. 'But you don't want to worry about this other girl. I'm sure of that. That's old history, bet you anything you like.'

Natasha tried to fight it, but she could feel herself being

swept up by this sudden tide of eloquence. Myra seemed to feel it too, because she stood up, suddenly animated.

'I know the type!' she said. 'I've met them. Bren's right, I bet what you want to do is—well, dress the part for starters . . .' She gestured dismissively at the crumpled demure cotton frock that Natasha was wearing. 'Makes you look sixteen, that does. You want to go home, put on some make-up, the way I showed you . . .'

'And some nice perfume,' Brenda put in.

'Put on some sexy undies, that always helps, gets you in the mood, gives you confidence . . .'

'And get some food in,' Brenda interjected. 'Turn the lights down low. Barry Manilow on the record player. Candles . . .'

'I can't do it.' Natasha, who had stood up during this inspiring exchange, slumped down again. Brenda and Myra regarded her fiercely.

'Don't be so wet. 'Course you can. Why wait? You seeing him tonight?'

She looked at Natasha closely as she said this; Natasha lowered her eyes, and Brenda hesitated, as if a new thought had suddenly come to her.

'Here,' she said. 'This isn't the first time, is it? I mean, you have . . .' Her voice trailed away. Natasha raised her eyes miserably.

'No,' she said 'I think that's part of the trouble. I've never . . .'

'Oh gawd,' said Myra.

CHAPTER ELEVEN

NATASHA stood in the middle of Sophie's drawing room, and surveyed it critically. She had obeyed her instructions, almost to the letter. It was seven o'clock, Alexis was already late. It was lucky he *was* late, because since leaving the club she had rushed round London like one possessed, and she had only just now completed the preparations.

First, the room. The blinds were half-lowered, one small lamp was lit. There were flowers on the tables, and on the dining table at the far end of the room were candles, already lit. She had laid two places with Sophie's best silver and prettiest china and glass. Out in the kitchen a salad was already prepared in a bowl, new potatoes were set, ready to cook, in a saucepan, and two fiendishly expensive fillet steaks, bought from Soho's French butcher, lay prepared under the grill. A bottle of claret that the man in the wine shop had claimed was superlative, stood on the dining table, already opened, so it had time to breathe.

The stereo was on, turned down low—not Barry Manilow, she did not dare risk that, not with Alexis—but a Chopin prelude. Natasha drew in her breath to steady herself; she hoped she could cope with all this. She was not a good cook, she'd probably burn the steaks; maybe Alexis loathed Chopin, he always seemed to be listening to Mozart.

In an agony of nerves she turned to the glass over the fireplace, and inspected her own reflection critically. Her hair was up; she had spent as long as she dared on her make-up, and then taken half of it off again, because she suddenly remembered Alexis saying he hated women with paint all over their faces. Now her eyes looked huge, and luminous, her skin very pale. She was wearing a black dress—she had never worn black before. The dress transformed her, she knew that. It curved over her slender hips, and emphasised her tiny waist. The neckline, cut low, left almost as little to the imagination as the costume she wore at the club. The underwear underneath lifted her breasts, cinched in her waist, and held up the sheer black stockings that gleamed on her legs. It too was black, of lace, threaded with red ribbon, and although it felt very uncomfortable at first, she was now growing accustomed to it. Myra was right; it did have an effect on her own feelings: knowing she tried to be desirable sharpened her own desires.

Now, standing in the room, feeling like an actress on set waiting for the curtain to go up, her body anticipated Alexis, but her mind was wracked with a feverish and inconclusive anxiety. Brenda might have been right; she, Natasha, might have been mistaken. So many words on the letter had been missing or torn—she might have mistaken its meaning. And then—Alexis had never sent it; perhaps he had changed his mind. After all, since he came to London he had flirted with her, and kissed her, and his assertion that it was all a game had not been entirely convincing. It would not be like Alexis to flirt with one woman if he loved another. So, maybe, there was hope.

She started. A key turned in the lock. Alexis came into the room. He stopped in the doorway and stared at her, an odd expression on his face. He was holding a briefcase, and for a moment he just stood there, clasping it in front of him, his eyes narrowing slightly. Then he dumped the case on a chair in an irritable manner, and—without greeting her—turned away and poured himself a drink. He poured himself a large whisky— Alexis, who never drank spirits! He poured a second glass, added water, and handed it to Natasha. Natasha was about to demur when something in Alexis' eyes reminded her. That wretched dinner party! Paul Vansittart had given her a whisky then, and she had taken it. Alexis had not looked too pleased then, and he didn't look too pleased now. Natasha took the glass without comment meekly.

Alexis looked round the room. She saw his gaze register the dim lighting, the candles, the table. She looked at him uncertainly. He appeared tired, and pale. He was looking at her now with a vague, slightly distant expression that did not bode well. All too often that expression meant trouble; it meant Alexis was controlling his emotions with difficulty, that—at any moment—he might fly into one of his terrifying rages. These had always alarmed her; bitter experience had taught her that Alexis' wrath was usually justified, and that his outbursts left her with an abiding sense of shame. Once, she would have sought to divert him; now she knew she felt too vulnerable even to attempt it. She lowered her gaze and took a sip of the whisky. At that moment the Chopin prelude came to an end; the needle scratched drily and repetitively over the record, and Natasha, grateful for the interruption, darted across, hesitated, and then turned the machine off. Alexis watched her.

'You've bought a new dress,' he said as she straighted up and reluctantly faced him. His eyes fell from her face to her neckline, down to the points of her high-heeled black shoes, and back up to her face again. A muscle moved in his cheek.

'It's an extremely provocative dress.'

'Oh . . .' Before she could stop herself Natasha lifted her hands to her bosom nervously. 'Is it?'

'We're dining here, are we?'

'Well, yes, I thought . . . I know I don't cook very well, but . . .'

'Who, I wonder, was it designed to provoke?'

'Why, you, of course.'

'I see.' He paused. 'Is this a new move in the game?'

'Yes,' said Natasha, grasping at the straw he offered. She smiled with what she knew was unconvincing brightness. 'It's a challenge. I'm bringing the Queen into play . . .'

'The King is virtually defenceless against the Queen. He can move only one square at a time. Whereas the Queen . . .'

'Can traverse the whole board,' Natasha finished, avoiding his gaze. 'On the other hand—I'm not very good at chess. You always out-maneouvre me.'

'At chess, possibly.'

Alexis' voice had an edge to it that increased her nervousness. Something was wrong, that was obvious, and she could not think what it was.

'So, tell me . . .' Alexis was regarding her intently. 'Should I be provoked before dinner, or after it?'

Natasha flushed. 'If you can choose the timing so nicely,' she said sharply, 'then the question doesn't arise. You're not provoked.'

Alexis smiled. He inclined his head slightly, as if to acknowledge she had scored a debating point.

'I'll rephrase the question,' he said. 'At what point should I—skilled and schooled in duplicity as I am—reveal the *extent* of my provocation? Before dinner, or after it? Not during it, I think, don't you?'

Natasha looked at him uncertainly. The way he inflected the word 'duplicity'—not one she would ever have associated with him—increased her nervousness. She set her mouth. As usual, Alexis was about ten moves ahead of her.

'After dinner, then,' she said.

'As you wish,' Alexis answered smoothly.

Natasha undercooked the steak and overcooked the potatoes; the salad was limp and the dressing tasteless. Alexis ate with apparent enjoyment, however, and tactfully ignored the fact that she picked at her food. The pudding, which she had bought ready-made in Soho, was oranges glazed in a sweet-sharp sauce with Cointreau. They were delicious, and Natasha, aware that the wine was going to her head, made an effort to eat them. The time passed, and as it passed her nervousness did not quite abate, but it slackened. Alexis was being very charming, and, though she watched him carefully, she thought she could detect no sign of his earlier anger. She could not be certain; he might have been disguising his emotions, holding them in check. But now, she was almost sure, it had passed. Perhaps he had simply been tired, worried about his work ... And also, she thought, her courage mounting, Alexis was not quite as firmly in control of the situation as he seemed to want her to believe. Once, when she crossed her legs, she saw he averted his gaze late and a little reluctantly, from the silk of her stockings. By the time she served the pudding she had discovered that, if she leaned forward a little, so her neckline became even more revelatory, Alexis tended to tangle his sentences, avoid her eyes, and fix his gaze on a spot some feet to the left of her shoulder. She smiled to herself, and looked at Alexis dreamily. He was talking, but she was not listening to his words. The wine had soothed her nerves, the room was dissolving into a wonderful golden haze, and, she thought, Alexis had the most beautiful mouth in the world. She would have liked, just now, to reach across the table, and ...

'You're not eating very much.'

'No.' She smiled at him and stretched langourously. 'It's this thing I'm wearing, under the dress. It's terribly tight. It's difficult to breathe, let alone eat ...'

Alexis froze. 'Thing? Under the dress? What thing?'

'Oh, it's a sort of corselet thing,' Natasha said daringly. 'You have to wear something like that with a dress like this ...'

'You do?'

'Mmmm. It's sort of all in one piece, and it's made of rather sheer black lace, with little frilly suspender things at the bottom. And it has whalebone, you see, so it sort of cinches you in, round the waist you know, and sort of lifts you up—well, elsewhere. And it has scarlet ribbon threaded through the lace, just here, over the . . . hips. It's called a Merry Widow.'

'A Merry Widow?' Alexis' eyes had a glazed expression. 'Black lace, you say?'

'Mmmm.'

'Good God!'

'And it's *extremely* difficult to get on, or off, by oneself. There are hundreds of little hooks and eyes, all the way up the back, and . . . But you must know what they look like.'

'I can't say I do.' Alexis' eyes narrowed. 'Of course, I read the Sunday supplements, which seem to contain the most extraordinary advertisements these days, and from personal experience, naturally, I . . .'

'Naturally . . .'

'However, I can't say I've ever encountered a Merry Widow. I wonder what the purpose of it is. I mean, you are very—slender. You hardly need to cinch yourself in . . .' His voice tailed away.

Natasha opened her eyes innocently wide.

'Oh, *that's* not the purpose. It's to make men's pulses beat faster. The woman in the shop told me so.'

'What extraordinary shops you seem to frequent these days,' Alexis said in a dry voice. He held out his wrist. 'Would you like to test her assertion?'

'What a good idea.' Natasha took his hand, and Alexis flinched. She pressed her fingers against his pulse. There was silence. 'Oh dear,' Natasha said at last. 'I'm afraid she's right, Alexis. I make it about 160 a minute. That can't be normal, can it? Do you feel all right? I expect you do of course. It's that metabolic condition you told me about once. Do you remember?'

Their eyes met. Natasha, who had kept her voice light, and tried to ignore the feelings that shot through her own body the moment she touched Alexis' hand, heard her own voice falter. She had raised her eyes to his teasingly; he met her gaze seriously, with a gravity and pain in his that caught at her heart. The memory of that day in his room rose clear in her mind; the image of Alexis' face as he had looked then mixed and dissolved with the face of the man before her. It was *then*, she thought, as the turmoil of the past weeks became suddenly clear to her. Of course; it was then she had known. How

slowly the mind kept pace with the heart. Alexis covered her
hand with his.

'Yes,' he said, his voice sad. 'I remember.'

'I'll make some coffee.'

Gently Natasha disengaged her hand, and turned away into
the kitchen. She could not go through with this now; she
knew it. She could not tease and cajole and play games any
more. She bent her head, dimly conscious that, behind her,
Alexis had moved from the table to a sofa. I shall make the
coffee, she said to herself, and then I shall simply go back in
there and tell him what I feel. I can't lie any more. It hurts too
much. Blindly, hardly conscious of what she was doing, she
put cups on a tray, and poured water on the coffee. Gripping
the tray tightly she went back. Alexis was sitting in the softly
lit room, his legs stretched out before him. As she came back,
he stood up, and reached to take the tray from her.

'Alexis . . .'

'No, let me. Natasha—sit down. He gestured to the sofa
beside him. 'Please. This is stupid. We are being very stupid. I
must talk to you . . .'

'Alexis, I . . .' But something in his manner stopped her, a
gravity and a gentleness that sent alarm coursing through her
body. She hesitated, looking at him, thinking wildly that this
was how someone must look when they brought bad news,
when they came to your door to tell you of an accident, an
illness. Her heart contracted with an instinctive animal fear;
something was wrong, deeply wrong. It was written in every
line of his face. She sat down, and after a pause, Alexis sat
beside her, leaving a wide space between them. He did not
pour out the coffee; he seemed to have forgotten its existence.
Slowly he brought the long narrow fingers of his hands
together, the pressure whitening the skin of his knuckles. Then
he relaxed them. He sat upright, not leaning back, not
meeting her gaze. When he spoke she could hear from his
voice that he did so with difficulty, that he chose every word
with care.

'Natasha. I want to tell you something, something I ought
to have told you before . . .'

Her heart leapt.

'Long ago,' he said, and the instant of hope died away.
'About your parents. And—about me.'

Natasha felt her blood suddenly cold. All the hints, all the
innuendoes of Paul Vansittart came rushing back into her

brain, as if the dam she had erected around them this past week had now been breached.

'My parents?'

'Yes . . . Natasha, I want you to understand this. I don't want you to be hurt. I want you to hear it from me, not——' he hesitated, 'someone else. And I . . . well, I'd better begin at the beginning. Your mother.'

'I know about my mother——' Natasha leaned forward impetuously. 'I've half known for years, anyway, I suppose, half guessed. I just didn't want to confront it, I think. Alexis, don't. I know she wasn't—well, that she probably wasn't very faithful to my father, but . . .'

'No, she wasn't.' Alexis glanced at her sharply.

'But that wasn't so very bad, was it? I mean, lots of women are unfaithful to their husbands. Lots of men to their wives. Maybe there were reasons, maybe they were just very unhappy together, maybe he . . .'

'Natasha, please listen.' Alexis stopped her, and at the quietness of his voice, all the energy went out of her. She leaned back against the cushions, her face pale, and after a pause, Alexis went on.

'Your mother was very beautiful,' he said slowly. 'She had quite a reputation, my parents always said, when Nico married her. He knew that, he knew what he was taking on. And she was very honest—if he had not known, she would have told him. Anyway. They married; I went to their wedding—I was about ten years old; it was one of the very few occasions I ever saw them.' He paused. 'Natasha. I want you to understand—I don't know if their marriage was a happy one or not—who can ever tell that? But I do know that according to my parents, to their friends, the marriage was not exactly a conventional one. It was . . .' He paused, and she caught a moment's distaste in his voice. 'A modern marriage. They came to an arrangement—each went his own way, no questions were asked, jealousy was not admitted. If they parted they always returned; they remained friends at least . . .'

Natasha leant forward, her mind leaping ahead of his measured words.

'Nico wasn't my father. Oh, that's it. Alexis—is that what you're trying to tell me?'

Alexis swung round to her, astonishment on his face.

'No, of course not. That's not what I'm saying at all. Of

course Nico was your father. You can't have doubted that? Why, you only have to look at a photograph, the resemblance is amazing ... Natasha, no. Please don't think that for a moment. There were long periods when they lived together, when they apparently were completely happy with each other. And then ...'

'Then what? Why?' Natasha stared at him. 'I don't understand. You could have told me all this long ago—it's not so very dreadful. I mind that it was like that, of course I mind. I wish it hadn't been. I wish that they had loved one another and married and ... If I remembered them better, perhaps. But Alexis, I hardly saw them, hardly knew them. I was so little when they died, and since then, you ...' She broke off.

Alexis' eyes were dark in the pallor of his face. At her words she saw his mouth twist a little. He waited, as if he knew what she had been about to say, and when she said nothing he turned away, fixing his eyes into the middle distance as if his eyes saw there, re-played, the events of which he then spoke.

'When I was nineteen,' he began, his voice very deliberate, 'I went up to Cambridge from boarding school. You were nearly seven. I had never seen you—I hadn't met your parents since their wedding. At that point your father had decided to return to England to live, and your mother was househunting—it was one of their periods of reconciliation, I suppose, although that makes it sound too dramatic. In fact, as far as I know, their comings and goings were quite amiable ...' He paused. 'Your mother had heard of a house, near Granchester. So, my first year, she arrived in Cambridge, and called in at Trinity. She introduced herself again to me, and said she would be very grateful, since I knew the area and she did not, if I would drive out and look at the house with her. I agreed.'

He broke off, looking down at his hands, and when Natasha did not speak, he cleared his throat and went on.

'We drove out to Granchester.' He hesitated. 'I was then very young and very inexperienced, certainly naïve, and I suspect, slightly puritanical. When we got to the house—I don't know how to put this. Your mother. She asked me to make love to her. Attempted to seduce me, I suppose ...'

'My *mother* ?'

'Natasha, please understand. It was farcical, really. I wasn't

remotely attracted to her. I'd had no idea what she intended.
When she made herself transparently clear, I—well, I wasn't
very sophisticated. I didn't know how a man extricates
himself from a situation like that without offending the
sensibilities of the woman concerned. And so, I'm afraid, I
was very blunt and insensitive and rude. I declined the
offer . . .'

Natasha stared at him. An image of Alexis as he must have
looked at nineteen rose up in her mind's eye; so tall, and so
beautiful. Her heart turned over; she felt an instant's wry
compunction for her mother.

'Was she—was she angry?'

'No.' Alexis glanced at her. 'No, she was not. She laughed.
She handled the whole thing with a grace of which I was
completely incapable. She said now she knew she must be
getting old because I was the first man ever to turn her down,
and that she'd go straight home and tell Nico what an
extremely honourable young cousin he had. I liked her, then.
So, we drove back to Cambridge, parted cheerfully and two
days later Nico turned up in my rooms at college.'

'Nico did?' The ghost of a smile came to Natasha's lips. She
had heard stories of her father's impulsive and Russian
temperament. 'What did he do, Alexis? Did he call you out?'

'No. He made a speech. A long, very involved and rather
Russian kind of speech, which became very emotional. All
about their marriage and how I would understand when I was
older. The vagaries of the heart. I was very moved and very
impressed—and flattered, I suppose. My own father had
always been a distant figure, and Nico spoke to me as if man
to man. I had Russian blood myself, he said, so he knew I
would understand him. I was completely overwhelmed; my
own parents couldn't have been more conventional, and here
was this wild romantic figure, this black sheep of the family,
talking to me about sex and love, men and women . . . it was
astonishing. I felt as if I'd found a blood brother. I couldn't
believe how tame my own life had been up until then, and I
immediately resolved to let my Russian nature come to the
surface—wine—women—I was going to kick over the
traces . . .'

'And did you, Alexis?' Natasha put in slyly.

'Well, yes, I did for a while, as it happens.' He gave her a
dark sideways glance, then his face sobered again. 'But that
came later. The point is, Nico made a request. He said he had

been touched by my behaviour, by my alleged honour, and that—if anything should ever happen to him—he wanted me to promise I would look after you. Take his place. Be a father to you.' Alexis paused. 'I agreed, of course, fervently. We opened a bottle of vodka and drank it between us. For me it was like a scene in a play—very romantic. Not the stuff of ordinary life at all. Six months later he and your mother were killed.'

There was a silence. He held his face averted from her, and Natasha looked at him curiously. When he did not speak, she reached her hand out to him.

'But Alexis,' she said. 'It's such a wonderful story. It doesn't make me sad, it makes me happy. I see them now, sense them—my parents—for the first time. I'm glad my father acted as he did.' She paused. 'But I don't understand. Why didn't you tell me before?'

Alexis ran his hand through his hair and gestured agitatedly.

'It was impossible at first, obviously. You were a little child—you'd just lost your parents, there were a hundred practical arrangements to make. I could never have managed without Sophie and Anne—I had to grow up myself, very fast. Then, later . . .' He paused. 'If you had asked, when you were in your teens—I think I would have told you. But you never did. I put it off. I was shy of you, and I decided, when you left school, when you came back to Cambridge to live, then . . .'

'But Alexis, that's nearly four *years* ago now.' Natasha stared at him in bewilderment. 'Surely you could have told me? When I was twenty-one—when you ceased to be my guardian. Why not then?'

'I know that was the obvious moment. I know that.' Alexis stood up abruptly. 'It was precisely then it was impossible.'

'But *why*, Alexis? I don't understand.'

'Very well.' He had begun to pace up and down the room. Now he came to a halt, and turned to face her.

'I had given your father a solemn promise that I should be as a father to you.' He paused, and then, seeming to steel himself, met her eyes. 'When you came of age I could not tell you that, because I knew I had failed in my promise. By then—I did not feel towards you as a father should feel.'

'You didn't . . .' Natasha stared at him, her face blank, her mind groping after his words. Alexis raised his hand, as if he could physically ward off her presence.

'No, please, Natasha,' he said. 'I know what you must be

thinking. I know you have—naturally—thought of me as a father. If I could have gone on as before, believe me I should have done. I tried. But it was such a lie, such a hypocrisy. I was living that lie, every day, and my ability to control my own feelings got weaker and weaker. I hate myself for that. I should never have come to London now, never have . . .' He broke off, his eyes dark with pain.

Slowly Natasha stood up. She looked across the room at him, seeing nothing but his face.

'You didn't feel to me as a father should?' she said carefully. 'But Alexis, you are not my father.'

'I had made a promise,' he said stubbornly.

'You fulfilled that promise. Alexis, listen to me. You've done more than enough. You've looked after me, made a home for me . . .'

'I promised to take your father's place.' Alexis interrupted her with a sudden savage gesture, as if he could bear the evasions no longer. 'How could I tell you that, Natasha, when I wanted to be your lover?'

Natasha, who had begun to move towards him as he spoke, stopped dead. Bewilderment and confusion dissolved in her mind like clouds before the sun; she felt hope light in her heart, and radiate through every vein in her body. Words were propelled to her lips on a tide of joy.

'But Alexis,' she cried, 'I love you.'

Alexis had turned away from her as she halted. At her words she saw his shoulders sag. He bent his head.

'I know you do, Natasha. I love you too. But I'm not talking about that kind of love. Oh, God. Please, Natasha, try to understand . . .'

'No, Alexis, I didn't mean . . .'

'I want you.' He turned back to her, his voice suddenly savage, as if, by being brutal, he would make her understand. 'In my bed. Sexually. The way a man wants a woman. I want it more than I've ever wanted anything in my life.'

'But Alexis . . .'

'Look——' He cut her off, his voice angry. 'Why do you think I'm telling you this now? I've managed to conceal it for the past two years longer—so why not conceal it now? I can't, because you have to understand. Because you need help. And because the last thing you need now is another lover . . .'

There was silence. Natasha stared at him in bewilderment. 'Another lover?'

'For God's sake . . .' He gave a gesture of exasperation. 'We have to try and get rid of all the lies first. It's the only way. Then perhaps I can help you, because it won't be under false pretences. I can't help and lie at the same time—not any more. I can't let you accept my help thinking it's offered entirely innocently—that I help you as I'd help Anne or William. It's not like that, and provided you understand that and . . .'

'Alexis—I don't know what you're *talking* about,' Natasha cried. 'What help? Why should I need help? Alexis, *listen*, you don't understand, you've got it all wrong, I . . .'

'I do understand.' He cut her off, his voice suddenly cold. 'Stop pretending, Natasha, there's no point. I've seen Ariana. I've talked to her, and Paul Vansittart this evening. That's why I was late.'

He moved away from her as he spoke, and slumped down in a chair as if exhausted. There was silence. Natasha looked before her into the shadows of the room, and the shadows seemed to detach themselves and begin to invade her own mind. She raised a hand to her forehead and pressed it hard against her skin.

'I know you've seen Ariana,' she began slowly. 'I came to the Library today. I wanted to talk to you—and then I changed my mind. I saw her go in as I was leaving . . .'

'Then why not say so, earlier?' He sighed. 'You see? All these lies and evasions—it shouldn't be necessary.' He leaned back against the cushions. 'I saw Ariana before that anyway. She came up to London three days ago.'

'Three days?' Natasha swung round. Pain cut through her like a knife. *So that was why he had not sent the letter: he had had no need. He had been with Ariana.*

'She came up on Thursday. She was working as a consultant on some book programme for the BBC. Paul Vansittart was appearing on the programme.'

'But you said he was in Italy. I thought . . .'

'He came back. The Italian thing fell through, I gather, Anyway, they met on Tuesday, and she moved in with him on Thursday. He has overcome his dislike for intellectual women, obviously . . .'

'*That's* why you were so odd tonight. So angry!' Natasha stepped forward accusingly. She felt blinded by pain and bewilderment, and a terrible violent jealousy so forceful it terrified her suddenly blazed in her mind. 'That was why. And then you . . .'

'Ariana's arrangements had nothing to do with it,' he said flatly. 'I can see they might upset you, of course, in the circumstances. If I could have avoided telling you, and hurting you, I would have done so.'

'Hurting me? Why should that hurt me? I don't care who Paul Vansittart is with, or why. I told you that . . .'

'I know you did,' he said, his voice quiet. 'And I believed you. But then it hadn't occurred to me that you could hide your feelings as well as I can. Now I know, you can stop. There's no need.'

'I'm not hiding anything. Anything!' She rounded on him furiously. 'I don't know what you're talking about. If you want to know what I truly think, I think they deserve each other. They make a fine pair. Good luck to them!'

'Natasha. This is beside the point.' He interrupted her impatiently. '*Listen* to me, will you? Concentrate. Now—who did you tell about the book you're writing?'

'My book?' The question took her totally by surprise. She stared at him, trying to push out of her mind the ugly jealous images that swarmed there suddenly like demons. 'I told nobody, except you. I didn't tell Paul. Oh . . .' She broke off, colouring. 'And I wrote a note to Ben Whitby, but that was nothing. I just said I was writing something, and might I show it to him to read when I finished it. He was the only publisher I've ever met, you see, and he'd been kind to me, and I thought . . .'

'How can you be so damn naïve?' Alexis gave a groan and ran his hands through his hair. 'I can't believe it. I've been here, for God's sake. In the same house. I didn't ask you about the book because I could see you wanted to keep it to yourself. I could understand that, respect that. But if you needed advice about a publisher, why the hell didn't you ask me?'

'Because I wanted to do it on my own,' Natasha said, indignation in her voice. 'Surely you can see that? I didn't want some publisher reading it as a favour, because I was your cousin . . .'

'Oh really?' Alexis' voice was as cold as ice. 'You didn't. How very scrupulous of you. Then perhaps you'd like to explain to me why you saw nothing wrong in contacting your lover's publisher?'

'*What?*'

'A man who, as I gather you knew, was involved in the past with your own mother—and a book . . .' He paused. 'A book which your lover asserts is based on material he's been gathering for the past three months. A book you had read, in draft form, and loyally and lovingly typed up for him.' Alexis met her eyes, his own glittering with anger. 'That may not be nepotism exactly, but if it's true I must say it's one of the nastiest examples of mutual exploitation I've heard in a long while. And, true or false, your lover is busily plastering the story all over London.'

There was a silence which seemed to Natasha to go on forever. Weakly she pressed her hand to her forehead.

'I don't believe this . . .'

'I can assure you it's true.'

'Who told you?'

Alexis shrugged. 'Ariana told me part of the story. I asked to see Vansittart. He told me the rest.'

'You saw him? You *asked* to see him? You went behind my back and listened to all that? You sat there and you . . . oh, it's horrible.' Natasha turned abruptly away. She could not even cry; every nerve in her body felt deadened and stunned. Alexis hesitated.

'I only saw him tonight. I had to see him—surely you can understand that? I thought it couldn't be true, that Ariana must have misunderstood. I thought I'd be able to stop him from spreading lies about you. And then . . .'

'And then you believed him!' Natasha swung round to face him again, anger blazing in her eyes. 'I hate you for that!'

'You're wrong.' Alexis reached for her arm, and she knocked him angrily away. His mouth set in a harsh line. 'If you want to know, I told Vansittart I thought it was a pack of lies, and that if one word of it, one word, got into the press, you'd sue for libel. That was what I said.'

'Oh did you?' Natasha heard her voice rise uncontrollably, so the words came out as an ugly taunt. 'Well you may have said that—you would. Anything to keep up appearances, anything to avoid gossip. But you didn't believe it all the same. You thought he might be telling the truth—you did—I can see it in your face, in your eyes. You thought I was like my mother—unprincipled. Ready to jump into bed with anyone. You didn't believe in me, and you didn't believe in my book . . .'

'That's not true. Stop this, damn it, Natasha . . .'

But Natasha could not stop; her heart was beating wildly. She heard her own voice rise.

'And then you came to me, and you told me—all that. All those things about my parents. Well, why should I believe them? Why should I trust you when you haven't a shred of trust and respect for me? After all, it's only words, isn't it? My word against Paul Vansittart's. Your version of what happened with my mother and father. That might be a lie—I can't ask them, can I? They're dead. So how do I know you've been telling me the truth? Maybe *you* lied. Maybe you didn't turn my mother down. Maybe that's why you feel so guilty now . . .'

Alexis hit her. He brought his arm up very fast, slapped her across the face, hard, with the palm of his hand. Natasha felt stinging pain; her head reeled back. The torrent of words stopped. For a moment, a second, her mind went black. Alexis gripped her by the arms painfully, and dragged her round to face him.

'Don't you ever say that,' he said furiously. 'Not ever. Not even when you're hysterical. Never, do you hear me? I won't even have you think it. For three *years* my life has been torn apart by what I felt for you, and you didn't even damn well notice. And then, when I tell you the truth, because I have to tell you, because you have to know, you turn round and throw it in my face. Natasha, I warn you . . .'

'Have to tell me. Have to?' Natasha lifted her face up to him, though she hardly saw his features she was so blinded still with anger and pain. 'Why did you have to tell me now—tonight, when you'd seen Paul? Because I need help and I have to know the truth before you can honourably give it to me? Because you can't bear to go on lying to me anymore? I don't believe you, Alexis—I don't believe a word. You thought I was a virgin before—that's why you kept quiet. Now you discover I'm not, so I'm easy game. No harm done. Join the queue.'

She spat the words out at him, and Alexis' eyes blazed green and dark in his pale face. Natasha, looking up at him, felt a mad exultation. She wished he would hit her again, choke off her words, anything; she wished he would hate her, because no matter how much he did he would never hate her as much as she hated herself. The words came, winging their way out of some ugly place in her mind, where she hurt

so much that all she could do, like an animal, was strike back
wildly, inflicting the same damage she felt. She knew she was
hurting herself more with every word she spoke, that she was
killing the very thing she most loved in the world, but she
could not stop, she was powerless to stop. She gripped Alexis'
jacket, and pulled him closer.

'Besides,' she went on, tauntingly, 'Ariana's gone, so you
haven't even that outlet now, have you, Alexis? So it makes
perfect convenient sense. I admire that, I admire your timing.
The minute she's out of the way you come back here and tell
me all this. You believed I'd prostitute myself and my work.
And it only made you want me more. You want me now . . .'
She tightened her grip on his lapels and banged her fists
impotently against his chest. 'I know you do. I can sense it.
Even when you're angry. Even when you hate me . . .'

'That's true.' A dangerous light came into Alexis' eyes.
'And I suppose it's the one way to stop you talking.'

He pulled her violently against him, forcing her head back,
his strong fingers pulling her hair so she cried out in pain. As
her lips parted he kissed her, harshly and angrily, forcing her
to respond. He hurt her; she could taste blood in her mouth,
and she reached up instinctively to push him away, to claw at
his skin, but he caught her hands, and imprisoned them
behind her, pulling her against him, so she was pressed
between his thighs, and she felt his body harden against her
belly. She felt herself go limp in his arms, as his violence
exorcised all the anger and pain which had built up in her,
and as he felt the fight in her die down he released her wrists,
and brought his hand up over her body, touching her,
clasping her.

His hand moved, across the small of her back, over her hip;
it rested there a moment, as his kiss grew more gentle and
more deep, and she sighed against his lips. Then it moved
round and down, to the soft warmth between her thighs, and
then up again, to the full curve of her breasts. She trembled,
and felt him shudder against her. He drew back a fraction,
kissing her face, her closed eyelids, and the withdrawal of his
mouth from hers made her give a tiny incoherent cry, and
instantly, blindly, he sought her lips again, parting them to
the warmth and sweetness of his tongue.

Natasha could not see or think; for a second he just held
her still, against the hammering of his heart, and the peace of
that moment the great black peace of it—seemed to assuage

all energy and all desire. Then the next instant, roughly and
with a man's impatience, he moved again, ran his hand over
the curve of her buttocks, grasped her hand and brought it
round between their thighs, so she felt his hard pulse against
her fingers, and at once the peace went, desire for him
sharpened and became imperative. He groaned against her
lips, moved his hand up to pull the neckline of her dress
lower, to cup her breasts from below against his palms. He
moved his mouth over her throat, and she thought through
the blackness that he said her name, over and over again, and
pressed his lips to the pulse that beat beneath her skin. He
bent her head back, his breath coming quickly, and lowered
his mouth to her breasts. She shuddered; her nipples hardened
under the moistness of his tongue; she felt his body move,
hard and demanding against her. Her dress had ridden up, he
held her so closely, so tightly, and now, in an agony of want
for him, she caught his hand and pressed it against her thigh,
moving it, under the silk of her skirt, so it rested for a
moment against the bare skin above her stocking.

She wanted then to be naked, to be without the impediments
of clothes, to touch him and be touched by him—to have him
know every curve and fissure of her body— because then, then,
he must know what she really felt, and how stupidly, blindly,
painfully, she had taunted him and lied to him.

'Alexis,' she murmured, against his lips, and she felt his
hand grow still. He moved it, relaxed his hold on her for a
moment, clasped her again to him, as if in desperation, sought
her mouth, and then, with an exclamation, drew back. He
held her, close but not touching him, so he could look down
into her face, and even as she looked at him she saw the fight,
the struggle to compose and control himself.

'Natasha,' he said, his breath ragged, his voice very low.
'Oh, Natasha. I have thought of this, of touching you as I
touch you now, so often. I drove it out of my thoughts, and it
invaded my dreams. I wanted it—if it were to happen, if it
could ever happen—to be, not tender necessarily, a man
cannot always be tender, though I should have liked to show
you . . .' His voice broke. 'I wanted it to be a free thing, joyful
perhaps . . . And now.' He raised his hands and gently,
regretfully, pressed them against her lips. 'Now it has been
born out of anger and violence and misunderstanding. I
always knew there was that danger, with you, with me. I
would have done almost anything to have prevented it.'

He bent his head, and kissed her forehead softly.

'I blame myself more than I can say. No, don't touch me—please, Natasha. I know what you must think. All those things I told you tonight, I hurt you, and you must think now that I took advantage of you. Believe me—if I hadn't lost my temper, this would never have happened. I wish with all my heart that it had not.'

'I don't wish that. I don't! Alexis . . .' She reached for him, and he stopped her, holding her hands sadly. 'No wait—I didn't mean the things I said,' she cried desperately. 'Alexis, believe me, I didn't mean them. I was so angry and jealous and hurt—I didn't know what I was saying . . .'

'It's all right. It doesn't matter, I know you were jealous, and I know how it feels. Oh, Natasha, don't, please . . .'

She began to cry; suddenly the tears which had refused to come earlier, now welled up. Sobs choked her throat and her chest; she could not speak. Her body trembled in a storm of weeping.

Alexis put his arms around her and just held her. When, eventually, she quietened, he dried her eyes, and took her hand, and led her into her bedroom. He helped her on to the bed.

'Try to sleep,' he said. 'You're exhausted. The strain of all this. Rest. Don't worry. My dear . . .' He lifted her feet on to the bed, and laid her back against the pillows. Natasha closed her eyes, and tears trickled under her eyelids; her mind darted wildly with pain.

'Sleep now. Please sleep . . .'

'Don't go. Alexis, don't leave me . . .'

He pressed her hand.

'I'll stay now, if you want. But it's all right, I promise I'll go in the morning.'

'I don't want you to go . . .'

'In the morning you will. It doesn't matter. I understand.'

She opened her eyes, though exhaustion pressed against her lids, and she longed to forget everything, all the pain, and just do as he said and sleep.

'You think I love Paul. I don't. You're wrong.'

'I don't think anything. I'm not capable of thinking. And neither are you. Sleep, Natasha . . .'

She shut her eyes.

'Lie beside me, Alexis . . .'

'No.'

'Please. I just want you to hold me. I'll sleep then . . .'

There was a silence; she felt sleep gather her on a tide, and buoy her up. She reached out a hand, blindly, into the darkness of the room.

'Please, Alexis, just this once.'

He did not answer her, but she heard him move. Very gently she felt the bed give as he lay down beside her. He lay carefully, not touching her, and Natasha sighed. She reached, and his hand found hers in the darkness. Then, wanting only the comfort of his arms, she turned on to her side so she was close to him. His arm came under her; he pillowed her head gently on his shoulder, and clasped her softly against his heart. Listening to its beat, first quick, then steadier, she let sleep engulf her. Its waves lifted her; they ebbed and flowed with the rise and fall of his breast. His name sighed on her lips; she fell asleep.

CHAPTER TWELVE

WHEN she woke the first thing she did was reach her hand across the bed, and the first thing she realised clearly was that Alexis had gone.

She sat up, instantly alert, and then sprang from the bed; she called his name; she ran through the rooms of the flat; he was not there. Her watch had stopped; the clock in Sophie's study told her it was still only eight in the morning. He couldn't have left; he couldn't. He had said he would leave, but he couldn't go, not without speaking to her, not now, it was impossible. Wildly, panic-stricken, she raced back to the little dressing room where he slept, and flung back the door. The bed was made; the curtains were pulled back; sunlight flooded the room. But his books were still by the bedside, and, when she pulled open the cuboard doors she saw, with a moan of relief, that his clothes were still there. Passionately she pressed one of his jackets against her face.

In a mad dislocation all the events of the past night leapt and darted in her mind. Then the self-hatred she had felt redoubled; it was incomprehensible to her that then—when it mattered so much—she could have said such wicked things, things that were the very opposite of what she meant or wanted to say. It was as if she had been unhinged, lunatic and she felt a moment's fear that the intensity of passion she felt, which should have propelled her towards goodness, clarity and light, had—by some trick, some twist—propelled her uncontrollably in the opposite direction, towards cruelty, lies and the dark.

Alexis, she said, into the rough woollen material of the jacket, and her mind offered up a silent prayer, an appeal to some deity, that wherever Alexis was now he would hear her thoughts and know. She concentrated her mind into a great effort of will, suddenly filled with the conviction that feeling could traverse distance, that the love and the guilt she felt was of such intensity that space was no barrier to it, and that Alexis, wherever and under whatever circumstances, must hear her now as clearly as if she stood by his side, took his hand, and spoke to him.

The effort of concentration calmed her mind, and filled her body with a powerful energy. Turning away from the cupboard, she closed the door, and left Alexis' room.

Then she took off the clothes she had worn the previous night—the costume—and packed them impatiently into a bag. She bathed, scrubbed the last of the make-up from her face, and put on her own, her ordinary clothes.

She went into Sophie's study, and sat staring in front of her, trying not to listen for footsteps, the turn of a key in the lock. She thought of what Alexis had told her the previous night, and she thought about her mother. She thought of her without shame or distress, and with affection. Alexis had said, and she believed him, that whatever else her mother might have been, she had been truthful; an eccentric kind of truth, perhaps, certainly not a conventional one—but still, she had been truthful. She picked up a pen and a piece of writing paper, and began, slowly at first, then more quickly, to write to Alexis.

Very deliberately she put from her mind all thoughts about his feelings. She knew if she began to investigate them, to ask herself exactly what he had meant and what he had implied, she would falter. If she allowed the image of Ariana, and the complexity of his involvement there, to interrupt her, it would arrest her completely, and she would lose her resolve, so she pushed that thought from her. She was not a man; if men could want two women at the same time—and in books they often did—or if a man could love one woman and simultaneously crave another, then that was their nature. She could not understand it, it was entirely foreign to her. But she would not think about it.

So, carefully, she began at the beginning, and went on to the end. She told Alexis how confused she had been, how she had not understood or admitted to herself, for a long while, her own feelings. She told him why she had gone to London, and what had happened there. She told him the truth about Paul Vansittart, and about her book. She told him about finding the scrap of his letter, and the pain and bitterness of the jealousy she had felt. She told him she loved him, of course.

The words were not very adequate, but they would have to suffice. At least, writing now in the clarity of the morning, she could tell him again what she had told him the night before and—this time—make sure there was no possibility of misunderstanding.

When she had finished the letter, she took the sheets of paper, sealed them in an envelope, wrote his name on the outside, and then laid it where he must see it, on his bed. Now, if he wanted to leave, if he went to pack, he could not do so without knowing the truth. She had no idea if that would stay him, or how he would react; she did not even let herself think of that. There was the letter; that was all.

Then she went back to the study, and without looking at it, picked up the typescript of her book, and put it into a large manila envelope. She paused. She had heard, once, of a woman who had written a novel, and dedicated it to her lover, and called it—*Instead of a Letter*. She might have done something like that; she could have left this for Alexis instead, because she knew if he read it, however bad it might be, he would see a little of what she felt, certainly that Paul Vansittart had lied. But the one was oblique; the other was direct; she preferred to leave him the letter.

At ten he had not returned, and she let herself out of the flat, clasping the heavy manila envelope. She would take it to Ben Whitby; she would explain to him; she would have done as much, then, as she could do. The thought freed her; her spirits lifted. The streets, the houses, the sky, sang to her of Alexis.

'And so,' she said, looking at the top of Ben Whitby's head, as he bent over his desk and riffled the pages of her typescript, 'I wanted to ask you if you would read it. Not publish it, of course. Not even consider it for publication—please don't think I even dreamed of that. But I thought you would tell me the truth—if there was anything there, or not. How I might try to improve. I'm sorry—I probably shouldn't have done that. You're very busy. There's no reason why you should bother.'

'It's my job.' He gave her a dry glance over his spectacles. 'I'm happy to read it. And then——' he shrugged. 'Which would you prefer, first novels being the problem they are— tact or brutality?'

'I'd like to know exactly what you think.' Natasha paused. 'Then I'll read it again, and try and learn.'

'And you think you'll bow to my judgment? Most writers don't.'

'I'll reserve the right to disagree. I did write it.'

'Fine.' He gave her a sharp glance. There was a little pause 'I owe you an apology,' he said then, his voice less brusque, his manner suddenly awkward. 'I mentioned you had written to me to Paul Vansittart, and when he asked why, I told him. It was extremely indiscreet of me, and I gather it's caused problems. I'm sorry about that. I had perhaps misunderstood your relationship with him, and I'd assumed . . .'

'It doesn't matter. I know all about that, Alexis told me last night.' She hesitated. 'I wanted to say—if it is embarrassing for you, in the circumstances, to look at my book, please say so. I shall understand.'

'Paul seems to feel there might be some overlap of material . . .' He looked at her closely. 'I told him I thought, from the little I knew of you, that that was extremely unlikely. I hope I was right?'

Natasha pressed her hands together. 'I typed up the first draft of Paul's book for him,' she said quietly. 'It was unfinished, just the first five or six chapters, and I have no idea how much he changes his books between drafts. But what I wrote bears no resemblance to the material of his I saw. None.' She hesitated. 'On the other hand, I should not have written it if I hadn't come to London to work for him, and if I hadn't gone to work at the club, and met two women there to whom he introduced me. So, in that sense, I owe him something. But the book is not really about them either.'

'Do you know what it is about? You might prefer not to say, of course. But in my experience, first novels . . .'

'No, I don't mind, and I do know. I don't think I realised when I was writing it, because I wrote it very fast, but I realise now. It's about my mother. A mother. About finding a mother.'

'I see.' His eyebrows lifted fractionally.

Natasha hesitated, wondering if she dared say any more, and then decided to risk it.

'You knew my own mother . . .'

'I loved your mother,' he corrected her firmly. He picked up a paper knife from his desk, and examined it, not looking up, as if momentarily he regretted the remark. Then he put the knife down, and raised his head with a smile. 'But that was a very long time ago. Before you were born. Before she married Nico.'

He paused, and she saw something cloud his eyes, some remembrance.

'She was a remarkable woman,' he said, abruptly, rising to his feet, indicating the interview was over. 'One of the most truthful people I ever met. I have her letters still. You don't remember her, I know. Perhaps, one day, you might like to read them.

'I should like that very much. If you wanted me to.' Natasha stood up. He held out his hand, and she shook it.

'I'm glad you brought me your book. I hope you won't regret it.'

'I'm glad too. And I shan't.'

He laughed, and she felt a moment's warm liking for him, a friendship.

At the door of his office, he paused. He glanced at her.

'Is Alexis in London?'

'Yes, he is. At the moment. We've been staying at Sophie's.'

'Oh, good,' he said vaguely. 'I haven't seen him for some years. Give him my regards—will you?' He paused. 'So— when I've read this work of yours, and I'll try and read it quickly, where should I contact you? There? Or are you going back to Cambridge?'

Natasha was flustered for a moment. Her plans had taken her this far and no further. She knew that he noted the sudden evasion in her face, for his eyes missed nothing.

'I haven't quite decided yet . . .' she said. 'I'm still working at the club, you see. I may stay here, or I may go home . . .'

'Well, leave both numbers with my secretary, would you?' He opened the door. 'Goodbye, Natasha.'

'Goodbye,' she said, and closed the door behind her.

Whitby's offices were in Bloomsbury Square. As Natasha came out of the house and into the street, the heat of noon hit her. The day was close, hotter than it had been all week, and the square had a dusty faded look. On the scorched grass in the gardens, secretaries from the nearby offices were already gathering to eat their picnic lunches. In the sunlight the chips of mica in the concrete pavings glittered like diamonds; she stood for a moment, irresolute, suddenly possessed with a wave of intense longing for Cambridge, for fields, grass, open spaces, willow trees and water. She thought of the river there, and its calmness; the slap of brown water against punts and under bridges; she thought of a particular bridge, and the evening she had stood on it, and wondered at her past stupidity and blindness. Then, when it had spoken so clearly, why had she not listened to the instinct of her heart? She hesitated, thinking of Alexis, wondering if he had returned, if he had read her letter, and the need to speak to him, to see him, swelled and beat in on her.

On the corner there was a telephone kiosk, and she hurried to it, and with trembling fingers, dialled the number of Sophie's flat. There was a click as systems connected, then the engaged tone. He was back then! Her heart leapt. She replaced the receiver, rested her head against the glass panes of the door, listening to the muffled roar of traffic and to the hammering of her own heart. She made herself count; to ten; to twenty. At thirty she picked the receiver up and dialled again.

This time the number rang, and went on ringing. Natasha bit her lip. He couldn't have left! Not in that small amount of time. It was impossible—perhaps she had dialled the wrong number. She dialled again frantically; again the number rang and rang. She would have let it ring for an eternity, mindlessly convinced that he must be there, or that he must come back, but a woman was outside waiting to make a call. She shuffled; she glared through the door; eventually she rapped imperiously on the glass. With a cry of exasperation and futile pain, Natasha banged the receiver down and left the kiosk. She stared around her in despair. She could go back to the flat, but what was the point? Alexis had left. All she could think was that she had to find him.

Trying to force herself to think, to be rational, she began to run in the direction of the nearest tube station. If he had left the flat then he might be going back to Cambridge. She stopped dead; the station—she would go to the station.

It took nearly an hour to reach Liverpool Street. Natasha had no memory of the journey, just a vision of crowded dirty platforms, stale air, of rushing up and down escalators. At Liverpool Street, there were comparatively few people, for it was the quiet hours in the middle of the day when few travelled. She took a time table; there were stopping trains he might be going to catch, or direct ones. She rushed from platform to platform; from the ticket office to the book-stall, and back to the platform. Frantically her eyes searched for the tall figure; they raked each passer-by; there was no one who even resembled him.

The telephone. Of course—she would try again. She might have missed him, he might be back at the flat, or—if he had caught an earlier train, on his way home. Sophie's number rang hollowly; there was no reply. Hands shaking, she dialled the Cambridge number. After a long pause, William answered.

'William, William,' she cried, now almost frantic. 'Has Alexis called? Is he home? Is he coming home?'

'Nat?' William's voice lifted. 'Where are you? We're missing you. No, he's not here, he hasn't rung . . .'

'Oh God . . .' Natasha rammed another ten pence in the slot. 'William, William, it's terribly important. If he comes back, or if he rings, tell him I called, will you? Tell him I must speak to him . . .' She paused, and then rested her head wearily against the wall of the kiosk. 'Tell him I have to go to the club, he'll know, and that if I don't see him there or at the flat tonight, I shall come home tomorrow. William, can you remember that? Will you make sure you tell him?'

'I'll tell him.'

'I love you, William. I miss you too. I've got to go now. Goodbye . . .' She hung up, feeling suddenly exhausted, hope seeping away from her heart. The dial tone rang in her ears.

The rest of the afternoon was like a nightmare; a succession of trains and buses and taxis, heat, dust, the sour smell of a city in mid-summer. She went everywhere she thought Alexis might possibly be; to the library, to his club, to his publishers. Between each halt she would telephone the flat, and each time no one answered.

At last, late, when it was almost evening, she went to Soho. Through the market, down the alleyway; she stood and faced the peeling green door. He might have come to see Paul Vansittart. Or Ariana. He might—it was possible. She rang the top bell. There was no answer. She rang all the other bells. Silence.

With a sob of frustration she turned, and then stopped. Of course, the club—it was her last hope. It was Saturday, and if Alexis were looking for her he would go there, he must do. She began to run, out of the alleyway, down the street, ducking past the tourists and foreigners who strolled along the narrow roads. Please, her mind cried, as she ran. *Please*, oh let him be there.

She flung back the door to the dressing rooms, half fell into the dimly lit passageway, and collided with a tall ample form.

'Oh Brenda, Brenda,' she cried, out of breath, clutching at her. 'Is Alexis here? Alexis, you remember? Has he been here? Has anyone been asking for me?'

'Hang on, slow down. . . . Get your breath back.' Brenda drew her to one side. She glanced over her shoulder, and lowered her voice. Natasha, looking up at her, her mind still whirling with anxiety and confusion, saw that her face was sober and worried. 'He's not here,' Brenda said. 'And he hasn't been. No one's asked for you. I've been here all afternoon.' She paused. 'Listen, Natasha, we've got a crisis . . .'

'A crisis?' Natasha stared at her, the pace of her mind slowing.

'Come into the dressing room. Quick. Before George sees you.'

Brenda grasped her arm, pushed back the door, and drew her inside. Natasha came to a halt, and stared across the room in amazement. Brenda positioned herself so her massive form had its back to the door, barring the entrance.

The room was in chaos. There were costumes all over the floor; someone had upset a case of make-up, and tubes, jars, and sticks of grease paint rolled underfoot. On the chair by the mirror, Myra was slumped. She was making a terrible noise, an awful gasping broken noise, as if she were chooking. Her arms were clutched around her stomach, and she was swaying back and forth. There were no tears on her face, and it took Natasha a moment to realise that she was not hurt or wounded, but that she was crying.

'He's dead,' she kept saying, over and over again. 'I know it. He's dead. Oh God. Oh God.'

Natasha felt her skin go cold; she stared for a second, horrorstruck, and then swung round to Brenda.

'What's happened?'

'It's her boy. Jonathan. The youngest one. There's been an accident—they just phoned . . .'

'Oh Myra . . .' Natasha forgot everything else as compassion flooded her heart. She crossed the room swiftly and knelt down beside Myra and put her arms around her. 'Oh Myra, I'm so sorry . . .'

'It's them railings.' Myra stopped her rocking for a second, and stared straight ahead of her. 'I've told him a thousand times, don't play on them, I said. Round my sister's. They're all rusty. He *promised* me. He said he wouldn't climb. I told her to get them fixed, warned her, but they're iron. Old. It costs money. Oh God . . .' She began rocking back and forth again, and Natasha lifted her white face and looked at

Brenda. She too was pale, suddenly aged, her face crumpled . . .

'Get a grip on yourself, Myra,' she said. 'Natasha, help me—I've told her. She won't listen. They've taken him round the hospital—she's got to go.'

'She's in shock.' Natasha turned back to Myra, and spoke very gently. 'Look, Myra. He'll be all right. I'm sure he will. If they've taken him to hospital, they'll know what to do. And you ought to be there, so, look, finish getting dressed, Brenda will help you. I've got some money, I'll go out and get a cab, you can go straight there—I'll come with you if you'd like . . .'

'They had to carry him.' Myra turned to her and gripped her hand. 'It was my other boy rang. Jonathan went all white, he said, and they couldn't see no blood, they couldn't bring him round. His breathing gone all funny . . .'

Natasha bit her lip; she pressed Myra's hand; she held her tight.

'The railings can't be very high, are they just round the house? It will be concussion, Myra, that's all—when he comes round he'll be fine. I'm sure he will—oh, Myra. Please—try and get dressed . . .'

Her words had some effect, though they sounded painfully inadequate to Natasha. Myra stood up, and clumsily, jerkily, her movements lacking all co-ordination, did up her skirt, pulled on a jumper. Then suddenly, she stopped, and doubled up as if she had been hit in the stomach.

'He'll fire me,' she said. 'That bastard. If I go. They're five foot the railings. Maybe more. Oh God . . .'

Natasha turned back to Brenda, her face pale with appeal.

'Brenda—what does she mean? Here, help me . . .'

Brenda left the door, and began to pick up the contents of Myra's handbag, which were scattered all over the table.

'She means him,' she said grimly. 'George. He hates her. Always has. He told her last time she was off, a few weeks back, when one of the kids was took bad with the chicken pox. If she was off again, he'd fire her. He would too.'

'Don't be ridiculous.' Natasha stood up. 'He wouldn't dare. He couldn't. And if he did, so what? There's plenty of other places Myra can work. She doesn't need him. Myra . . .' She turned back to her again pleadingly. 'Forget it. Forget him. He's not important. Look, let me go and get a taxi . . .'

'You don't understand . . .' Myra's voice rose in a wail. 'He means it. And it's not just him. He'll put the word out, round the street. That I'm unreliable, that I don't turn up. The jobs'll go—I've seen it happen. I'm not as young as I was . . .'

Even as she spoke there was a hammering on the door; George's voice came through its panels.

'What's going on? You got some trouble in there?'

Myra began to shake. She sat down again, as if her legs could not hold her. Natasha hesitated, then marched across and opened the door. George stood there, full-square, looking at her belligerently.

'Yes, we have,' Natasha said. 'Myra's son has been hurt in a fall. He's been taken to hospital. She's leaving. Now.'

'Not if she wants her job, she ain't.' George made as if to push into the room, and Natasha raised her arms, blocking his path.

'Did you hear what I said? Her son's been hurt in an accident.'

'I heard. And she heard. Now get out of my way, you.'

'Don't you dare to push me!' Natasha glared at him furiously. 'You get out of the way. Myra's leaving, and I'm going to get her a cab.' George hesitated, but he did not attempt to push Natasha again. He sneered.

'Got you defending her now, has she? You stupid little tart. She won't put one over on me. I've heard it all before. Son in an accident? Leave it out. If she don't open the show she's out. I've had enough of her and her bleeding kids. If I put the word round—well, she knows what'll happen.'

The malevolence in his eyes so disgusted Natasha that all she wanted to do was turn and run away. But she forced herself to face him.

'You need someone for the opening number? Is that the problem?'

'Yes. It is. And Brenda can't cover for her neither, so don't start suggesting it. She closes the show. She's star attraction—not trash, like this one.'

'So without Myra you're short of one number. Is that it?'

'Yes, it is.' George turned his gaze from Myra to Natasha. Half hypnotised she stared into his pale blue eyes; they were bloodshot, slightly protuberant. He was enjoying himself, she realised. All Natasha could think was that she had to get Myra out of there. She let her hands fall from the doorway.

'I'll do the number,' she said.

George began to laugh. 'You? You've got to be joking . . .'

'I'll do the number. I've seen it. I know it. Brenda will help

me. I'll do it—if you get out of the way. If you leave Myra
alone.'

There was silence for a moment. Natasha heard a swift
intake of breath from Brenda. George's eyes focused on her
own face, and then he passed his tongue over his lips.

'I might be willing to give it a try . . .' he began slowly. His
manner was truculent; Natasha knew he wanted to agree, but
hated to lose face.

' 'Course you will, George.' Brenda suddenly spoke up, her
voice low and mocking. 'You're a gentleman, George, we all
know that. After all, if anything bad come of all this, and
word got round the street you hadn't let Myra go, well, that
wouldn't look too good, would it, George?' She paused
meaningfully. 'What would your mates have to say to that,
George? Eh?'

George's eyes fell. He backed off. Myra stood up. She
walked across the room, and Brenda followed her.

'All right,' George said. 'But she better be in here Monday,
that's all.'

Myra's sleeve brushed Natasha's arm; she walked out of the
room like a sleep walker, looking neither to left nor right.
Brenda went with her.

'I'll get the cab,' she said to Natasha. 'You better start
getting ready.'

They disappeared down the passage. George still hovered.

'And you better come up with the goods,' he added.

Natasha slammed the door in his face.

She stood behind the red curtains, then, because her legs were
shaking so much, she sat down on a small wooden chair.
From beyond the curtains she could hear voices, male voices,
and the clink of glasses. Musak throbbed; she had five
minutes. It had happened so fast, so very fast, and now, trying
to remember how it had happened, Natasha found she could
remember nothing. The scene in the dressing room was a blur,
she could remember only the expression in George's eyes, and
the sudden clarity of what she must do, which had then
seemed very simple and very clear, and now seemed simple no
longer. She wanted to cry, and found she could not; she felt
like retching.

It doesn't matter, she kept saying to herself. What I'm
doing is not much more than thousands of women do on
Mediterranean beaches every summer. It's no different.

Hardly different. Three minutes and it will be over. It's just taking your clothes off, that's all. That's not so terrible. Just listen to the music, time it right, keep moving, don't look at anyone.

She understood now, she thought, the reason for Myra's contemptuous disdain when she did her number, the reason all the girls ignored their audience, because she knew that if she could not do that she would never get through it. She felt shamed, shamed for herself and shamed for the men who watched her, who paid money for the privilege, who bought a woman to undress for them.

I can't do it, she thought. I can't. I can't go through with it. I just can't.

'Natasha, love.' A hand touched her arm.

Natasha swung round sharply.

'Sssh, it's all right, love. It's me, Brenda.'

In the dim light, Natasha saw her now, huge, resilient, at that moment supremely comforting. She grabbed her hand. Brenda bent down beside her.

'Myra's all right, love. She got a cab straight off. She'll be in the hospital now . . .' She paused. 'How about you? Can you go through with it?'

Natasha hesitated, but Brenda seemed not to notice. She swore.

'Old Fascist. Expect he couldn't believe his luck when you spoke up. He's had his eye on you, right from the start. Likes them young, he does.' She pressed Natasha's hand gently. 'If it's him you're worried about, I'll fix him. I know just how to distract him. I do, even if I am getting on.' She paused, and looked at Natasha meaningfully. 'He won't be back till you're off, I guarantee you . . .'

Natasha smiled wanly. 'Oh, Brenda,' she said.

'There's no one out front you know, no one you'll ever set eyes on again, so you're home and laughing.' She grinned. 'There's nothing to it. I've had a look, there's about twenty blokes out there, that's all. They're ordinary men, they want to see a pretty girl, have a bit of fun, and for most of them paying for it is the only way they're going to get it. Just forget about them. Pretend you're alone. Pretend it's your bloke out there and you're dancing for him. That's what some of the girls do—I done it. When I started.' She paused, her face suddenly serious. 'I thought of him, you know, the one what give me the silk stockings. I'd think, he's back from

Birmingham now, and he's out there watching. It's him I'm doing it for. Just him.'

There was a little silence. Natasha regarded her closely. Brenda's face looked very old in the half light; the make-up clung to the creases and ravages of her face. Pity turned in Natasha's heart. She thought of her letter to Alexis; it had not brought him to her, but those revelations mattered far more than any physical ones. She had done that; she could do this. She pressed Brenda's hand, and stood up.

'I'm okay now,' she said. 'Thank you, Brenda.'

The musak had stopped; the spotlights came on beyond the red curtain. Brenda winked.

'Over to you, love,' she whispered. 'I'll go and fix George . . .'

She disappeared, and Natasha turned to face the curtains. She clenched her hands, and stepped up on to the tiny stairs that led on to the platform. There was a badly recorded drum-roll; George had theatrical instincts.

The lights in the club went down; the spots shone through the thin red silk on to Natasha's pale skin; she lifted her hand to the curtain. In the machine the tape, as it always did, hitched, clicked, re-engaged. From beyond the curtain, the buzz of conversation died away.

The music chosen for the numbers was not remarkable for the subtlety of its message. Myra's music was sung throatily, by a woman; it had a weird throbbing synthesizer backing, and consisted largely of the refrain, *I Want You*, repeated at varying levels of decibels.

It began. Natasha felt instantly a blessed sense of disassociation take over; she pushed the curtain aside and stepped forward into the light.

At first, half blinded, she could see nothing. She stood still for a second, a half-second, an eternity, then, tentatively at first, gradually more confidently, she began to move. Somewhere, a million miles away behind the music she heard a sigh, soft as the sea washing a beach. *I want you, and I need you*, cried the voice, and Natasha moved her hips.

Slowly, taking her time, letting her hands move gently over her body, she began to dance. It was easy, not hard at all. She was quite alone, and then she was not alone, for Alexis was there, and she was dancing for him, slowly, gracefully, her body at one with the beat; and her dancing had a purpose, which was not to tease at all—how stupid she had been to think of it like that—no, it was to reveal, to show him, that she was a woman, that she was herself. Alexis, she said, with her straying hands and the sway of her back and the bend of her throat, Alexis; and the cheap costume she wore felt transformed under the touch of her fingers, so it was not a costume, not black nylon poorly made so it scratched her skin, but a veil between her and him, a veil which she chose to remove because she wished him to see her as she was: bared of all defences.

But it must not be done quickly, this unveiling, because it was a ritual and also a game between them, a game she controlled, for it was she who danced, she who moved to the music. So, slowly, she lifted the thin material and eased it over her skin, then let it fall again, then eased it just a little more, watching as its darkness moved and rippled like water over the pallor of her skin. *Alexis*, she thought, as it slipped from her like silk, and she held it loose in front of her, concealing her thighs, her stomach, her breasts, because she wanted to preserve the mystery a little longer, just a little. *Alexis*, she said to herself, as she let it fall at last to the floor, and the sigh came again, like the sea from the grey world beyond her.

The throb of the music grew stronger, and her feet and her hands and her back, her whole body moved at one with it. She bent at the waist, so her hair fell forward in a dark curtain, then straightened again, running her hand slowly up the sides of her back, arching her throat, lifting her hair from the nape of her neck. She turned her back then, on the greyness, as she had seen Myra do, reaching for the front fastening of this tiny garment she now wanted to be rid of. It undid; she held the material tight in her hands, and an extraordinary sense of power surged through her. She was herself, and yet not herself. She was Natasha and Myra and any other woman, capable of wildness and also gentleness and consolation. She turned, lifting her face, hearing the sigh as she bared her breasts, and as she did so, she saw Alexis.

He was lit, for an instant, by the flare of a match near him. He was standing, quite still, near the door, and had perhaps just come in, or had been there since the beginning. The match died; her feet faltered and stopped. Her eyes, accustomed now to the lights, saw him still and saw also the others. Pale faces raised to her; it was they who sighed.

The music continued. Natasha could not move; she felt frozen like a statue, a piece of marble, paralysed as if her nerves had been severed at the neck. Move, said her mind, *move*; and nothing happened.

She stared across the room at Alexis, seeing it all now, the blue cigarette smoke drifting, the glasses half drunk, the man in front of him, wearing a red tie, and Alexis' face, expressionless, staring back at her. The shame came back then, suddenly and violently, washing up her body like a wave. Alexis had his arms folded; as she looked at him, he unfolded them and stepped forward, and the panic she instantly felt freed her from paralysis.

She stepped back, sharply, covering her breasts with her hands; the music was reaching its climax as she got to the curtain. Irrationally, suddenly remembering Myra, and her pride in her costume, she bent and picked it up, clutching it in front of her. The lights went out as she fumbled for the curtain; the music stopped. From behind her she heard voices, a mocking shout, some applause.

Hazel was standing there, waiting to go on, clutching her hair brush and her teddy bear, adjusting her skimpy gym tunic.

'Mucked it up a bit?' she said cheerfully. 'Don't fret. Happens to everyone some time. Here—sit down. Have a sip of that—it's mine, but you have it.'

She pushed a glass into Natasha's hand, and tilted it against her lips. It was brandy, and Natasha nearly choked as she swallowed it. The tape hitched and clicked and a male voice of great cheerfulness began to sing *The Teddy Bears' Picnic*.

'Hey up. I'm on. 'Scuse . . .' Hazel nipped smartly through the curtain, as Natasha, who wanted to cry, began to laugh helplessly.

She had her bar costume there, back-stage, and now, feverishly, she began to put it on, her fingers slipping on the hooks and eyes, while Hazel's shadow leaped against the curtains behind her. God, they would *not* do up, she could get them as far as the waist and no further. All her mind was concentrated just on them, she would not let herself *think* . . .

'Have you nothing else to wear?' A cold voice spoke by her ear. Natasha jumped violently. 'Evidently not. I suppose it is preferable to the other. Turn around. I might be able to assist you.'

'Alexis,' she began in a low voice, shaking, as his cold hands came around her waist and her bare breasts brushed against his dark jacket.

'Turn around.'

Alexis caught her arm, and wrenched her about, not very gently, so her back was to him. He then did up the hooks and eyes with swift efficiency.

'Keep still. There.' He turned her round to face him, keeping a firm grip on her arm. He had gone back to wearing his spectacles. They caught the light now, so that she could not see his eyes or read his expression. But his mouth was tight. He was handling her impersonally as if she were a doll; misery welled up in Natasha's heart. After that long terrible day she felt the last of her hopes fall away.

'I think we'd better leave, don't you? Now.'

'I can't ...' she said, her voice little more than a whisper. 'I'm supposed to go back and work in the bar.'

'You're never working here again. In the bar or on stage. Out.'

He began to pull her towards the dressing room, and Natasha followed him without more protest, like a dead thing.

Alexis opened the dressing room door, to reveal Brenda making the final adjustments to her tassels. Natasha looked at her wanly; she wanted to cry, and she felt that at any moment she might just begin to laugh and not be able to stop.

'Do you have a jacket or something?'

'Here's your mac, love.' Brenda handed her a carrier bag, and the raincoat. 'Your clothes is in there. Change later.' She gave Natasha a wink. 'You done lovely,' she went on. 'George didn't see nothing so he's none the wiser. And Myra just rang. He's okay, her Jonathan. It's just concussion, like you said. Keeping him in tonight, just for observation—they done the X-rays and all. He knows all about it ...' She inclined her head towards Alexis. 'Old friends we are, him and me. He come round looking for you, so I told him.'

'Thank you, Brenda.' Natasha pressed her hand. She put on the mac, and picked up the carrier bag. 'You're sure he's all right? Oh, I'm so glad ...' She turned round slowly, to find Alexis waiting. His hands were thrust deep in the pockets of nis dark suit; his face betrayed nothing.

'Good night, Brenda.' Alexis held out his hand formally. Brenda stared at it for a moment, and then shook it.

'You want to look after her,' she said to him, a little sharply. 'She's plucky. But she's only a kid.'

'I thought that once. Now I'm not sure I'd agree with you,' Alexis replied. 'Goodbye, Brenda. And thank you.'

Brenda——' Natasha hesitated. Brenda held out her arms, and Natasha kissed her. The embrace was brief, and warm, and it made the tears even closer. Gently Natasha detached herself, Alexis gripped her by the arm, and propelled her out into the corridor. He seemed to be in a hurry, and that confused her, because there seemed to her no point in ever hurrying again. If Alexis had responded to her letter in any way he would have indicated it by now. He had not then, and so she could feel a terrible dead lethargy take possession of her, a relaxation of the will. She didn't care where they went now, or what happened.

In the corridor, head bent, she felt Alexis hesitate for a second, and then continue forward, his grip on her arm tightening. When she looked up she understood the reason for his haste.

Perhaps Alexis had thought they might avoid him, but if so, they had failed. At the end of the corridor, swaying slightly on his feet, blocking the exit, was Paul Vansittart.

And from the malice and delight on his face, she knew at once that he, as well as Alexis, had witnessed her performance.

CHAPTER THIRTEEN

ALEXIS came to a halt about a foot in front of him, moving slightly so that Natasha was just behind him. He looked straight at Paul, and the novelist looked straight at him. He did not move, or attempt to get out of their way. Natasha, watching them, could sense the antagonism between them: it crackled like electricity in the air. Alexis spoke first, his voice icily polite.

'Excuse me. Would you mind moving to one side? You're blocking the way.'

'No? Am I?' Paul Vansittart smiled at Alexis innocently. His breath was coming fast, as if he had been running, or were nervous, though his face bore the cocky arrogant expression it took on when he had been drinking.

'But I'm a fan.' His eyes swivelled round to Natasha. 'I've come round to pay my respects, to congratulate the little artiste. Natasha, sweetie, you were doing so well—what went wrong? Did something put you off?'

'I don't think Natasha is terribly interested in your opinion,' Alexis said, with deceptive mildness. 'Would you mind moving aside?'

'Things *have* changed ...' Paul smiled insolently at Natasha, ignoring Alexis completely. 'She was very interested in my opinions last week. Couldn't get enough of them, could you, Natasha? I was quite drained, Alexis, *spent*, giving your little niece my opinions. But that was before she decided to write a book, of course. Tell me, Natasha, how *is* the book?'

'It's finished,' Natasha said, flatly, hoping he would give up and go. But he did not. He did not move. Beside her she was dimly conscious that Alexis transferred his weight slightly on his feet, and that he removed his right hand from his jacket pocket.

'Paul,' he said, his voice perfectly even. 'I'm afraid, if you don't move then I shall have to move you. Which is it to be?'

Natasha knew that voice, heard the danger in the calmness of its tone, but the novelist, who knew Alexis less well, did not. He laughed.

'I might have known it,' he said. 'Finished? But then you're a quick worker, aren't you, Natasha? And you had the first five chapters off pat—that must have helped. Tell me, who are you going to screw to get your follow-up? Is it a hot read—a good read? Is it as good as your tits?'

Alexis moved—so fast Natasha hardly saw what happened. One second he was standing quite still, the next his left hand shot forward, caught Paul Vansittart by the shirt front, and lifted him bodily in the air, slamming him back against the door behind him.

'Tell me,' Alexis said, his voice still quite calm, as if his question was of purely academic interest. 'Are you drunk? Very drunk? I don't want this to be an unfair contest, and I'd just like to be sure you're sober before I knock you down.'

Paul struggled impotently in his grasp. 'Sod off, Lydiard,' he said. 'I've had one Scotch, and if you want to make an issue of that stupid little tart then come outside and do it . . .'

'Fine.' Alexis released him as suddenly as he had caught him up, and Paul reeled back, momentarily off-balance. 'Much more seemly. Outside then. After you.'

'Look, this is stupid . . .' Paul regained his balance, he looked at Alexis, and Natasha saw he registered the spectacles. He lifted his hand, palm forward in a calming gesture. 'What's the point in fighting?' he began, his voice taking on a conciliatory whine. 'She's plagiarised me— obviously I'm angry. So—let the lawyers sort it out. There's no need to lose our tempers . . .'

'I haven't lost mine.'

'After all, look at it this way, Alexis. You win some, you lose some. I've got your mistress, you've got mine—and I've warmed her up for you just nicely . . .'

'Alexis . . .'

Natasha cried out as she saw Paul's fist bunch and lift. It curved through the air, aiming at the glasses, but it never made contact, because while his arm was still in mid-arc, Alexis' upper-cut connected with his jaw. It was a clean, perfectly timed blow; Paul's head swung back; he went down like a nine pin. He lay there, groggily on the floor, half on his back and half on his side, shaking his head from side to side in a puzzled way as if wondering what hit him. Alexis stepped back; his knuckles were cut, and he brushed the blood from them absent-mindedly. His face was very pale; his eyes glittered.

'Vansittart,' he said, 'I'd just like to be sure you knew why I did that. You do understand, I hope?'

Paul's mouth was bleeding. He spat, and raised his head; the left side of his face was starting to swell up, but his eyes focused on Alexis maliciously.

'I understand,' he said thickly. 'It's because of her. That stupid ignorant little bitch. You just can't stand the thought that I had her first . . .'

'You're wrong.' Alexis bent. He spoke very distinctly. 'Your insults to Natasha aren't important—not really. Because they're lies, from beginning to end. So they can't hurt her, and they certainly can't hurt me, which I suspect was their main intention. Cowards are always indirect. No—I'd like you to think of it as fundamentally a blow against your writing—against the loathsome, tenth-rate, prurient trash that you seem so eager to dump on your unfortunate readership. Please don't try and get up, your present posture suits you. Just think of it as that, will you, Vansittart? A reply, long overdue, from all the people, not just Natasha, that you've exploited and corrupted and maimed in order to produce your cheap, best-selling lies . . .'

'You . . .' Paul was struggling to get to his feet. He finally managed it, and stood there swaying, his face swollen and pugnacious, hatred in his eyes. 'You . . . don't you speak to me, don't you dare to talk to me about my books. Leave my books out of it—what do you know . . .'

'I wish we could leave them out of it,' Alexis smiled at him charmingly. 'I wish we could consign them to oblivion forever. Unfortunately, just now, that's not possible.' He paused. 'Do you know,' he went on reflectively, and Natasha saw that, being Alexis, he spoke without malice, which made his words all the more deadly. 'Do you know, there was a time when I thought you just might have the makings of a novelist? Through the mish-mash of other writers' styles, behind the third-hand plots cobbled together by your unfortunate researchers, behind the echoes of all those florid writers you admire—there was, once, just a glimmer of originality. And you lost it. And then you got really desperate. You started piling it on—the lewdness, the smut, the cheap sensationalism, fiction paraded as fact . . .' He paused. 'You see, if you are going to tell lies, or write them, the least you can do is work at them—make them that bit more convincing. Your lies are sloppy, pathetic. I despise the way in which you contaminate every emotion—every human feeling you set out to describe. I despise the way you cheapen and brutalise the act of love. I despise your work—not you. And I imagine you despise yourself, everything you write is riddled with masochism and self-loathing . . .'

'I loathe *you*.' Blood and saliva trickled down Paul Vansittart's chin. 'I loathe you, Lydiard, I loathe your class and your type and your accent and your conceit. I loathe the dried up cant you talk. . . . And I loathe *her*. A typical, devious, scheming bitch of a woman . . .'

He looked up at Alexis as he said this, and with a lurch of disgust and pity, Natasha realised that, punch-drunk as he was, he wanted Alexis to hit him again; he was trying to be provocative, but really he was pleading, with an awful, sick, perverted desperation behind the bluster and the abuse. Alexis must have seen it too, because he did not touch him. He stepped back a pace, and took Natasha's arm.

'Well, yes,' he said. 'Let's not repeat things. That's where we came in, I think. We despise each other. You despise Natasha—because she wouldn't go to bed with you. Just ask yourself this. Wouldn't you have despised her a lot more, if she had? Why chase so compulsively what you don't really want?'

He moved as he said this, speaking in a low voice, and pushed Vansittart gently to one side. The novelist looked at him in a dazed fashion. As Alexis opened the door behind him, he reached out a hand and grasped Alexis' arm with an urgency and a desperation.

'Lydiard,' he said hoarsely. 'Wait . . . Alexis . . .'

Alexis hesitated; he looked at Paul intently, as if something suddenly had become clear to him, and Natasha saw compassion in his eyes. Then, gently, he released Vansittart's hand. The writer slumped back against the doorpost.

'I'm sorry,' Alexis said, his voice very quiet. 'You must know that's impossible.' Then, drawing Natasha after him, he went out into the alleyway, and the door swung shut behind them.

They walked for a little way in silence, Alexis keeping his face averted, while Natasha stumbled to keep up with him. Suddenly Alexis stopped.

'I shouldn't have done that,' he said. 'I shouldn't have said those things, and I shouldn't have hit him. But I hadn't realised. It was stupid of me—I should have known . . .'

Natasha came to a halt in front of him, and looked up into his face.

'I see now,' she said slowly. 'I didn't realise either. It wasn't me he wanted, was it? Ever? Nor Ariana. He's with her now because she was your mistress. It's the next best thing to you. But it was you he wanted, all along, wasn't it, Alexis?'

'Ariana was never my mistress,' Alexis said absently. 'I don't have a mistress.' He paused. 'But I wish I hadn't done that. It was cruel and uncharitable, and I should have known better . . .' He sighed, and Natasha, whose heart had begun to beat very fast, and who was telling herself that that was a very selfish reaction and she had better ignore it, reached tentatively for his hand.

'There's a lot of things I wish I hadn't done too,' she said, in a small voice. 'Maybe we're a bad influence on each other.'

'Do you think so?' Alexis turned his attention back to her, and gradually the worried crease between his brows was erased. He looked down into her face, his eyes cleared, and gradually an expression of the greatest happiness began to radiate his features. He clasped her hand. 'Maybe we'd better reform,' he said. 'We could reform each other.'

'You'd have the lion's share of the work,' Natasha said wryly.

'Nonsense.' He tucked her hand under his arm, and pulled her close. Then side by side, in step, they began to walk again, neither speaking. As they walked Natasha felt utterly at peace, and utterly happy. She could have gone on walking, just like that, saying nothing at all, all night. After a while, Alexis came to a halt again.

'Where are we going?' he demanded.

'I haven't the least idea.'

'Nor have I. I found your letter. I've been looking for you all day.'

'I've been looking for you.'

'Natasha.' He bent, and gathered her in his arms, and kissed her forehead very gently. Then he straightened up, turned, and began to look distractedly up and down the street.

'What are you *doing*, Alexis?' she asked eventually.

'Doing? Doing? I'm looking for a taxi, of course. If it were not ten o'clock at night I'd be looking for a priest or a registrar, but as it is and this is London, alas, and not Las Vegas, I'm looking for a taxi.'

'Las Vegas?' Natasha's voice came out as a whisper.

'You can get married in Las Vegas twenty-four hours a day. It's a horrible place, but it has that one advantage.'

'Married?'

'Well of course married. I told you I found your letter, didn't I? If I'd found you this afternoon we could have done it then, by special licence. But I didn't so we'll have to wait until tomorrow. So I thought now we'll go back to the flat and ... except that's the wrong way round, isn't it?' Alexis looked momentarily perplexed. 'After all, we're pledged to reform each other. However, I don't think we'll bother about the niceties, do you? Not now. Oh look——' He leapt into the road with a commanding gesture, and a vehicle screeched to a halt. Alexis opened its door and helped her in.

'You see?' he said. He leaned back in the seat, removed his glasses, and put his arm around her. 'A taxi. I knew one would come.'

'Where to?' The driver turned, peered through the glass partition, and raised his eyes patiently to the heavens. There was a long pause before he got his answer, and he tactfully turned his back.

'Wimpole Street,' Alexis managed, at last. 'And could you hurry?'

He reached for her in the half light, pushing her back so he pinned her with his weight, his easy strength, against her bedroom door. His hand came under her hair, grasping her tightly round the nape of her neck, lifting her face to his. He looked down into her eyes, and watching her face, slowly and deliberately loosened, with his other hand, the tie of her coat, and ran it up over her body in one slow firm caress. Fire shot through her; her lips parted with a low moan; her eyelids fluttered then closed with a deep langour.

'Yes,' Alexis said, and brought his mouth down hard upon hers.

Blindly she sought him, reached for him, moving her hands over the hard planes of his body, moving them back and forth, back and forth in the same compulsive trajectory. He moved then, trapping her between his body and the door, resting his arms on either side of her, so that first only their mouths were joined, and then, gradually, as he leaned against her, their bodies, so her breasts were crushed against his chest, and his hard thigh parted her legs. Heat built in her, as it built in him, a feverish heat. She trembled, and Alexis began very slowly, first to undo her stockings, then the fastening of the costume she wore, until it was all undone, and he could slip his hand under it, to her back, to the curve of her buttocks, and lift her, so she was pressed against the hard pulse of him.

He lifted her then, and carried her to the bed, and removed the costume. When she was naked, he stood for a moment, looking down at her, and she exalted in his gaze, seeing it travel from the lift and curve of her full breasts, over her slender waist to the tiny triangle of dark hair between her thighs. He was still dressed, but his arousal was obvious; she watched, the eroticism of the moment heightened by the raggedness of his breathing, the urgency of his movements, as he roughly tore off his clothes. He turned back to her, naked, and knowing him at last, she trembled and reached up her arms to him. He bent, lay beside her, flesh against flesh, and slowly, carefully, guided her blind hand over his body, his body which felt so miraculously alive, which pulsed and responded to the first shyness of her touch. He groaned then, bending her back, arching her against him, his hands fiercely lifting her breasts to the caress of his tongue and the suck of his mouth.

She let his hands find all the secret shelters, the moist soft places of her body, and she cried out as he touched her, offering her breasts, the pulse that beat so fast in her throat, her opened mouth, to the gathering fierceness of his kisses. But his kisses alone, his caresses, could not assuage now the want that she felt for him, it sharpened, it built, it located itself, so she cried out as he parted her thighs, lifted her legs a little, straddled her.

He had not spoken; he had gone beyond her into some dark wild place, she could see it in the clouding and intentness of his gaze, as he lifted himself above her, waiting a moment, looking down into her face. Male, in control; she had a second of fear at his strangeness, his domination. He was poised to thrust against her, and into her, she felt the throb and demand of his flesh against her thighs; still, a moment, he waited, touching her just very lightly, where she most craved him, and with a strange low muffled crooning sound that she could hardly believe came from her own lips, she reached for him, lifted herself up to him, moist and open to his thrust.

Saying something, half groaning, he pushed into the channels of her body, held back, pushed again; pain exploded behind her eyes like white light, she could not contain him, she was wounded. And then, miraculously, as she felt him fill her, the wound healed, his every movement, gentle and slow at first, then harder, more demanding, then tender and gentle once more, beat through her body, and sang in her blood. Slowly, instinctively, she began to move against him, feeling her body flower darkly and begin to tremble, to move to the rhythm of his.

Heat built in her; the passages of her body began to move against the deep fierce plunging of his flesh. He drew her on, pushing her further, and then, when he seemed so deep in her he must rend her whole body, he bent to her parted mouth, his tongue between her lips, his breath against hers, and at that twin joining, something inside her seemed to break, to implode with the ecstasy of it. She cried out, clutching him, feeling his whole body stiffen and shudder. He came against the contraction of her womb, crying out as she did, at this joining, this consummation.

So Alexis found her at last, and she him. Afterwards they slept a little, the deep sweet peaceful sleep of satiation, and then, waking up, discovered they were not satiated at all, and so made love again, and slept and made love. The night passed, and most of the next morning, but time had no meaning, the world had contracted to the limits of this, their bed, within which there was a new world of touch and exploration, embraces were hours, kisses were minutes.

Natasha grew bolder—Alexis said more abandoned—though neither boldness nor abandonment seemed to displease him. At last, some time in the afternoon, Natasha lay back on the pillows, her hair dishevelled, her body silken with sweat; she slept, and in her sleep she dreamed of the things Alexis had said to her, his mouth against her throat, in the heat of his passion that night.

When she opened her eyes, Alexis lay beside her, propped up on one elbow, looking down into her face.

She looked up into the greenish depths of his eyes.

'That letter you found,' he said. 'It was to you, you know. The last word was not "missed", it was "mistakenly". "I have mistakenly tried"—something like that. You have a deplorable effect on my grammar.'

'Good.'

He laughed, and rolled over on to his back, folding his hands under his head. He stared up at the ceiling.

'We were going to get married today.'

'I know. But there's not much of today left, and besides,

I've remembered. It's Sunday. I'm sure you can't get married on a Sunday . . .'

'Tomorrow then . . .'

'Or we could wait.'

'I don't think so.'

She glanced at him teasingly. 'We could do it in Cambridge, and I could wear a white dress and William could be page-boy . . .'

'William would loathe that. As you perfectly well know.'

'Oh, all right then. Tomorrow. But I'd like William to be there, and Anne, and Brenda, and Myra . . .'

'Let's invite the world,' Alexis said grandly. He paused. 'Oh, I have bought us a house. Near Granchester. It's very beautiful—but if you don't like it, or you want to be somewhere else, we'll sell it, and buy another.'

'Alexis!' She turned to him, her eyes wide. 'You bought a house? For us? When?'

'I don't know . . .' He gestured vaguely. 'A month or two ago. And I didn't know it would be for us—I just hoped it might.'

'But . . .' She stared at him, and then began to laugh softly. 'You are quite mad, you know. Why did you do that, then?'

'Well, I loved you. It seemed reasonable. And I had decided I'd had enough of self-restraint, and if I wasn't to go entirely mad, or suddenly grab you and rape you in the middle of Great Court, I'd better do something about it. So, I was steeling myself. For a formal declaration.'

'Oh Alexis,' she said, bending to kiss him. 'I do love you.'

The telephone began to ring. They let it ring for a long while, and eventually, reluctantly, while Alexis cursed, Natasha went into the drawing-room to answer it.

When she came back, she stood at the side of the bed, and looked down at him.

'Alexis . . .' she said.

'Mmmm,' he answered, drawing back the sheet.

'Do books and babies go well together, do you think?'

'Wonderfully,' he replied, drawing her down beside him.

'Because that was Ben. He's going to publish my book.'

'Natasha!' He sat up excitedly, and put his arm around her. 'I was sure he would. I'm so glad. Are you happy?'

'Well yes——' she began slowly. 'I am. But I can't really concentrate on that now. Tomorrow maybe. Or the day after. I . . .'

He touched her, and she sighed, and slid down against the warmth of his body. They lay side by side, and gently she reached up her hands, and held his face, and looked a long while into his eyes.

'Do you love me, Alexis?'

'But of course. I shall always love you. There it is. A fact. Like—oh, I don't know—gravity, or the rotation of the planets, or $E = mc^2$, or . . .'

'Then *why* didn't you say so?'

'I'm not very good with words. You may have noticed. Too reticent. Too easily deflected. Too likely to get impassioned . . .'

'I don't mind your being impassioned——'

'There were a lot of other things I wanted to say to you as well . . . but I'm better with actions.'

He moved his hand as he spoke, and Natasha felt her body tremble.

'Darling,' he said, and he ran his hand softly down from her breasts to the curve of her stomach; Natasha sighed happily. She moved her own hand, and felt his instant response.

'Darling,' she answered, her voice husky but measured. 'I'm not going to let you off, and you're not going to distract me. I love you, Alexis, and you can damn well tell me . . . oh . . .'

'What, darling?'

'All those things . . .' She moaned a little.

'Very well.' He moved swiftly, so his weight was upon her 'It's inordinately simple. About three years ago, when you were still technically my ward, which complicated matters, I came home from college one day, where I had spent many miserable hours trying to concentrate on my seminars and exorcising from my mind the visions of you which kept distracting me shamelessly from the matter in hand—and you were in the garden. You were wearing a white dress, and as I came out, you straightened up, and looked at me, and the sun was behind you, it lit your hair, and you took my hand, and laughed, and said something, I don't remember what—and I knew then, both that I loved you, and that, with a fierceness I would not have believed possible . . .'

'Then?' Natasha wound her arms around his neck. 'I remember that day! I remember thinking then that . . .'

'Don't interrupt,' he said, and he kissed her for a while, then lifted his head again. 'Now where was I? Oh yes. With a fierceness I would not have believed possible, I realised that I wanted you, and that I wanted to . . .'

So saying, he lowered his mouth to her ear, and spoke into it softly, and as he spoke he suited the action to the word, the word to the action, until at last, long after hers, his own control broke, his voice faltered, and they both moved, with joy in the knowledge, far beyond words.

ROMANCE

Next month's romances from Mills & Boon

Each month, you can choose from a world of variety in romance with Mills & Boon. These are the new titles to look out for next month.

DON'T PLAY GAMES Emma Darcy
A WORLD OF DIFFERENCE Sandra Field
AGE OF CONSENT Victoria Gordon
OUTCAST LOVERS Sarah Holland
TIME FUSE Penny Jordan
ACAPULCO MOONLIGHT Marjorie Lewty
ECLIPSE OF THE HEART Mary Lyons
DREAMS TO KEEP Leigh Michaels
IMPASSE Margaret Pargeter
A SECRET PLEASURE Flora Kidd

Buy them from your usual paperback stockist, or write to: Mills & Boon Reader Service, P.O. Box 236, Thornton Rd, Croydon, Surrey CR9 3RU, England. Readers in South Africa-write to: Mills & Boon Reader Service of Southern Africa, Private Bag X3010 Randburg, 2125.

Mills & Boon
the rose of romance

The perfect holiday romance.

ACT OF BETRAYAL
Sara Craven

MAN HUNT
Charlotte Lamb

YOU OWE ME
Penny Jordan

LOVERS IN THE AFTERNOON
Carole Mortimer

Have a more romantic holiday this summer with the
Mills & Boon holiday pack.

Four brand new titles, attractively packaged for only £4.40.

The holiday pack is published on the 14th June. Look out for it
where you buy Mills & Boon.

The Rose of Romance

Twice as romantic.

'Hidden in the Flame' is a compelling, involving story of love and revolution in South America, and twice the length of a Mills & Boon romance.

Anne Mather is a best-selling author, world-renowned for more than 90 romantic novels.

'Hidden in the Flame' is published on 10th May. Twice the romance for just £2.95.

The Rose of Romance